Seven Graves, Two Harbors

SEVEN GRAVES, TWO HARBORS

Dennis Herschbach

NORTH STAR PRESS OF ST. CLOUD, INC.
Saint Cloud, Minnesota

Dedication

This book is dedicated to my wife, Vicky Schaefer,
who supports all of my writing endeavors
and encourages me when I begin to doubt myself.

ISBN 978-0-87839-702-0

First Edition: June 2013

Printed in the United States of America

Published by
North Star Press of St. Cloud, Inc.
P.O. Box 451
St. Cloud, Minnesota 56302

www.northstarpress.com Facebook - North Star Press Twitter - North Star Press

Acknowledgements

Special thanks to several people who have been key to the publication of *Seven Graves, Two Harbors*:

To Elizabeth Brunsvold, Patricia Sohler, and my wife Vicky, who read my manuscript and made valuable contributions with their advice.

To my many friends in the writing community who offer their encouragement.

To the staff of North Star Press for accepting my manuscript and for all the work they did in publishing the book. They are a great group of people with whom to work.

Chapter One

The bar stool George "Skinny" Tomlinson sat on was old. Its red vinyl cover was torn in two places, and the yellowed foam stuffing of the cushion hung out in ragged pieces. He gulped the last swallow of the beer he had been nursing, slid off the stool, and jostled his way through the crowd of drunks to the men's room.

The place smelled of stale urine and rancid beer. He finished his job at the yellow-crusted, cracked porcelain urinal and pushed his way back to his stool where he sat alone. He wasn't a stranger in the dive, but as usual everyone ignored him.

That was the way Skinny's evening went: drink a couple of beers, hit the men's room, come back to the bar, drink a couple more beers. He became more disheveled as the evening progressed until half of his red-plaid flannel shirt hung out over his pants, and his cap sat crooked on his head.

By ten thirty he was ready to call it a day, gave up his stool, and wobbled to the door. He almost toppled off the top step, caught himself on the rusty railing and made it to his pickup. Through his alcohol fog, he glanced at his front license plate. It wasn't the customary Minnesota plate but was a glaring black on white. The first two letters read WP, a whiskey plate. He had been arrested twice for DWI in the last five years. The last time, his blood alcohol registered .25 percent, and the courts had mandated he place the lettered stigma on his truck's license plates.

Skinny rankled at the idea. Because of those two letters, law enforcement could pull him over for no cause other than to check his state of sobriety. Right now there was no way he would pass a breathalyzer test. That would mean the loss of his driver's license, or worse, jail time.

Just as he was about to open the driver's-side door, he felt a hand on his shoulder, and he spun around.

"Hi, Skinny."

It took Skinny a moment to focus on the man's face, but then he grinned.

"What the heck are you doing up here in Isabella? You're a long way from home, aren't you?" the man asked.

Skinny was glad to see a face he recognized. "I was dealing with business and stopped for a cold one on the way home. I guess time got away from me. I'm heading back to Two Harbors now," he said with slurred speech. Then he added, "What're you doing here?"

"I was fishing on Silver Island Lake this evening and stopped for the same reason you did. Problem is, now my truck's battery is dead. Can't even get the engine to grunt. I was kinda hoping I could catch a ride into town with you."

Skinny wobbled, steadying himself by grabbing the man's arm. "Hey, it'd be nice to have company on the way home. Jump in."

The two men crawled up into the pickup cab, Skinny having the harder time of it. He turned the ignition key and the rattletrap coughed twice and started. They pulled out of the dirt parking lot, and he turned right.

"Hey, Skinny, you okay to drive? Two Harbors is the other way."

Skinny snorted. "Did you see my plates? Whiskey plates. I get caught driving in this condition again, I'm hung. I'm going up to where the Whyte Road takes off from the main highway. Hardly anybody uses that trail anymore, especially the deputies. I figure by the time we get back onto Highway 2, I'll be sobered up enough."

"Tell you what, Skinny. Why don't you let me drive? That way we don't have to take that dirt trail they call a road. I've only had a beer. I'm sober."

Skinny looked at the man through eyes that drooped to mere slits. "What'ya think? I'm too drunk to drive? Hell, I've gotten home in worse shape than this before," Skinny slurred at him.

"Come on, Skinny," the man said. "I don't want to end up wrapped around some tree. Why don't you let me drive? I'll be gentle with your truck." He laughed, trying to disarm Skinny.

"Nobody drives for me," Skinny said belligerently. "You think I can't drive my own truck? You're like all the rest of them, always putting me down like I'm nothing. Well I'm going to show you. Not too long and I'll have enough money to buy you and the rest of Lake County. Then people will change their tunes. They'll have to if they want any favors from me."

The man tried to talk Skinny down from his rant. "Ah, come on, Skinny. You know you're three sheets to the wind. I can have us back in Two Harbors in forty minutes. By that time, you'd be good to go. I'd get off at my place, and you could take the wheel. Don't you think?"

Just then they saw a neon sign ahead. It flashed on and off, "T RRY'S." Skinny pulled into the parking lot and slammed on his brakes.

"Get the hell out of my pickup. Get out, now! Find a ride back with somebody else."

Reluctantly, the man opened the truck door and stepped out onto the gravel surface.

"Come on, Skinny. Be reasonable and give me the keys. You know darn well you're in no shape to be driving. Otherwise you wouldn't be taking the back way home."

Skinny peeled out of the parking lot, letting the forward motion of his truck slam the passenger door shut and leaving the man standing alone.

Two miles down the highway Skinny turned off the pavement onto the Whyte Road and tried, not too successfully, to avoid the potholes on the neglected logging trail. After twenty miles of fighting the deteriorated condition of the road and the blackness of the night, he was becoming so tired he could hardly hold his head up. The sky lit up with a flash of lightning, rain started to pelt down, and Skinny's windshield wipers had a difficult time keeping up with the deluge.

Good thing I'm getting close to the highway. Should be only about five or six miles from the intersection. He glanced in his rearview mirror.

"Damn," he said to himself. "Where'd that car come from? It would be just my luck to have a county deputy out here on a night like this."

Another streak of lightning slashed through the sky, and the rain continued to pour down.

Chapter Two

THE RED-FADED-TO-ORANGE PICKUP sat nose down in the ditch. Its driver's-side door had been left open, and as Lake County Deputy Sheriff Jeff DeAngelo looked in, he could see water pooled in a couple of places on the floor. He reached in and felt the seat—wet. The old-timer he had spoken with a few miles back said they had a real soaker three days ago, but since then the weather had been sunny. Evidently, the pickup had been sitting there for a while. Jeff looked around for any human sign—nothing.

He had been on a routine patrol when he decided to cut through to Highway 2 via the Whyte Road, which was some thirty miles north of Two Harbors, a small town on the North Shore of Lake Superior. The Whyte was one of several single-lane roads built on abandoned railroad beds that crisscrossed the wilderness. It connected four or five houses called Whyte with another cluster of buildings twenty miles away, Jordan Landing. These two sites—they couldn't really be called villages—were isolated by swamps, bogs, and wooded ridges. Every week Jeff swung through the area to check for any emergency needing to be reported.

As he looked at the stricken vehicle partially buried in the swampy ditch, he thought that someone must have had a long walk out to the highway. Jeff moved to the back of the pickup and jotted down its license plate number, WP 2A30. *Whiskey plate,* he thought. He walked back to his squad car, a white Ford Explorer with "LAKE COUNTY SHERIFF'S DEPARTMENT" stenciled on its side.

"Hi, Jaredine," he said into the two-way. "I need a check on a Minnesota license plate, number WP 2A30."

He listened, then answered the dispatcher, "No, this isn't a traffic stop, just a pickup truck in the ditch. Looks like it probably belongs to Skinny Tomlinson, but I want to be sure."

After a pause, he answered again, "Thanks, Jaredine. I thought it was his. Well, he's probably with a buddy somewhere and maybe is still in the bag. You know him."

Jeff hung up and jotted down a few notes to report the next morning to Sheriff Johnson. Before leaving, he shut the door of Skinny's battered truck.

IT HAD BEEN OVER A YEAR SINCE Deidre Johnson, sheriff of Lake County, was gunned down at Gooseberry State Park. Her wounds had pretty much healed, but the scars, both physical and psychological, remained. She paced around her office, trying to organize her thoughts before the morning shift. Through her office window, she could see that most of the deputies had arrived. They were helping themselves to the coffee and sweet rolls always on hand for the short time they were together each morning.

With an effort to get on with the day's work, she picked up a notepad and headed for the conference table in the other room.

"Okay, guys, let's get this over with so we can start the day and the nightshift can go home and catch some sleep," she announced.

The deputies all settled into their accustomed chairs, and the meeting started.

"Does anybody have anything significant to report?" she wanted to know.

Before anyone else could speak up, Jeff pulled out his notepad. "Yesterday, I was taking the Whyte Road between Isabella and Highway 2, and I came across something. At first I thought it not so strange, knowing the person involved, but the more I mull it over, I feel like things don't add up.

"Skinny Tomlinson's truck is buried in a ditch about five miles from the highway. It's just before the old logging road off to the left. I didn't think much of it, knowing his drinking history, but the driver's-side door had been left wide open, and the front seat was soaked from a rainstorm that hit three days ago. All signs of footprints were washed away, so I couldn't tell in which direction he might have walked.

"He had to have plowed into the ditch at least three days ago, and being that his truck had been abandoned the way it was, I thought we better look into the matter."

"Ah, you know Skinny," chimed in Pete. "He's driven that old pickup into more ditches than we can count. I'll bet he turns up in a day or two after he's sobered up. I think that guy has more lives than a cat."

Jeff argued back. "I'd tend to agree with you, and yes, he does have quite a reputation around here. But something just didn't seem right when I was at the scene. Nothing particular that I can tell you, just not right."

"We can't go on assumptions about people, but then we can't do much if things just don't seem right," Deidre interjected into the conversation. "Nevertheless, I think we should take this situation seriously. Skinny deserves as much concern as the next person, and if he's in some kind of trouble, we have to be there for him.

"Jeff, would you stay after our meeting? I'm going to have you do some checking around to see if anyone has seen him in the last day or two.

"Does anyone else have anything significant to report?" Some shook their heads. Others sat in silence. "Good. Let's get to our assignments, or in the case of those who worked the nightshift, to bed.

"Jeff, let's go to my office."

Jeff entered first and Deidre pulled the door shut behind them.

"What do you think, Jeff?" she wanted to know. "My guess is that Skinny's off on a real bender this time and will show up in a day or two. But we have to do some checking in the meantime.

"I have to go to the northern end of the county today, up to Isabella. I'll stop in at a few places while I'm there. Is it worth the effort to check out the bars in town?"

Jeff thought a minute before answering. "I know we have to go on facts, but I tell you, something just didn't seem right when I was checking out his pickup. I think we should begin looking, if only because of my gut feeling. I know it's Skinny, but we'd feel pretty terrible if we could have helped him and didn't.

"Give me today to nose around. If I don't come up with anything, we can drop it until something more concrete does."

"I'll drive up the Whyte Road to see if his pickup is still there. Chances are he's already had somebody pull him out. Knowing Skinny, he doesn't want this reported," Deidre offered.

Jeff turned to leave, and over his shoulder he said, "Thanks, Deidre. Maybe you're right and this will end up being a waste of our time, but I don't think so."

Chapter Three

Last December, in the middle of a nor'easter, Ed Beirmont had moved into a house near Lake Superior about two miles up the shore from Two Harbors. It was as though he had appeared from nowhere. Because all his neighbors chose to avoid the winds and the snow by holing up indoors, they didn't notice any activity at the place next door. When the storm subsided after two days, there was Ed, plowing out his driveway.

To call the building he bought a "house" was stretching it. Most people would say it was more of a shack, with one room serving as a living room, dining room, and kitchen. There was one bedroom and a bath off to the side, and a large screened-in porch on the lakeside.

When he erected a pole building that seemed to be half the size of a football field, his neighbors thought he was a little crazy, but no one questioned him. Ed was six-foot-four and about two-hundred-fifty pounds, none of it fat. Everyone thought of him as a gentle giant, although no one really knew him. He was a loner.

Above the double door of his building, he put up a sign, "Ed's Plumbing Contracting." His neighbors noticed several delivery trucks arrive, but they always drove into the warehouse where their cargo could be unloaded behind closed doors.

After about three months, people began to talk. They seldom saw Ed working, but he always seemed to have plenty of money and drove a shiny new F-250 Ford pickup. He spent a great deal of time in the bars and taverns in the area, especially a notoriously rough place ten miles up Highway 2, the Big Noise Tavern. He was out drinking almost every night of the week, and word was that he could drink all night and not pass out.

People who frequented the bars and dives had a different impression of Ed than did his neighbors. They said he was the life of the party after he had a few drinks in him, striking up conversations with everybody, buying drinks for the house, and hanging with some of the toughest and dirtiest characters in the county.

He seemed to take a special interest in Skinny Tomlinson. Most people were happy when Ed sat drinking with him. That meant the rest of them wouldn't be bothered by Skinny's talk about the large sum of money he was on the verge of inheriting, or his ranting about the authorities, who forced him to drive with a WP license plate.

Ed did a few small plumbing jobs around town, and his customers raved about how fast he worked and what a good job he did for them. During the day he made himself visible, driving the streets, always in a hurry, always looking as though he was heading for another job. Many days Skinny rode with him, but no one ever saw him helping Ed. All they did was cruise around.

JEFF STARTED HIS SEARCH FOR SKINNY at the Pub Bar and Grill.

"Hi, Jeff," the bartender, Betty, greeted him. She was a transplant in Two Harbors, having moved into town from Jordan Landing. She said she had gotten tired of having no one to talk to and that the nights alone were too long so far up in the woods.

"What can I do for you today? I know you're not here for a drink," she said, pointing at his badge.

"We're looking for Skinny Tomlinson. His pickup's been sitting in a ditch off the Whyte Road for a few days, and no one has reported seeing him lately."

Before he could go on, Betty interrupted. "You know Skinny. He's holed up with one of the boys somewhere in the woods, probably drunk to the gills. When he runs out of booze, he'll show up. He always does."

"I know, but we have to check it out. He usually doesn't go missing for this long. When was the last time you saw him here?"

Betty thought for a second, her face screwed up as though by physical effort she could jar her memory.

"Gosh, Jeff, I'm not sure. Now that you mention it, he hasn't been around for quite a while, maybe over a week. Wish I could give you a better answer, but we've been so busy every night he might have been here, and I missed seeing him."

"Thanks, Betty. Next time I'll leave my uniform at home." He gave a short wave as he went out the door.

It was the same at every bar he went to. Jeff stopped at the one liquor store in town, but no one there could remember seeing Skinny for at least a week, maybe more. Wherever he went, the answer was always the same.

"You know Skinny. He's on a bender and will show up pretty soon, looking like he's been pulled through a knothole."

ON HER WAY UP TO ISABELLA, Deidre swung off Highway 2 onto the Whyte Road. She had a difficult time maneuvering around the obstacles. Not only were there deep holes she had to dodge, but the corduroy logs laid down by the railroad company in the early 1900s were working their way to the surface. Here and there the jagged end of a timber stuck up through the dirt.

It took a good twenty minutes to travel the five miles to Skinny's truck. When she arrived, she pulled out her evidence kit and stretched a pair of rubber gloves onto her hands.

By this time, so many have had their hands on the truck I doubt we'll get much in the way of prints, but you never know, she thought.

The door of the truck was still unlocked. She opened it and looked inside. The first thing she noticed was a scuffed shoe lying on the floor. It was a brown loafer, and its mate was nowhere to be found. She looked under the seat but found nothing. Deidre placed the shoe in an evidence bag and labeled the time, date, and the location where it had been found.

I suppose he dropped the other one outside of some bar. Deidre smiled at the image of Skinny staggering around with only one shoe on his feet.

She tilted the seat forward and sifted through a collection of burger wrappings, clothing and junk. She was about to give up looking for anything of interest when she spotted a small plastic bag a quarter-full of white powder that stuck together in a clump. She bagged and labeled it as evidence.

Other than those two finds, she could see nothing that might cause her to believe that anything was amiss. Deidre took the keys from the ignition, locked the doors of the truck, and placed the keys in a separate evidence bag.

It took another twenty minutes to return to the highway, but when she turned north on her way to Isabella, Deidre became lost in the beauty of the forest. In most places it came down to the roadway that had been built long before wide rights-of-way were mandated. A few miles up the road a cow moose and her calf stepped out from the brush. Deidre stopped her vehicle to allow them to cross in front of her. She remembered the patrolman who hadn't given a moose the right-of-way and ended up with its front legs through his windshield and in his lap.

Several minutes later she stopped at one of the two taverns in the area, Friendly Jane's. She climbed the rotting wooden stairs and opened the door. The stench of stale beer swept over her, and she had to force herself to enter the dark confines of the bar.

"Yeah, what do you want?" Jane snarled. In the past she and Deidre had had problems. Jane liked to sell beer to kids from town. "I ain't sold nothin' to underagers."

Deidre had the urge to do more than question the woman, but she calmly asked, "I'm trying to track down Skinny Tomlinson. Can you remember when you last saw him?"

"I don't keep track of my customers," Jane shot back. "What they do is their business, not mine." Then she asked "He in some kind of trouble? Run over somebody or something?"

Deidre took Jane's question as an opportunity to get an answer. "No, we found his truck in a ditch on the Whyte Road. It's been a few days, but he hasn't shown up. Have you seen him?"

Jane contemplated whether she'd answer. "Yeah, he was in here last Saturday night. Got himself pretty smashed. The last I saw him he went outside, and a big guy came up behind him. I thought Skinny was in trouble, but they got into his pickup and drove off toward Isabella. An hour later the big guy showed again, got into his own pickup and drove away. That's all I know, and that's all I'm tellin' you."

Deidre thanked her and stepped outside. The first thing she did before getting into her Explorer was to take a deep breath of fresh air.

After driving another forty miles, Deidre saw the sign, "ISABELLA, POP. 113," and she thought that was being generous. She pulled into the parking lot of a business housed in a paint-peeling, leaning-to-one-side two-story building. The neon sign read "T RRY'S," and beneath the large letters in smaller painted print: "LIVE BAIT, GROCERIES, ON SALE LIQUOR, OFF SALE LIQUOR."

When Deidre opened the door, it nudged a bell that announced her presence, and the grizzled proprietor came out of the back room. His unshaven face broke into a smile when he recognized her, revealing several gaps created by missing teeth. Beneath his rugged veneer, however, his features belied intelligence and caring.

He carried a plastic bag filled with four or five fresh fish heads, and Deidre wondered what he was intending to do with them.

"Deidre, what can I do for you today? Is this official business or just a visit?"

She smiled back. "No, Terry, I'm afraid this is official. We'll have to visit another time."

Terry had been a successful college professor until he started to hear unfriendly voices in his head. Gradually the voices became louder, more demanding, until he could no longer function in the classroom. Eventually he lost everything: his professorship, his friendships, his marriage, even his property.

Terry became a streetperson, self-medicating his condition with cheap wine and booze to kill the voices long enough so he could sleep. He lived under a bridge in Minneapolis, sometimes going days without food. As the months passed, his health became more and more of an issue, and he hung onto life by a thin thread of reality. After a third trip to the emergency room at Hennepin General and countless arrests for public drunkenness and vagrancy, Terry was at the limit of his endurance.

One morning he was found lying in the gutter beside a downtown theater, where he had regurgitated and aspirated the fetid contents of his stomach. He had defecated in his underwear, his hair was snarled with dirt and grime, and it had been weeks, or perhaps longer, since he had last bathed. During his time spent on the streets, most of his teeth had either fallen out or been knocked out.

The paramedics who came could barely stand touching him, but they transported him to the ER. This time he was so soiled his clothes had to be cut and peeled from his cracked and bleeding skin. The ER nurses had to take turns working on him, each shift lasting only as long as they could hold their breath. Two of them couldn't control themselves and vomited in the sink. Terry was as close to death as a human could be.

With the assistance of Social Services, his three children were able to convince a judge to have him involuntarily committed for psychiatric treatment. The diagnosis was a type of psychosis that was treatable, but too much damage had been done. There was no way for him to go back to the college where he had once been an esteemed professor, no way for him to put his marriage back together.

Medication killed the voices and returned his sanity, but Terry wanted no more of academia, no more of the city and its commotion. As a young man he had vacationed in the northland, fishing the lakes and streams near Isabella. He returned to the happy place of his youth, bought a rundown tavern, and now lived contentedly in the remoteness of pine trees and lakes.

"I'm trying to track down Skinny Tomlinson. I think you know him, don't you?" Deidre asked.

"Oh, sure, everyone knows Skinny. What's he done, been involved in a hit and run? That old pickup of his looks like it's had its share of fender benders," and Terry sort of chuckled and held up the bag he was holding. "Suppose you're wondering about these. Don't worry, fish head soup's not on the menu." He walked over to a bait tank full of leeches and dumped the bag's contents in with a splash.

Deidre looked over the edge of the tank and shrank back in revulsion. Hundreds of small, black leeches were attacking the heads before they had a chance to settle to the bottom. In one corner of the tank lay an older head with leeches slithering in and out of every exposed cranial cavity. It was nearly stripped bare of any semblance of flesh.

Terry looked in at the sight. "Well, they gotta eat, too," he said matter-of-factly. "But what about Skinny? Has he gotten himself in trouble with the law?"

"No, nothing like that. His pickup's been sitting in a ditch off the Whyte Road for a few days, and he's not around. Is there any chance you've seen him lately?"

Terry answered without hesitation. "I haven't seen him, but I know he went by here last Saturday. Some big guy came in about eleven o'clock at night. He said he had hitched a ride with Skinny, but Skinny was so drunk he was afraid to ride with him. Skinny dumped him off at my place."

"Did you recognize this man?" Deidre wanted to know.

"He's been in here a couple of times on his way back from fishing. He always kept to himself, had one beer, and left. Like I said, he was a big guy, well over six feet and pretty brawny," Terry added.

"What did he do when he got here?" Deidre wanted to know.

"He just walked in and bellowed in a loud voice, 'Is anybody going back to Friendly Jane's Tavern? I need a ride.' One of my regulars was just leaving, and he said to come along, and they left together. I saw the truck lights head back down the highway toward Friendly Jane's. That's the last I thought of it until now." Terry added, "Sure hope Skinny's okay. I know a little bit about the life he's living. He must feel alone all the time, even when there is a crowd around. I know I did. Being a drunk is a lonely life."

Deidre thanked Terry for his help and continued down the highway to the next community, where she had a scheduled meeting with the township board.

Chapter Four

By late afternoon, Deidre had returned to her office in Two Harbors. She called Jeff, on patrol at the Two Harbors ore docks.

"Jeff, I wonder if you'd have a minute to stop by my office before your shift's done. We've got to decide what to do about Skinny's truck."

Shortly before Deidre was ready to close up shop for the day, Jeff knocked on her door and walked in without waiting for an invitation. He sat down with a sigh. "These ten hour shifts are killers when nothing's going on, but I'm not complaining. After last summer, you and I have had enough excitement to last a lifetime, don't you think?"

Deidre nodded.

"Did you find out anything about Skinny?" she inquired.

"Not a thing. Seems like nobody's seen him for a week or so. How about you?"

"About a week ago he was at Friendly Jane's, and the same night he drove by Terry's place. Actually, he stopped in the parking lot but didn't go in. On the way to Isabella this morning, I stopped at his truck and looked it over. I found one shoe. More troubling, I found a small plastic bag with a white powder in it. I sent it in to be analyzed. Should have the results back in a day or two. Do you know if Skinny was a heavy user?"

Jeff looked surprised. "I don't think he ever used. Not that he hasn't, but all I ever heard about him was that he couldn't lay off the beer and booze. I can check around to see if anybody knows anything about him being on drugs."

Deidre scribbled a message to herself on a notepad.

"I was thinking what would have happened to him if he had wandered away from his pickup that night. His truck went into the ditch near a big beaver pond. What if he stumbled into it while he was drunk and drowned? I know those ponds are filled with leeches. Terry told me one time that he traps his own, and his favorite places are those same kinds of ponds. When I was at Terry's, I looked into one of his bait tanks. There must have been a thousand leeches in it, and he threw in a few fish heads to feed them. It was one of the grossest things I've seen. The leeches were all over the heads, slithering into every hole and crease. I almost lost my lunch right there. If Skinny fell into one of those ponds and drowned, he's probably on his way to being skeletonized by now. It's a pretty gruesome thought, I know, but it could have happened."

Jeff wrinkled up his nose. "Sounds like a job for Search and Rescue if you ask me," he chuckled. "Seriously, why don't we have them go up there tomorrow and drag the pond? If he's in there, they should be able to find him, even if they only find bones."

Deidre jotted another note to herself and glanced at the wall clock. "Quitting time, let's get out of here."

She locked her office door behind them as they left.

DEIDRE PULLED INTO THE SPACE by her garage and parked alongside the car already there. She had expected John a little later, but then she looked at her watch. She was the late one. She took her time walking up the curving sidewalk bordered by a variety of irises. Along the way she stopped by a peony bush and stooped to smell the bloom. How things had changed over the past year.

John Erickson, the FBI agent with whom she had worked on the terrorist case, had started out as a burr under her saddle. Her first impression of him was that he was another male chauvinist who thought women should be relegated to domestic duties. Deidre smiled when she thought how wrong her first impression had been.

Over the course of the terrorist operation, she had come to realize he was a caring and trustworthy man, someone she could be close to, someone who would not expect her to give up her personhood. During the months of the investigation, she had realized she was falling in love for the first time.

Then came the day when her path converged with the path of a known terrorist, and she was forced into a deadly conflict at Gooseberry State Park. During the melee that ensued, she had been seriously wounded. Her last memory of that day was of John cradling her in his arms and saying, "No, not now."

But she survived the near-fatal gunshot wound and had been hospitalized for weeks afterward. The two discovered they shared more than a working relationship, and now they shared a lot of time together. They were what some called an item.

As Deidre moved up the path, she noticed her neighbor's curtain pulled back a crack. Mrs. Olson kept an eye on everything that happened. Deidre waved, and the curtain dropped back into place.

She picked a few flowers to put on the supper table, humming a tune softly to herself. She had planted several types of flowers so no matter what part of the growing season, something was in bloom. Today, they were irises, and she cut off several of the long-stemmed blooms, enjoying the peace and beauty of her backyard.

Deidre opened the back door to her house. As she walked into the kitchen, she saw John bent over the range, intent on whatever he was stirring. He turned and smiled.

"I got here before you, so I thought I'd throw supper together for us. Remember what you fixed the first night I came over? We had stroganoff. That's what I fixed tonight. Hope that's okay?"

Deidre placed the flowers on the counter and hugged him from behind. "Perfect," she said as she laid her head on his back.

The evening went far better than the first time John had been to her home. That night they had gotten into a squabble over work and jurisdiction. It ended with Deidre asking him to leave. This night their parting was difficult, and John stayed much later than he had intended.

"How about lunch tomorrow?" he asked as he was about to leave.

"I don't think I can," Deidre answered, an exaggerated pout on her face. "I've got something to try to clear up tomorrow. It's probably nothing, but I have to check it out to be sure.

"I'd like to go out for supper, though. How about that gourmet place down the shore? I'll buy."

"Sounds good," John responded. "I'll meet you at six, but I'm buying."

"We'll see," Deidre challenged him, and they hugged.

Chapter Five

Early in the morning Deidre called the captain of the Lake County Search and Rescue Team. The phone rang several times before he picked up.

"Hey, Scott," she greeted him. "Is there any chance you could spare this afternoon to do some search work? We haven't had any luck tracking down a missing person. His truck's sitting up on the Whyte Road near a fairly large beaver pond. I'm wondering if you could go up there and drag it to see if he might have fallen in."

Scott jumped at the opportunity. "Anything to get away from this office," he said. "We'll try to get there by noon, but we might be a little late. What kind of equipment do you think we'll need? If it's a beaver pond, I assume our big rig won't be of much use."

Deidre thought for a moment. "Make sure you bring hip boots for each person. There isn't much of a bottom in those ponds. I think you can get a fourteen-foot aluminum boat to the water. That'd give you a stable enough platform to work from. Other than that, just your dragging hooks, I guess."

Deidre knew Scott well. He was in his element when he could be outside, no matter what the circumstances. She knew he'd be prompt and eager to spend the time doing what he considered meaningful work.

"Good, I'm going to call Denny's Towing and have him pull the pickup back to town, so I'll meet you up there."

Before she could hang up, Scott asked, "Can you tell me who you're looking for, or is that confidential?"

"No, that's okay," Deidre answered. "The truck belongs to Skinny Tomlinson. I'm afraid he might have driven into the ditch while he was drunk, got mixed up, and fallen into the pond."

"I know Skinny," Scott laughed. "He's probably drunker than a skunk and holed up some place. He'll come crawling out of the woods when he hasn't got anything left to drink."

Deidre leaned back in her chair. "That's what everybody says, but we have to make an effort to find him. It's only right."

She said goodbye to Scott and hung up. Then she opened a folder on her desk marked "Jill Marie Moore." Inside were two reports, one from the county coroner, the other an ER report.

JILL MOORE HAD LEFT HOME at nine o'clock in the evening. Her parents had asked where she was going and she had responded, "With friends."

They pushed the issue. "What friends, and where are you going?"

"Just friends," she snapped back at them. "We're going to ride around." She slammed the door, stomped down the steps to the sidewalk, and got in a car that peeled away, leaving burn marks on the street.

Mr. and Mrs. Moore looked at each other in despair. Jill had become so irritable and short with them lately, and frankly, they felt they had lost control of their only child.

After a moment's silence, Mrs. Moore laid her head on her husband's shoulder. "We've got to stop fooling ourselves. Our daughter shows all the signs of using some kind of drug. Her physical appearance and behavior have changed so fast. You know it as well as I do. What are we going to do?" she blurted out between sobs.

"There's only one thing to do, confront her. I've put off saying this for too long, not wanting to cause you distress, but I think we have to set up an intervention group. Do you agree?"

Mrs. Moore nodded.

By ten o'clock, Mr. Moore had called his friend, who was the director of Human Services for Lake County. He in turn had called the Moores' pastor, two of Jill's teachers, the principal of her school, and a personal friend, a recovering alcoholic who was skilled at leading intervention groups. Even though it was quick notice, all agreed to meet at the Moores' home at noon the next day.

Shortly after eleven that night, before they had gone to bed, the parents heard a car pull up in front of their house. They heard a car door open. Mr. Moore rushed to the window in time to see his daughter either fall out of or be pushed from the car. She crumpled in a heap on the boulevard grass, and the car sped away before he could recover from his shock and before he got a good look at it.

Both parents rushed out to help their daughter, but she was totally unresponsive to their revival attempts. Mr. Moore swept his daughter up in his arms and carried her to their car. Mrs. Moore cradled her daughter in her arms as they rushed to the hospital which was only a few blocks away.

Once again, Mr. Moore took his daughter in his arms and carried her into the ER.

"Anyone, we need help right now!" he screamed. "My daughter's had a seizure, and I'm afraid she is dying. Help us!"

An attendant on duty grabbed a gurney and wheeled it over to where Mr. Moore stood. They placed her on the white-sheeted stretcher and wheeled it down the hall and into an unoccupied room.

The nurse on duty buzzed for the doctor and his team, reporting a code blue.

The Moores were swept aside as a young doctor and a crew of three nurses quickly split open Jill's clothing, allowing them access to her chest.

"Her pulse is 150 and irregular," one nurse reported. "BP 200 over 100 and rising."

Another nurse had already started an IV, and the doctor ordered medication meant to decrease Jill's heart rate and lower her blood pressure. Still, her vital signs continued to be out of control. Before an hour had passed, Jill died on the table in front of her parents, and the medical team stood with their heads bowed in silence. They had failed.

After escorting Jill's parents to a waiting room where a nurse stayed with them, the ER doctor called the coroner.

"Per, we had a young lady die in ER tonight. I think you should come take a look. Several things don't seem right for a seventeen-year-old. I've recorded the time of death but haven't put down a cause yet. I want your opinion before I put my name on this one."

The doctor listened for several seconds, and then spoke into the phone. "Thanks, Per. Fifteen minutes? I'll be here when you arrive."

DEIDRE LOOKED AT THE PICTURE of the girl stapled to the upper left-hand corner of the manila folder. She sighed. Jill was shown smiling broadly, her teeth gleaming white, and her long blond hair shining in the camera flash. Deidre thought she was beautiful.

She lifted out the ER report and studied the notations. The report began with a series of routine questions answered by the admitting nurse.

Under the section labeled "vital statistics" was a type-written paragraph.

The patient was admitted to the Lake Side Hospital ER in a comatose state. Her parents were present. The patient's temperature was acutely high and her respiration more than twice what is normal for a girl her age. The patient's blood pressure as recorded was dangerously high, and the patient's body did not respond to attempts to lower her BP. The patient exhibited muscle tremors consistent with convulsive motion. It was noted that the patient was sweating profusely. The patient went into cardiac arrest, and attempts to resuscitate her were unsuccessful. Noted was a bruise surrounding a small puncture wound consistent with a needle mark on the inside of her left forearm, proximal to her elbow.

Deidre put aside the ER report and picked up the hand-written page from the coroner's office. Some of the data overlapped with that of the ER staff, but one line in the summary stood out.

The finding of this office is that symptoms prior to death are consistent with a drug overdose, specifically methamphetamine. A blood sample has been sent to the State Crime Lab for toxicology testing. The results of such testing are expected back in six weeks, at which time an official cause of death will be entered.

Deidre laid the paper down and closed the folder. She lifted the phone receiver and called the Moores. Mr. Moore answered.

"This is Sheriff Johnson," Deidre began. "First, let me offer my deepest condolences for your loss. I know I can speak for all of the staff in my office in saying how sorry we are concerning your daughter's death."

Mr. Moore didn't respond, so Deidre continued.

"I would like to speak with you and your wife about the circumstances that led up to your taking Jill to the hospital. Would it be all right if I came to your home later this afternoon?"

After clearing his throat, Mr. Moore said, "Today would be a bad day. We have relatives traveling to be with us, and they'll be arriving about that time. Could you come tomorrow mid-morning?"

Deidre could sense the man's pain, and it troubled her to be infringing on his privacy. "Of course, would ten-thirty be okay with you?"

He answered with his voice barely audible. "Yes. Thank you for your concern," and Deidre heard the click as he hung up.

Chapter Six

DEIDRE PULLED OFF THE HIGHWAY onto the Whyte Road at eleven forty-five. Slowing to a crawl to avoid damaging her Explorer, she drove over the pitted and rock-strewn road and reached Skinny's truck fifteen minutes later. Scott and the Search and Rescue Team hadn't arrived yet, so she stepped out of her truck with the thought of soaking up the sights and smells of the forest.

As she slowly walked up the road, the wind caused a loose piece of paper to fly up and catch on an overhanging branch of a jack pine. Deidre pulled it from the tree and was ready to crumple it, but before she could, she realized it was a blank sales receipt. At the top of the document was the name of a company: ED'S PLUMBING CONTRACTING.

Deidre thought it odd that Ed would recently have driven this back road. She placed the receipt in a plastic bag and put it in her SUV. It wasn't much, but it was something she would want to check out.

The rattle of vehicles coming down the road caused Deidre to turn. She saw Scott and his crew approaching in their orange-colored vehicles. One pulled a boat trailer that swayed from side to side each time it traversed a hole in the road, and water from the puddles sprayed outward from the wheels. Bringing up the rear of the parade was Denny's tow truck.

Scott rolled down his window. "I guess we're pretty close to being on time. So this is where Skinny went in. I'd say that's one big beaver pond. I've seen lakes smaller than this."

Deidre smiled. "Thanks for coming at the drop of a hat, Scott. You might have trouble getting to the water with your boat. There's a lot of mud to wade through. I hope your guys brought hip boots, or it's going to be a long, smelly ride home."

"Looks like loon shit to me," Scott added, referring to the decaying mass of vegetation that always accumulated on the bottom of beaver ponds. In most cases it was several feet thick and reeked of decomposition.

Deidre had to laugh. "I wanted to say that, but I didn't want you to think I was crude."

The banter continued as the crew removed the retaining straps from the boat and hoisted it off the trailer rack. It was a fourteen-foot aluminum boat, one that four men could easily lift and carry. They set the boat down, donned their waders, and lifted the boat again. Deidre didn't volunteer. She had no desire to wade through the muck of the beaver pond.

The four-man team made their way down the bank to the water's edge. The boat was not heavy, but the footing was difficult, and they took turns stumbling over humps of sedge and other lowland plants.

"Damn, this stuff is hard," one of the men cursed as he sprawled on his hands and knees, dropping his corner of the boat. "Why didn't you tell me we'd be in a beaver pond? I would'a stayed home."

Scott laughed. "I didn't tell you, 'cause I knew you'd have had an excuse."

The team, lugging the aluminum boat through the muck, reached the water in a few minutes, and Deidre saw them launch the boat.

She turned her attention to Denny, who had backed his wrecker up to the rear of Skinny's truck. He was on his hands and knees looking under the pickup, trying to access the best place to attach his tow cable.

"Do you see anything under there that looks at all suspicious?" she wanted to know.

"Can't see a thing," he grunted back. "The edge of the road got scraped clean when he nosed over." Denny stood up. "I think the best way to get it out will be to hook onto the frame and bring it out the way he went in. Once I get it up on the road, maybe you can steer while I pull it back a ways. Give enough room to get my truck up front. Then I'll be able to get the lift under its front wheels."

Deidre had brought the keys to Skinny's pickup with her, and she walked back to her vehicle to retrieve them. As she did, she looked out at the pond. Scott's crew was in the boat, one man pulling on a pair of oars. The others were tossing grappling hooks into the water and slowly pulling them toward the boat.

Scott hollered, "We've just brought up a bone. Looks like it could be a leg bone. There probably are other pieces of the skeleton near the same spot," and he flung the hook out again. This time Deidre could see him bring up an object.

"It's a piece of a spinal column," Scott hollered again, and he tossed the hook into the same area for a third time.

By Scott's reaction, it was plain to Deidre that he had snagged something again, and she watched intently as the object broke the surface of the water. Even from where she stood, she could easily make out a set of antlers attached to a skull.

"Just a damn deer head," Scott yelled to her, a hint of disappointment in his voice.

"You can toss the head but bring in the other bones. Unless Skinny sprouted horns, that's not him," she yelled back. "We should have the others checked out just in case."

Deidre watched for another few seconds as the crew probed more distant parts of the pond, and then she picked up the keys for the stranded pickup. As she walked back to the vehicle, she put on a pair of rubber gloves.

I might have missed something the other day. No use contaminating evidence if I can help it, she thought.

By the time she got there, Denny had already hooked the cable to the pickup's frame.

"I'm all set, Deidre. You'll have to turn on the ignition or the steering wheel will remain locked. Try to start it, if you can. That way it will be easier to maneuver once it's on the road."

Deidre slid into the driver's seat and tried the ignition. The starter motor spun but grabbed nothing. She tried again. This time the worn cogs of the starter caught the flywheel, and the truck's engine turned over enough for it to cough once, backfire, and start. It wasn't running smoothly, threatening to die at any moment, but Deidre kept nursing it back to life with gentle pressure on the gas pedal. She felt the cable from the tow truck tighten, and Skinny's truck slowly moved backwards out of the ditch.

Denny unhooked the cable and motioned for Deidre to pull over to the side. Then he turned his truck around on the narrow road and pulled ahead of her. While he hooked up to the battered old truck so he could tow it into town, Deidre stood off to the side and watched the rescue squad pull the boat back through the muck and up onto the road. She reached inside it and lifted the two pieces of bone, placed them in a clean plastic bag, then stripped off her gloves.

"I doubt if these are human, but we better have an expert check them out," she said to no one in particular. The men were busy trying to remove their waders without getting the smelly muck on themselves. With practiced efficiency, they loaded the boat onto their trailer and cinched it down, then threw the waders into the hull. They had no intention of bringing the smell into the truck's cab.

During the ride back to town, Deidre had time to think about what to do next. She decided she should talk to Ed Beirmont. He fit the description of the man who was with Skinny the night he disappeared, and the sales receipt she had found by Skinny's truck was a link. Not a strong link, but a link.

And she thought of the coming evening with John.

Chapter Seven

THE FEELING DEIDRE HAD as she walked into the restaurant that evening was so different from the first time she and John had dined there. Then, it was all about business. Now, she was hardly able to not run to the table where he sat. She wasn't surprised that her heart did a flip when she saw him.

When John saw her, he stood and took a step toward her, a broad grin on his face. His eyes were fixed on her. He gave Deidre a big hug before helping her to be seated. As they scanned the menu, John reached out and took hold of her hand.

"May I order you something to drink?" he asked.

"The usual," she answered.

A courtly waiter came to their table and asked if they'd like to begin with something from the bar. Wine perhaps?

John answered for both of them. "We'd each like a glass of Riesling, your better wine, Chateau St. Marie."

As the waiter left to get their drinks, John laughed and said, "I guess we're a couple. I even know what you drink." The waiter returned with the wine, and they lifted their glasses in a toast.

"To us."

"To us," Deidre echoed.

After dinner, they ordered dessert and talked for a half-hour over cooled cups of coffee. Deidre objected, but John paid the bill. He agreed to allow her to leave the tip, and the hostess thanked them as they walked out the door.

Once they were outside, Deidre stopped, breathed in the fresh air wafting off Lake Superior, and looked at the golden orb of a moon rising over the lake.

"There's a paved path down to the Lake Walk. The night is so beautiful, why don't we take a stroll along the shore?" John suggested.

Hand-in-hand, they made their way down to the boardwalk at the water's edge. They walked in silence for many minutes.

Suddenly, John stopped and wrapped his arms around Deidre, and she looked up into his face. "I don't know what I'd do without you," he said. "That day you were shot, I thought I'd lost you forever. All I can remember is cradling you and rocking back and forth. I was almost paralyzed with fear. If Ben hadn't taken over, I don't know what would have happened."

Deidre held her fingers to his lips. "That's in the past, John. Let's move on and not look back. The important thing is that we're here, and everything is about as perfect as it can be."

"I know," John said, still holding her close. "But every day I worry about what you might be facing. The law enforcement field is changing so fast. It seems that every day I read about a small town cop being ambushed by some wacko. Please don't take any chances. Okay? That's all I ask."

"John, what happened last year was a one-in-a-million case. I'll probably work until I retire and never encounter what happened last summer again. But I will be careful, I promise," and she squeezed him tightly.

WHEN SHE WOKE THE NEXT MORNING, the glow still hadn't worn off, and Deidre moved around her kitchen humming a show tune. Then she remembered her scheduled meeting with the Moores, and the glow went out.

She made toast and washed it down with a cup of coffee. As she got ready for work, she pondered what to say to the grieving parents. Halfway through brushing her teeth, she lowered her toothbrush, looked in the mirror, and said, "Damn it all, anyway!"

Deidre stopped at her office and straightened her desk. When her deputies had all arrived, she conducted the morning debriefing and then looked through Jill's file folder again.

At ten-thirty, Deidre pulled up in front of the Moores' home. It was laborious getting out of her Explorer, and even more difficult to climb the cement steps leading up the bank from the boulevard to their front door. Hesitantly, she rang the bell. Mr. Moore answered it and invited her in.

Every seat in the living room was occupied, and Deidre assumed the people were relatives and friends. Mr. Moore introduced them one by one. When he finished, he looked at his wife.

"I think it'd be best if we went into the den, don't you, dear?"

Mrs. Moore only nodded and then wiped her nose with a well-used tissue. She stood, appearing to be unsteady on her feet, and walked into the adjoining room. Mr. Moore signaled for Deidre to follow her. He came quietly behind and closed the heavy wooden door.

The den was comfortable. A sofa rested under the window, with two lounging chairs, one on either side. Mrs. Moore sat down on one end of the sofa, and Mr. Moore motioned for Deidre to sit on the other. He pulled up a straight-back chair so the three could face each other and converse.

Deidre spoke first. "Mr. and Mrs. Moore—" but before she could finish he interrupted.

"Please, Sheriff, call us Lydia and Mike. This is going to be hard enough without formalities. We appreciate that this must be a difficult task for you."

Deidre started over. "Lydia and Mike, I am so sorry for what's happened. Your grief is beyond my comprehension, but please realize, I have to ask you some questions, some that might seem hurtful. Forgive me for making you go through this again."

Lydia looked catatonic. Her eyes were sunken and her face had a flat affect. She looked washed out, colorless, lifeless.

Deidre said, "I have some personal questions to ask you about Jill, and I'd appreciate your answering as honestly as you can."

Both Lydia and Mike pursed their lips but nodded.

"Can you tell me what your relationship with your daughter was like?"

The pair sat in silence, and Deidre didn't rush them. She allowed the seconds to pass until it seemed the Moores might not be able to utter one word. Then Lydia spoke first, her voice quavering. "We loved her so much." She buried her face in her hands, her shoulders convulsing, and then looked up. "She was a wonderful child, always happy, always lively. When she was in elementary school, her teachers always commented on how bright and alert she was, and how kind she was to others. When she was in middle school we received the same reports. Other students seemed to be attracted to her, because she was friendly toward them, even the most unpopular classmates." Lydia blew her nose. "At home she was always smiling. She'd hug us and tell us how much she loved us. That's how she was until part way through this past school year. Between Thanksgiving and Christmas she started to change." Lydia's chin puckered and her words quit flowing.

Deidre waited.

"About that time we noticed a change in Jill," Mike continued for his wife. She seldom smiled, and began spending most of her time alone in her room. We found out she'd broken up with her boyfriend and assumed that was the problem. When Lydia tried to comfort her, Jill said she didn't care about him and to get off her back."

Deidre interrupted. "Will you tell me the name of Jill's ex-boyfriend?"

Mike nodded. "Peter, Peter Wilson. They had so much fun together, always on the go to this or that school event. We liked him very much."

Deidre wrote his name down in her notebook.

Mike continued. "Things went from bad to worse. Jill became more morose and withdrawn, and her mother and I felt like we were losing touch with her. By March she hardly talked to us. At mealtimes she'd push the food around on her plate and leave it hardly eaten."

Mike stopped to regain his composure.

Deidre cleared her throat and asked, "Did she still associate with her friends?"

Lydia shook her head. "That's when we really began to worry. She used to be so popular. Her friends were always here, eating and playing games or studying. By mid-winter, we never saw them anymore. They just stopped coming. I asked Jill about them, but she'd snarl at me, tell me to keep my nose out of her life. When I tried to press the issue, she became even more belligerent and stomped out the door." She used the damp tissue.

After a moment, Lydia continued. "Not long ago we saw her leaning into an open car window and talking to what looked to be an older man. They looked like they were arguing. When Jill came home that evening, I asked her who she'd been talking to. All she said was, 'A friend,' and continued up the stairs to her room. I heard her slam her bedroom door.

"The evening she died, Mike and I had decided we needed to confront her about the possibility that she was using drugs. With the help of the county's Human Resource Office, we had set up an intervention to be held at noon the next day. If only we had acted sooner, she might still be alive."

Lydia broke down and wept into the soggy tissue.

Deidre sat quietly to allow both parents to gather themselves. She asked as gently as she could, "Can you describe the car Jill was leaning on, or can you tell me anything about the man driving the car?"

They both shook their heads.

"If you can, I'd like you to write down the names of Jill's friends."

Mike walked over to his desk and picked up a pad of paper.

"We thought you'd want to speak with her friends, so we made a list this morning while my brother and his wife were in the kitchen fixing breakfast. As for a description of the man, from the angle we were looking, we couldn't see inside the car. The other windows weren't rolled down and were darkly tinted. We really couldn't see much at all."

Deidre noted that on her tablet. "Thank you so much for taking the time to see me this morning," she said gently. "We'll keep you informed about any developments as far as Jill's death is concerned. Her toxicology report should be ready in a little over five weeks. Then we'll have a definite answer about the cause of death. You do know that the coroner suspects her death was caused by a drug overdose, don't you?"

"Yes, we read that in the newspaper. I suppose the reporter was only doing his job, but it was hurtful to see it in print."

Mike put his arms around Lydia, and she wept onto his shoulder. Deidre thanked them again and said she could let herself out.

Chapter Eight

Deidre descended the steps from the Moores' home with her head down. The anguish displayed by the parents made her visit one of the worst she had experienced during her career as a law enforcement officer. Her mind was on their pain as she pulled away from the curb and headed out of town to Ed Beirmont's place on the lake.

As she pulled into his driveway, a huge dog, a Great Dane she thought, came bounding out to greet her. Deidre opened her window a crack, gingerly stuck her fingers through the opening, and was rewarded by the feel of the dog's tongue eagerly licking them. Its tail was wagging so hard his whole body moved with it. Deidre pushed the door open against the dog's bulk. It was tall enough to look her in the eye through the driver's-side window.

Just as she was about to step out of the car, Ed poked his head out of his warehouse. "Sam, get over here, now!" he yelled at the dog, and Sam loped over to his master, who ruffled his ears. It was evident there was a bond between the two.

"Hi, Ed," Deidre said extending her hand, "I'm Sheriff Deidre Johnson. Do you have a few minutes? I'd like to ask you a question or two, if you don't mind."

Ed shook her hand, his large mitt engulfing hers. "Of course," he answered, looking down at her and squarely into her eyes. "Let's go up to my porch where we can sit down."

Sam bounded ahead and up the stairs to the deck before them. It was clear who ruled the roost in this house. Ed indicated with a sweep of his hand for Deidre to take a seat, and she sat facing the lake. The view was phenomenal.

"So, what do want to know, Sheriff?"

"For the past week, we've been trying to discover the whereabouts of George Tomlinson. Most people around here call him Skinny. He's been seen riding around with you quite often, and I thought you might have some idea if he's out of town."

"Yeah, I pick up Skinny once in a while. He's a pretty lonely guy. Funny, when somebody with few social graces is ignored they respond by becoming even more obnoxious. If you get Skinny away from the bars and talk to him, he really isn't all that bad of a guy. I haven't seen him for a few days myself. Do you think something's happened to him?" Ed looked concerned.

"We don't know. His pickup was found in the ditch off the Whyte Road, and he hasn't been seen since. I know he's done this kind of thing before, but he's never dropped out of sight this long.

"I had a talk with Friendly Jane. She says she saw you get in the truck with Skinny, and he drove away. Do you remember that?"

Ed puffed out his cheeks before he answered. "That was the last time I saw him. I stopped to have a beer on my way home from fishing, and Skinny was staggering out of the tavern. He was in no shape to drive home, so I made up an excuse to go with him, told him that the battery of my pickup was dead.

"But when he started out, he turned onto Highway 2 going the opposite way from town. I thought he was so blitzed he didn't know where he was, but he wanted to take the roundabout way through Whyte. I tried to get him to let me drive, but he kicked me out of his truck at Terry's tavern, said to find another ride home. He told me he was heading for the Whyte."

"Did anyone see you fishing?" Deidre wanted to know.

"There wasn't anyone else on the lake. I was up at Silver Island. Not many people get back there, especially late in the evening. It was dark by the time I came off the lake."

"One last thing, Ed. When I was waiting for the tow truck by Skinny's pickup, the wind kicked up a piece of paper, and I picked it up. It was a blank sales receipt, one of yours. Were you with Skinny when his truck went into the ditch?"

Ed looked Deidre square in the face, and without hesitating, answered, "No. I told you, he kicked me out of his truck at Terry's. I caught a ride back to Friendly's place and took my truck home."

Deidre studied him for a moment, and he didn't flinch. "How do you suppose a copy of your sales receipt ended up by his truck?"

"That I can't answer," Ed stated flatly, still looking directly at Deidre.

She stood and offered her hand again, this time not shocked at its size.

"Thanks, Ed. Let me know if Skinny shows up on your doorstep," and she walked down the stairs to her SUV.

SHE HARDLY HAD ENOUGH TIME to return to her office and sit down when her phone rang.

"Hello, Sheriff Johnson speaking."

"Good afternoon, Sheriff. This is Mac McAlpine from the Lake Superior Drug and Gang Task Force in Duluth calling. How are things on your end of the district?"

Mac was a detective who had worked for the Duluth police force for twenty years, but three years ago he took on a new responsibility. He still worked out of the Duluth office but now was in charge of an area that covered approximately a quarter of the state. His salary was paid by tax dollars from four counties, and his force consisted of members of the Duluth SWAT team when he needed them, three of his own officers, and sometimes officers "on loan" from other forces. Deidre was on good terms with Mac. Her office and his had worked together on four sting operations since she had become sheriff.

Deidre knew this wasn't a social call, but she answered his inquiry about Lake County's goings on. "Not too bad, something every day, but overall, pretty calm. What's up with this call? I assume you aren't totally interested in what's happening in Lake County."

Mac cleared his throat. "I heard you had a death the other night in Two Harbors due to a probable overdose. Have you discovered anything we might be interested in hearing about?"

Deidre paused. "We can't move too fast until the tox screen gets back. I've started to put together a profile of the dead girl, and we'll certainly share the info with you. Jeff, Deputy DeAngelo, is our liaison to your group. I think you meet next week, if my calendar is correct. He'll be there."

Mac wasn't done. "I'm wondering if I could meet with the two of you before then to discuss a matter of mutual concern. If I drive up tomorrow, could we meet in your office?"

There goes my lunch hour, she thought. "Sure, that would be okay. I have an hour free from twelve o'clock to one, if that fits your schedule."

Mac agreed, and Deidre jotted down a note to herself to talk to Jeff about the meeting.

CHAPTER NINE

THE NEXT MORNING DEIDRE CALLED the high school office, asking permission to speak to a number of students, including Peter Wilson, Jill's ex-boyfriend. At first the principal was reluctant to talk with her.

"I'm not sure you can do that without parental permission," he hedged. "I could get in serious trouble if we start giving out their schedules and pulling them from class. Why do you want to speak with them?"

Deidre was used to people stonewalling her. "There's no need to worry. I'm not trying to interrogate any of them, and it's their choice if they want to speak to me. All I'm looking for is some background information concerning Jill Moore."

"Ah, yes" the principal intoned. "That poor girl. Have the doctors determined what kind of seizure she suffered? "

Deidre played along. "No, the final report won't be complete for a few weeks."

"I suppose it'll be all right, but each student must be informed they don't have to talk to you."

Deidre agreed, and after driving to the outskirts of Two Harbors where the school was located, she walked into the principal's office.

"Hi, Deidre," the secretary greeted her. "The principal said you'd be here, but I didn't think it'd be this quickly. Is something serious going on?"

"No," Deidre lied. "Just a minor incident I'd like to get a handle on. Would you give me these students' schedules, and I'll find them?" she said as she handed her a list.

It took the secretary a few minutes to pull the files up on her computer and print them off. She filled the time by talking. “Isn’t it a shame about Jill Moore? I’m sure her parents are heartbroken.” She continued to prattle on. “Whatever could have caused a young girl to die so suddenly of a stroke? Just bad luck, I guess.”

Deidre didn’t take time to correct her. Rumors were going to fly in a small town, and she couldn’t stop them. The secretary handed Deidre the schedules. “They’re all in school today, so you should be able to find them without much difficulty.”

“Thanks,” Deidre answered and started down the hall.

First on her list was Peter, and she knocked on the door to the biology lab where he was in the process of dissecting a frog. The teacher answered and called over her shoulder. “Peter Wilson, someone is here to see you.”

Peter came to the door with a bewildered look on his face.

“Hi, Peter. I’m Sheriff Johnson. I’d like you to come with me to the guidance counselor’s office. I have a couple of questions I’d like to ask you about Jill Moore. I think it’d be best if we spoke somewhere in private.”

Deidre saw tears well up in Peter’s eyes, but she couldn’t tell if they were tears of grief or fear. He followed her down the hall.

In the private meeting room, Peter took a seat. He was nervous and fidgety, looking at the tabletop and picking at his fingernails.

“Try to relax, Peter. You’re in no trouble. I only want to find out about Jill, what kind of person she was, what kind of friend. I know it’ll be difficult to talk about her, but please bear with me. Also, I’ve been asked to tell you you can return to class if you’re uncomfortable speaking with me. You aren’t required to answer my questions.”

Peter looked up and tried to smile. “No, that’s okay. I’ll try to answer your questions as best I can, but you must realize, I have,” and he paused, “I had lost touch with Jill these last few months.”

"I understand you and Jill were considered to be going together, boyfriend and girlfriend. Is that right?"

Peter nodded without raising his eyes.

"How long did that relationship last?"

"We started going together in seventh grade. Not really going together, I suppose, but you know, we were really good friends. Then as we got older and could go out on dates, we were together most of the time, at least until last fall," Peter said in a barely audible voice.

"Then what happened?" Deidre pushed him.

"I don't know. Jill seemed to not be herself. We used to have so much fun together, but then she became irritable and cranky. She'd go off like a bomb over the least little thing. A couple of times I saw her riding around with some guys I didn't know, and when I asked her about them, she started screaming at me that I didn't own her, and it was none of my business.

"After that I stayed away from her, and she never talked to me again, no 'goodbye' or 'I'm sorry' or anything." Peter sobbed into his hands, and Deidre shoved a box of tissues toward him.

"I know this is tough, but I have one more question. Do you think Jill was using drugs?"

Peter looked up. "I don't know anything about drugs." Deidre noticed how his eyes darted away from her to the corner of the room. "I suppose she could have, but I doubt it," he mumbled and hung his head again.

"Thanks for your help, Peter. Why don't you go to the washroom and rinse your face. Then you can return to class."

Deidre followed him to the door, then walked down the hall to find the first of Jill's girlfriends on her list. The girl, Amanda, looked shocked when she saw who wanted to speak to her. She and Deidre went to the same office, where she had spoken with Peter.

"Amanda, I'm Sheriff Johnson," she introduced herself. Amanda squirmed. "Please try to relax. You're not in trouble. I just want to ask you some questions about your friend, Jill. I'm so sorry about what happened to her. You must miss her very much."

Amanda burst into tears before Deidre could begin her questioning.

"Try to calm down, Amanda." She waited until the sobs turned to sniffles. "I understand you and Jill were close friends. Is that right?"

Amanda nodded. She blew her nose and said, "We were. I haven't seen much of her for a few months, even though we were in many of the same classes."

"Can you tell me what happened that caused the two of you to drift apart?"

Amanda shrugged. "I guess she found new friends or something. We didn't have much to talk about anymore."

"This is a sensitive question. Did Jill use drugs?"

Amanda's eyes opened wide. "No," she blurted out "and neither do I."

"No one's accusing you of using, but Jill showed many signs of having started. Why do you think Jill wasn't?"

Like Peter had done before her, Amanda broke off eye contact. "I just don't think so."

For the rest of the morning, Deidre questioned one former friend after another. Two of them, when they were told they didn't have to speak to her, requested that Deidre allow them to return to class. By the time she finished with the last name on her list, she knew no more than when she had started. Everyone agreed Jill's personality had changed last fall, but no one would admit to a suspicion she was using drugs. To Deidre, it was almost as though they were afraid to say anything about the subject.

By noon Deidre was back in her office. Jeff was waiting for her, as was Mac MacAlpine, the head of the Lake Superior Drug and Gang Task Force. The receptionist had poured each of them a cup of coffee and let them into Deidre's office. They put their cups down and stood to meet her.

"Hi, guys. Sorry I'm a few minutes late, but there were a number of people for me to interview today. So what can we do for you today, Mac?" she said getting straight to the point.

"Well, I heard through the grapevine you paid a visit to Ed Beirmont yesterday. From what I heard it made him pretty nervous."

"Maybe he should be," Deidre said, her eyes narrowing.

"Why? What's he done that you're interested in him?"

Deidre felt her face beginning to flush, something she didn't like, but she disliked being put on the spot for her investigative work even more. "Why are you asking about a case in Lake County?" she parried.

"Look, Deidre. I'll meet you straight on. The Task Force has been working on what we suspect is an extensive drug operation in the area. It involves a gang from Chicago that moved part of its operation to Minneapolis. It has spread its range to St. Cloud and Duluth. Now we suspect something significant is going on in the wilderness north of here. Ed is a person of interest to us. He set himself up in Two Harbors. If you have proof of his being involved in that girl's death, by all means arrest him. But if you don't have a rock solid case against him, leave him alone."

Deidre blinked. "Um, Mac, that's not why I went to see him. We have a man who's been missing for a week. His truck was found in a ditch on an almost abandoned road north of here. All indications are that Ed Beirmont was the last to see him before he disappeared. Also, I found a paper from Ed's sales receipt book by the truck. That's what I talked to him about."

"Have you found a body or any evidence of a crime having been committed? Second, even if you do, do you have any direct evidence that this guy Beirmont is involved? Just what are you thinking of charging him with?"

The air between them was beginning to become charged.

"Do you expect me to just forget about a possible missing person?"

"I'm not saying that, Deidre. If you have solid evidence Beirmont committed a crime, arrest him. Otherwise, please don't push him too hard. This is one person we don't want to scare off. We think Beirmont is up to his eyeballs with this drug ring. We hope he'll lead us to bigger fish. If you keep hounding his hind end, he might get nervous and pull out of here. Then we'd have to start over. All I'm saying is keep an eye on him, but don't try strong-arm tactics. This guy's been around the block a few times, and he covers his backside really well. I'm asking that you back off unless you're dead certain he's done something to your missing man. Agreed?"

Deidre let out her breath. *The same thing all over again.* "So you want me to back away and cool my heels while you people come in and do all the work?" she asked, her voice rising.

"No, not at all, Deidre. We want to work jointly with you on this problem. I know you have other cases on your plate, but we need each other on this one. We need you to continue investigating your missing person, as well as the possible death by overdose of the girl. Just be sensitive about Ed's situation, and please keep us informed. Your department has strengths in your area, just as we have assets that can be valuable to you as well. Both sides will benefit if we work together rather than each doing our own thing. Agreed?"

Without waiting for her answer, Mac stood and extended his hand. "Thanks, Deidre. Let's start meeting on a regular basis. I'll call next week, and we can arrange another meeting if it seems warranted—that is, if it's okay with you."

Deidre shook his hand and walked him to the door. When he had left, she turned to Jeff. "Well, you were certainly talkative today."

"I thought you two heavyweights did just fine," he grinned. "We can work with them, believe me."

CHAPTER TEN

JILL'S FUNERAL WAS HELD ON THE WEDNESDAY following her death. As expected, it was a sad affair attended by hundreds of friends and relatives. The grief of her former friends, Peter, Amanda, and the others, was inconsolable, and they wept openly during the service. Afterward they stayed together in a small cluster, talking in lowered voices. Every few seconds one of them would give a furtive glance over his or her shoulder as if expecting someone to be eavesdropping on their conversation.

The next week Deidre received a report from the lab about the small plastic bag of white powder she had found in Skinny's truck. It contained cocaine that had been cut to dilute its potency.

Five weeks after Skinny disappeared and Jill died, Skinny had still not been found, neither dead nor alive. It was as though he had dropped off the face of the earth.

Deidre found a note on her desk when she returned to her office one day. It read:

Deidre, the tox results came in on Jill Moore. Stop by Per Johnson's as soon as you get the chance. You'll be interested.

She had known Per from the time she was a little girl. He didn't fit the image of a coroner at all. He was almost as large around his belly as he was tall, and he laughed at every joke, and better yet, remembered them all. But he was good at what he did, and Deidre thought his effervescence was at times a diversion from the tragedies he often encountered.

She walked down the street to his office. He was an old physician who had retained his independent status, refusing to join with any clinic. Per was near retirement and treated his long-faithful patients, not taking on any new ones. His office was empty when she walked into the waiting room.

"Well, Deidre, how are you? Glad you could stop by. Have a seat," he said, motioning to a chair by his desk. "I know you'll want to get this over with as soon as we can. Here is the report on Jill's tests."

As Deidre craned her neck sideways to read the report, Per insisted on reading it aloud. There were several bits of data that were of no interest to her, glucose level, uric acid level, and the like.

Deidre's eyes scanned down the page ahead of what Per was reading. Alcohol: 0.00, cocaine: trace, methamphetamines—Deidre's eyes widened in surprise. The quantity was double anything she had seen recorded. The report summarized the data, "Cause of death: four times the lethal dosage."

Deidre let the air out of her lungs. She looked at Per, who had just finished his oral reading. He shook his head. "Things are different than they used to be. This job used to be interesting, but not anymore. It hurts so much to see young lives wasted, ended for no reason. Used to be, the only thing I was called out for was to verify the death of someone who had died alone. Now it's murder, drug cases like this, suicides." He shook his head again.

Per chuckled. "I remember many years ago when I got a call placed from Big Jimbo's tavern up in Brimson. There were two bachelor brothers who lived in a shack up there, foul-smelling guys who drank way too much. It was the first of the month, when they would have just received their assistance checks, or maybe it was

Social Security. Well, I guess it really doesn't matter one way or the other. One of them called me—it was about eleven o'clock at night. He was crying and carrying on, and I eventually made out that his brother had died. He wanted me to come up and verify the death so the body could be taken to the funeral home. He was calling from Big Jimbo's, because they had no phone in their shack, or electricity for that matter.

"Well, I dressed and drove all the way up to Brimson, picked him up at the tavern, and drove to their shack. He led the way, and I came behind with a flashlight. Remember, they didn't have electricity. We got into their cabin, and the stench was almost more than I could take, smelled like someone had been dead in there for a week. Sure enough, there lay his brother on his bed, his hands folded on his chest as if he were ready for the casket.

"I shined my light on his face, and one eye popped open and looked at me. The brother who had called me let out a whoop. 'Hallelujah,' he screamed. 'My brother's been resurrected. I sure never thought he'd make it.'

"I couldn't stop laughing. The dead man had received his check and had been on a two-day drunk. He passed out on his bed and couldn't wake up."

Per sat quietly after that, just shaking his head. Then he looked up and lamented, "Those kind of characters are gone."

Deidre laughed at the image Per's story had conjured up. She patted his shoulder as she left his office, Jill's report in a folder under her arm.

She returned to her office and studied the report again. A question haunted her. How could a person administer such a lethal dose to herself, unless she had little experience with it and had taken a copious amount of the drug in one injection? That didn't make sense to her.

A reporter for the local paper found out how Jill had died. That wasn't surprising, because her death certificate became a part of the public record. Later in the day, the reporter contacted Deidre to interview her about Jill's death. She tried to be as tactful as she could to respect Jill's family, but the next day the paper's headlines blared TEENAGE GIRL DIES OF METH OVERDOSE.

The article went on to question the effectiveness of the police and of Deidre's department.

By this time everyone had pretty much forgotten about Skinny. Rumors abounded as to what had happened to him: he had fallen into the beaver pond while he was drunk, he had faked his death and ran away to start a new life, he had been kidnapped by mobsters, even that he had been raptured up to heaven, although hardly anyone believed that of Skinny.

Chapter Eleven

As he promised at their first meeting, Mac was diligent about contacting Deidre. He called as soon as the news broke about Jill's toxicology report, and they met in her office the next day.

"I have to admit," Deidre confessed. "We aren't making much progress on our end. There are plenty of rumors flying around about some big operation going on up here, but as soon as we start questioning people, they clam up. We can't get a thing out of them.

"I'm starting to believe everyone's too afraid to say anything. If that's true, somebody's carrying an awfully big stick out there." Mac shook his head in disbelief.

"Since Jill's death, things have been really quiet around here," Deidre offered. "It's almost like the calm before a storm. I told you the guy who went missing left a half ounce of cocaine in his truck. It had been cut way down so it was pretty low grade, but still, it was coke. Since then we haven't been able to link it to anybody. Could he have bought it off a pusher in Duluth and then forgot about it when he went on a drunk?"

"Could be, but I don't think so," Mac responded. "It doesn't fit with what's sold on the streets there, and second, your guy's name hasn't come up in any of our busts. I think he got the drugs from around here. All we can find out is something pretty big has been in operation for some time. We don't know exactly where or what it is. I wish something would break to give us a clue as to what's going on.

"By the way, what's happening with Ed Beirmont? Have you seen him lately?"

Deidre shrugged. "Ed's an enigma. He has a business that does no business. He has money all the time, and he hangs out in some of the worst dives. Ed seems to be everyone's friend and nobody's friend at the same time. Every time I think we have something to haul his fanny in for, he pulls back. It is as though he walks a fine line between legit and not. My deputies have watched him, trying to catch him driving drunk or committing some other infraction, but they've never been able to find a reason to stop him. He always drives the speed limit, stops at stop signs, signals before turning, everything. We've wondered how he does it. Seems like he can drink forever and not get drunk."

Mac looked at Deidre. "We've had our eye on him too, and like you, we can never pin him down to anything illegal. Just wait him out. Sooner or later he'll slip up."

Before ending the unproductive meeting, the two law enforcement officers agreed that they should meet once a week, if for no other reason than to support each other.

"DEIDRE, HOW ARE YOU? It's been ages since I've seen you. It looks as though you healed up pretty well."

Deidre had decided to stop at one of the local restaurants for coffee. She and her close friend, David Craine, reached for the door handle at the same time. As they walked to where a host waited for them, she could see he still walked with a pronounced limp.

"The question is, David, how are *you*?"

"Not as good as I could be, but I'm not complaining. I could just as well be six feet under." He sort of laughed.

David had been involved in the catastrophe at Gooseberry Park last summer. He had fallen from a cliff while being pursued by terrorists intent on destroying the ore docks in Two Harbors.

Deidre had gotten there too late to prevent him from falling from the twenty-foot cliff to the rocks below. As she stood looking down at his crumpled body, she'd been shot in the chest by one of his pursuers.

David Craine had been her teacher in high school, had rescued her from an abusive home, had been her encourager, and now they were bonded by a common traumatic experience.

"Care to sit with me?" he asked Deidre. "I'm in town for today while they go over my boat at the Knife River marina. I'll buy."

Deidre laughed. "I'll flip you for it," she said.

As they finished their caramel rolls and sat enjoying a second cup of coffee, David became serious. "I read about that Moore girl in the paper. Sad, isn't it?"

Deidre nodded. "You taught back in the late sixties." she said. "Wasn't that when drug use among teenagers exploded?"

"Yes. I was teaching when all of this destructive stuff hit the schools in our area. It was more like the early seventies, maybe '72. I remember how unsophisticated the kids were when they started experimenting with drugs. They took anything and everything they could get their hands on without any concern for the results. One day in my classroom, a boy passed out and fell out of his seat."

"It must have been difficult for you to get a handle on what was happening to those kids. What did you do?"

David shrugged. "What could we do? I remember the start of one school year in particular. I took attendance and called out the name 'Jessie.' A tenth-grade girl hunched over her desk unenthusiastically flicked her hand up. She was a total mess, dark eye shadow smeared on her face, bright red lipstick, and her hair looked like she had combed it with a rake. I'll never forget her appearance: ragged jeans and a tie-dyed tee shirt. She looked stoned, but I had no solid evidence to accuse her. I felt so sorry for her, but what could I do?"

"There are symptoms you could have looked for, you know," Deidre started to instruct, but David cut her off.

"Later, we were trained to spot those symptoms: change in behavior, in appearance, and so on. One student, after he dried out, chastised us and asked why we hadn't seen what he was doing and stopped him. I told him I had never seen him act differently. I had nothing with which to compare. Anyway, this Jessie dropped out of school after three weeks, and I forgot about her. Next year, on the first day of class, a very attractive blond girl walked in and confidently chose a seat. She sat waiting patiently for class to begin. I checked attendance, and called out, 'Jessie.' The blond raised her hand and looked straight at me, a slight smile on her face. All I could do was stare as the realization of who that girl was hit me. I could have hugged her. She had been given a second chance and had taken it. I never asked what had transpired to cause her to go straight, but she never went back to her old ways. I still see her in town once in a while."

Deidre looked into her coffee cup. "Well, Jill will never get that chance. It's too bad her life ended this way. What a waste." They both sat in silence for a time.

"On that happy note, I'd better get back to work. Where are you off to?" she asked David.

"I'm meeting some friends at the marina and we're heading over to the Apostle Islands for a few days of fun. You and John should join me someday. We'd have a ball."

Deidre left a tip on the table. "I wonder when either of us will have a chance to get away, but when we do, you've got a deal. I'm not sure how long I can keep this up and retain my sanity. The job gets a little more demanding every day."

David shook her hand, placed his other hand on her shoulder, and said, "I'm proud of you Deidre."

"Thanks" was all she could say as tears welled up in her eyes.

Chapter Twelve

The folder containing Skinny's information was eventually filed away. Deidre had other incidents needing her immediate attention, but she never totally forgot about him, or Jill for that matter.

All of her inquiries about Jill's activities reached dead ends. Either no one knew what had happened, or no one was talking.

Autumn arrived, and an early frost, along with an unusual dry spell, prematurely turned the maple leaves several hues of red, orange, and yellow. They fell early, leaving the trees and bushes denuded. This made for perfect hunting conditions when grouse season opened the second weekend of September.

The Monday after the season opener Deidre was working at her desk. Her receptionist came to her door. "There are two men outside who want to speak with you," she said. "They want to report something unusual they found in the woods yesterday."

"Buzz them in," she said, wondering what they might have found that would prompt them to take time to stop at her office. Deidre heard the familiar sound of the electronically controlled doors unlocking and locking, and the men were ushered into the secure space of the sheriff's offices and meeting rooms.

The taller of the two men extended his hand. "I'm Gust Anderson, and dis here's my nephew, Eric," he said, his voice carrying a thick Norwegian accent.

Deidre shook hands with both men.

"The receptionist said you ran across something unusual yesterday. Were you hunting?" she asked, expecting them to have a poaching incident to report. She was prepared to refer them to the area's conservation officer.

"Ya," Gust replied. "We were up on da Whyte Road after grouse yesterday."

Deidre's head snapped up, and her eyes widened with interest at the mention of the Whyte Road.

"Usually we walk da old logging roads until we reach a swamp, but dis fall has been so dry dat we was able to cross what had been too wet in other years. We were able to cross t'ree ridges and must have followed da last one for about a mile."

Gust went on to tell about what a beautiful day it had been. The leaves had smelled so nice when they crunched under their feet, and the dried ferns rustled in the afternoon breeze. Deidre was getting a little antsy, wanting him to get to the point, but she told herself to be patient. Most people eventually got to where they were going with their story.

She looked at Eric and could see that he was getting irritated at the older man for dragging things out so long. Gust continued. "Well, you see, we was back about four miles off da road by dat time, and we came upon an old backhoe parked on the ridge. Pretty strange, don't ya tink?"

"Yes. Yes, that's strange, but I don't—"

Before she could finish her sentence, Eric spoke up. "That's not all of it. We looked the machine over, and other than being rusty, it looked to be in good shape. It was covered with fallen leaves, and it didn't look like it had been moved in awhile. The thing is, we noticed how shiny the rams extending from the hydraulic cylinders were, as if they had been used from time to time. They were still slippery with hydraulic fluid when I felt them."

Deidre started to say that still wasn't a crime, but Eric cut her off again.

"Uncle Gust and I didn't think too much of that. We commented that they must have driven it in when the swamps were frozen in the winter. We walked another hundred yards, and that's what we came to tell you about."

Deidre was exasperated. "What?" she wanted to know.

"This is going to sound crazy, but I think we found some graves."

Deidre sat upright. Eric had her undivided attention.

"What do you mean? Were there headstones, crosses or what?"

"Nothing like that. There was a place where the dirt was mounded up under the leaves. We cleared them away and underneath, the dirt was still bare. Nothing was growing on it. The weird thing about it was its dimensions, about four feet by six feet.

"We started looking around the area, and we found six more spots that were about the same size, except that they weren't mounded up. They were sunk in, like you see at a cemetery after a newly made grave has settled for a few months.

"I remember after my grandma died, we had to go back and add more fill to level the ground. That's what they reminded me of."

Deidre was shocked. "Do you think you could take us to that same spot?"

This time Gust answered. "It'd be easy, so long as we don't get a lot of rain in da meantime. How soon do you want to go? Eric and I have the week off, and we were planning on huntin' the whole time."

She looked at her watch. It was already after noon, and by the time her deputies loaded up the county's ATVs and drove to the Whyte Road, the sun would be low in the sky. It would be dark by the time they reached the backhoe.

"Can you be out front of the Law Enforcement Center at eight tomorrow morning?" she asked.

"Oh, ya," Gust answered for the two of them. "I live in town, and Eric is staying with me. We'll be here den." He stood to leave.

"By the way," Deidre stopped them. "Do you by any chance own an all-terrain vehicle, an ATV you could take back to the site? I can't let you use the county's machines, and it would be great if you could ride in on your own."

"Oh, sure," Gust smiled. "We don't hunt dat way, but we do have a couple, and we can trailer dem up dere."

"That would help us a lot if you will." Then she thought of one more question. "Have you told anyone else about your find?"

"No. We had breakfast and came to see you without talking to anyone," Eric answered.

Deidre breathed a sigh of relief. "Good. Please don't speak to anyone about this until we have a chance to find out what is buried on that ridge."

After the two men left, she got on the phone with the manager of the county garage.

"Jim, I need you to load up two ATVs on a trailer. Then, if you will, set a couple of number two long-handled shovels out where we can get at them in the morning. You might as well set out a pick and a grub hoe, too."

Deidre listened while Jim talked. "No, I think that will be all we need. Just doing some gardening," she laughed into the phone.

BY AFTERNOON SHE WAS ABOUT to close up shop. John was coming for dinner, and she had some grocery shopping to do on her way home. As usually happened, when she was almost to her office door, her phone rang. With a sigh, she retraced her steps and answered it.

"Hello, Sheriff Johnson?" a timid voice asked.

"Yes, this is she," Deidre answered. "How may I help you?" Impatiently, she looked at the clock on the wall.

"This is Peter, Peter Wilson." There was a long pause on his end. "I was Jill Moore's boyfriend. You talked to me shortly after she died." Deidre slowly sat down in her swivel chair. "I'd like to talk to you, if you still want to know about Jill."

The air went out of Deidre's lungs, silently she hoped. "Yes, of course I'd like to, Peter. Do you want to come to my office right now? I'll wait for you."

Peter responded too quickly. "No!" Then he caught himself. "No, I want to meet where no one will see me talking to you, maybe after school someplace."

"I'm afraid I'm awfully busy tomorrow, Peter. Is there any chance we could meet in the early evening?"

"I, I suppose we could."

Deidre felt like she had a fish on a very weak line, and she didn't want it to break. "You said you didn't want anyone to see you talking to me. Why don't I pick you up someplace with my personal car? We could drive some place where we can talk without any interference. Does that sound okay?"

There was a long stretch of silence, and Deidre thought for a moment he had hung up.

"Peter, are you still there," she asked quietly.

"Yeah, yeah, I'm here. I'd feel better if we took my dad's Highlander. It has tinted windows, and I could pick you up somewhere you could jump in, and we could be off."

Does this kid think we're in a James Bond movie, or what? Deidre thought, but she didn't want to scare him off.

"Sure, that will be fine, Peter. Where would you like to meet me?"

"Park your car on Ninth Street. Act like you're out for a walk and take the alley between there and the railroad tracks. I'll drive down the same alley at 7:30. It will be dark, and you can get in my car without much chance of anyone seeing you. It is a dark gray Toyota Highlander."

This kid's been watching too much television, she thought. But she agreed with his wishes. "I'll see you at 7:30 tomorrow night."

Deidre smiled a crooked smile and shook her head as she hung up the phone. *But he wants to talk about Jill, and that's something.*

Chapter Thirteen

Deidre always disliked wearing her uniform in public when she was off duty, but rather than going home to change clothes, today she stopped at the grocery store decked out in her work attire.

As she walked down the aisle she heard a little boy exclaim to his mother, "Mom, she's got a gun!"

Deidre stifled a laugh, wondering how the mother would answer.

"Yes, she's a police officer. She has to carry a gun."

"Do you think she has ever shot anyone?" the boy went on.

"I don't know," and as the boy tried to pull away in an attempt to approach Deidre, the mother said, "but let's not ask her right now. Okay?"

"But, Mom, I want to know."

Deidre kept walking. She didn't need to cope with a four-year-old. Shrimp fettuccini with veggies was on the menu for tonight. She picked up the ingredients and headed home. John was waiting for her. This time Mrs. Olson waved and smiled as Deidre proceeded up the walk. She waved back.

John met her at the door with a big hug. "I've got the pasta boiling. Are you as starved as I am?"

Deidre poked him in the ribs. "Is all you think of is eating? There must be something else," she said playfully.

"Okay, I do think of something else, but let's eat first." He laughed and his eyes sparkled. "I brought a bottle of Chardonnay to have with our meal, and a wonderful dessert wine for after dinner, while we sit in front of the fireplace. It feels so good to meet you at the door."

"It's good to know you'll be here to meet me," Deidre said, looking up into his face.

Just then the pasta water boiled over and the liquid hissed as it hit the hot burner. Both of them scrambled to turn the heat down under the foaming pot.

"That certainly ruined the moment," John complained.

"Later," Deidre said.

THE NEXT MORNING WHEN DEIDRE'S alarm rang, she rolled over in bed and wrapped her free arm around John. He stirred beside her and opened his eyes.

"Do we have to get up?" he groused, and made no move to get out of bed. Instead, he pulled the down comforter higher up over their bare shoulders.

Deidre kissed him, and said, "Not everybody in this room has today off. I've got a full day ahead. I can't even be home tonight. Got a date with another man," she joked.

They showered at the same time, and Deidre was grateful she had two bathrooms. She couldn't imagine juggling her makeup and hairdryer while John was taking up so much of the limited space. She hummed as the hair dryer did its work.

At breakfast, John wondered what made her day so busy. Deidre wouldn't have shared her day's schedule with anyone else, but John was special, and anyway, he was FBI. She knew he wouldn't talk. Deidre filled him in on the latest developments.

She kissed John before she left, knowing he wouldn't be there that night when she returned home. On the way out, she waved goodbye to Mrs. Olson.

Deidre arrived at the Law Enforcement Center as her deputies were filing in for the morning briefing/debriefing. Fortunately, it had been a slow night, and no one had anything of substance to report. After ten minutes, Deidre dismissed everyone but Jeff.

"I had an unusual report yesterday. Two hunters found what they think might be graves in the woods near Whyte. Jump in my squad with me, and I'll fill you in as we drive up to the county garage. Jim's supposed to have a couple of ATVs loaded on a trailer. I told him to have some digging tools ready."

After Deidre relayed to Jeff what the hunters had told her, he sat in silence for a few seconds.

"Skinny?" he asked. Deidre shrugged.

Jim had everything ready to go when she and Jeff arrived. She backed up until the towing ball of her SUV was aligned under the hitch. Jeff lowered it over the ball, secured the safety chains and plugged in the trailer's light system. While he was doing that, Jim helped load the shovels and picks into the back of the Explorer.

"Good luck with your gardening," he called out as they drove away, and he returned to the shop to work on a snowplow blade he knew would be needed in only a few weeks.

Deidre and Jeff pulled up in front of the Center at the same time Gust and Eric arrived.

"Gust, you lead the way. You know where we're going."

She followed him out of town and up Highway 2 with Gust driving a little under the posted speed limit of fifty-five miles an hour. She pictured him worrying about getting a speeding ticket because the sheriff was following close behind, and the thought brought a smile to her face. She and Jeff rode in silence, neither quite awake yet, both wondering what they would find when they dug into the soil.

It took them almost an hour to reach the Whyte Road and another twenty minutes to reach the logging road Gust and his nephew had used. Jeff tilted the trailer bed so the ATVs could be driven off. By the time they had unloaded the machines, Gust and Eric had theirs on the road as well. They tied the shovels and other tools to the back carrier of Deidre's ride and started down the trail with Gust leading the way and Eric taking up the rear.

Deidre could understand why Gust had gone into detail about walking in the leaves and enjoying the sights and smells. She inhaled deeply, and wished she weren't on the job. Gust stopped after a mile or so.

"Dis is as far as we used to be able to go," he explained. The low area we're going to cross usually is way too wet to get through, but with all the dry weather we've had, you can see it's dry as a bone."

He eased into the rough area that had been swamp, and with his vehicle in low gear he climbed the next ridge. When they reached the third ridge, Gust turned west, followed it for several minutes and pulled up alongside the backhoe. He was right. It was totally out of place.

"Dere it is," Gust announced as though he thought Deidre hadn't believed him. "The other things I told you about are over dere," and he pointed a little farther down the ridge.

Deidre looked where he pointed, and there was no mistaking the shape and size of the mound that rose slightly above the ground around it. Gust motored over to the spot before Deidre could stop him.

"Let's back out of here before we get off. We should do a thorough search of the ground before we start walking around."

The four of them formed a line, shoulder to shoulder, and they slowly walked the area, heads bowed and eyes on the ground. It didn't surprise Deidre that they found nothing. The dry leaves were layered upon each other, hiding anything that might be lying underneath.

Deidre got down on her hands and knees and scraped the leaves off the mound. As Gust had said, the soil beneath was bare—mineral soil. It was evident it had been turned over not too long ago. She sifted the leaves through her fingers, making sure there was nothing hidden that might be valuable evidence. She found nothing.

"Well Jeff, it's time to roll up our sleeves and dig. Be careful, though. Let's take it a shallow layer at a time."

Like many ridges, this one was a leftover from the last glacial age. Rivers of water had run under the ice sheets, carrying gravel and dirt in their currents. The gravel was deposited in eskers, which might be thought of as upside down river beds left as ridges under the ice instead of eroded channels.

When the ice melted, it left behind mounds of gravel and sand that usually ran parallel to each other like those they had crossed to reach this site. They became covered with vegetation, and trees sprouted along their length. The areas between the ridges remained wet swampland during all but the driest of years.

Deidre and Jeff had no trouble sinking their shovels into the loose soil, and painstakingly, they removed it inches at a time. By eleven o'clock, they were down five feet and had found nothing. Deidre was about ready to give up when Jeff's shovel met resistance. He tried again, this time not pushing his shovel in as deeply. For a second he spotted something red, and then the soil caved in around the place from where he had scooped up the last shovelful of gravel.

"Deidre, something is down there. My shovel got hung up on it, and it moved."

"Was it a root? These maples can send them down quite a ways." She didn't want to get too excited.

"No, I'm sure it wasn't a root. I got a glimpse of red before the dirt spilled back into the hole," Jeff said excitedly as he began to gently scrape away the last layer of soil.

"There, it's a piece of red-and-white cloth. Easy now," he said more to himself than to the others. "You can see it better now."

Gust and Eric both leaned over the hole just as the stench began to rise. They both turned their backs and took deep breaths. Deidre knelt down beside the piece of exposed cloth, holding her breath as best she could.

"I think we better put on some rubber gloves. This looks like it's going to be messy," Deidre advised as she stood up to take in the situation.

Jeff climbed out of the hole and went to a pack strapped to his ATV. He threw a pair of durable gloves down to Deidre, pulled on his own, and climbed back down beside her.

"Let's clear the dirt away with our hands," Deidre suggested, holding her breath. They began clawing the dirt, working their way up what appeared to be a shirt.

The deteriorated fabric practically fell apart exposing a putrid mess underneath, and it took all of their willpower to continue the grisly task. Using extreme care, they reached what seemed to be the collar of a shirt.

"I'm not sure I want to see what comes next," Jeff gasped between breaths.

"I know, but we have to keep going. We know what we are going to find, but I need a look to be sure."

They meticulously cleared away the dirt. It was unmistakable; there was a face above the frayed collar of the shirt. Its eyes had deteriorated to nothing but holes, and what had been lips were shrunken back. Two ragged rows of teeth were exposed, and they could see that several were missing from the body's jaws. There was no mistaking, this was a grave.

"I think we've found Skinny," Deidre mused. Jeff stood atop the hole, looking down at the body.

"Let's stop digging until we have more equipment to process the dirt we've removed. I don't want to miss any clues. Try not to disturb the sides of the excavation," Deidre cautioned.

She crawled out of the hole, and thinking out loud said, "I think we have discovered a graveyard, and it's going to take a lot more manpower than what we have in our department to process what's here."

She turned to Gust and Eric. "Thank you so much for coming to me. I'm sorry your hunting trip has been ruined, but you have done a great service by taking the time."

"Ya, well what else could we do?" Gust answered as if he made finds like this everyday.

"I think you and Eric should take your ATVs out to the road and load up. When you get to town, please don't talk to anyone about this. The media will find out soon enough, and then this place will become a three ring circus."

Eric nodded and climbed onto his machine. He and Gust rode away without looking back. In a few munutes Deidre could hear them disappearing in the distance. She turned to Jeff.

"I'm afraid we have a mess on our hands. The two of us can't handle this, so I want you to stay here to keep watch on these graves. I'll go out to my Explorer and call for help. These graves will have to be guarded day and night until the bodies are exhumed, and I don't feel comfortable having one person do that. Hang tight, I won't be long."

As Deidre rode out of the woods, she couldn't help but think of how isolated this part of the state was. Cell phones had no coverage, and most areas didn't even have landlines. There were people living up here who didn't have electricity. She knew of a reclusive ex-physics professor who lived a few miles from where they had left the trailers. He had rigged up a small wind generator and some solar panels that provided him and his partner with a barely adequate electrical supply. Otherwise, most of the people lived by nineteenth-century standards.

Deidre reached her truck in less time than she remembered it taking to get into the woods. She picked up her radio transmitter.

"This is Sheriff Johnson. I need back up. We are on the Whyte Road, about six miles in from Highway 2. Find out which deputies are closest, and send two of them to me. I'll be waiting for them on the road."

Deidre received a confirmation and then began pacing, wondering what her next move should be. There was no link to a drug-related crime yet. However, something like this find, if the other suspect graves really did contain bodies, could point to some type of gang activity. Or maybe a serial killer was at work in her county. Should she call in the Bureau of Criminal Aprehension? What about the FBI? She mulled these questions while she waited.

It was nearly three o'clock when the first deputy arrived.

"What's happening?" he asked.

Deidre saw his puzzled look. "Jeff and I found a body in the woods. I'll wait until the other deputy arrives so I don't have to repeat myself. I'll say this, it isn't pretty."

She wondered how Jeff was coping with being left far back in the woods at the macabre scene. She imagined him standing with his back to a tree and flinching at the sound of every snapping twig or rustle of leaves. Someone could be hiding only a few feet away behind a balsam fir tree and not be seen.

Another deputy arrived within fifteen minutes. They gathered around Deidre, sensing something out of the ordinary had been discovered in this remote setting. They looked at her questioningly.

"We've got the possibility of a real mess four miles back in," she announced. "I want each of you to take your long gun with you.

I know most of you have a shotgun in your squad, but if you have a rifle, bring that along as well. I'll fill you in as we drive to the site. Jeff is back there alone, and I don't want to leave him in that situation any longer than necessary."

It was a wild ride. One deputy sat on the rear rack of the ATV and the other sat on the front. Deidre drove and talked above the sound of the engine. She traveled slowly so the deputies weren't thrown off of what at times resembled a bucking bronco. When she hit particularly rough spots in the trail, it was all the men could do to hold onto their seats. They were an odd sight, three people on a machine built for one, with guns bristling in every direction.

"Hang on, guys!" she shouted when the machine reared up and over a fallen tree trunk.

Finally, they arrived at the grave, and Jeff stepped out from behind a windfall to greet them.

"Glad to see you," he said as he put his arm around the shoulder of one of the deputies. "I'm usually not squeamish, but this place had me spooked, at least when I was alone."

Deidre explained what she wanted them to do. "One of you give Jeff and me a ride out to the road, then bring the machine back in. That way there will be two ATVs for you. I want you to guard this site. I'll send out another crew to relieve you, but they probably won't get here until after dark. We've been over the trail so many times I don't think they'll have any trouble finding their way. Try to get a good night's rest when you get home. We're going to need all the manpower we can muster over the next few days. You might not be back here, but you'll be needed to cover the rest of the county. I'll be calling in some help. I hope by tomorrow evening to have finished digging up this body and to begin on the other suspected graves. Be sure to stay alert. Whoever did this isn't going to be happy with what we've found."

One of the deputies climbed onto the four wheeler and started the engine. Deidre sat on the front, and Jeff rode the back. It was a slow ride out to the road.

CHAPTER FOURTEEN

BY THE TIME DEIDRE AND JEFF pulled into Two Harbors, Deidre's head was spinning as she tried to organize her thoughts. It was almost five o'clock. The first thing she would do was enlist the help of the State Bureau of Criminal Apprehension. Then she had to set up a watch schedule at the grave site. She thought she better put the FBI on alert. Finally, she had her clandestine meeting with Peter Wilson scheduled for that evening.

"Jeff, I hate to ask you to do this. I'd like you to get your gear together and return to the area for the night. I need you to make sure the shift changes go smoothly. I'd like you to stay there until our work is done."

Deidre virtually ran up the stairs to her office and immediately went to her phone to call the BCA. It rang several times before a receptionist answered.

"Hello. You have reached the Minnesota BCA. This is Amy speaking. How may I direct your call?"

Deidre explained her situation as briefly as she could, and the receptionist transferred her call. A woman answered.

"This is Melissa Sobranski of the homicide division. How may I be of assistance?"

"I'm Sheriff Deidre Johnson of Lake County," she began, and then she told her story in as much detail as she could.

"This is far more than we are equipped to handle," she said after relating all the facts she could, "both personnel wise and also monetarily. I think we'll need the services of a forensic pathologist as well as manpower to help unearth the graves."

Deidre could almost feel the tension rising on the other end of the line.

"I'm going to get on this right now. We have a crack pathologist skilled at field work. We'll also be bringing two assistants to help with the excavations. I'll call you first thing in the morning to give you an approximate time we will arrive."

Deidre thanked her and hung up. She quickly made out a new shift schedule to allow for the site to be adequately guarded and called the affected deputies.

"Hello, Bill? I know you're scheduled to work the night shift, but I need to see you in the office as soon as you can get here." She quickly dialed another deputy, making the same request. When they gathered, she shared with them what had happened during the day. "Take along what you need to camp out tonight. Pack a lunch and a couple of thermoses of hot coffee for each of you. It's supposed to get down to the high twenties so bring enough warm gear. Also, bring a tarp or something to protect you in case we have bad weather. The forecast looks good, but you might need something to keep the frost off. I don't expect you'll be sleeping, but it might be good to bring along sleeping bags. They're easy to climb into with your clothes on, and they'll keep you warm.

"Arm yourself. I'd suggest taking at least one rifle and two shotguns. There'll be a shift to relieve you in the morning. Any questions?"

The two deputies looked at each other, questioningly, but no one said a word.

"Good. Have a great time camping," Deidre said and sent them off.

She looked at her watch. It was already seven-ten, too late to call the FBI and almost time to meet Peter. She changed into civvies she kept in her office for emergencies and went down to the parking lot.

DEIDRE GOT INTO HER OWN CAR and drove to Ninth Street, where she parked in the middle of the block. Her car was partially hidden in the shadow of an overhanging elm tree. She stepped out of her vehicle and quickly walked down the sidewalk to the alley. It was a dirt road a half-block long that took a ninety degree turn to the right, running parallel to Ninth Street. As she walked up the oiled byway, a car pulled up behind her.

Through its open window, Peter urged her, "Quick, get in!"

She opened the door and noticed that the dome light didn't come on. She jumped in and Peter drove away. He exited the alley and followed back streets until they were heading out of town toward the fairgrounds, which were deserted at that time of the year. He parked near the building that normally housed 4H projects.

Now what? Deidre thought, as Peter checked his mirror to make sure no one had followed them. *This kid definitely has to get a life.*

"What is it that you have to tell me, Peter?" Deidre said, opening the conversation.

He picked at his fingernails. "No one is talking to you because they are all afraid."

"Afraid of what?" Deidre pressured.

"Afraid we'll end up like Jill. There are some awful things going on out there, and no one dares talk about them."

Deidre thought he sounded like a delusional teenager, and she was about to suggest that they return to his home and have a talk with his parents.

Peter said, "Jill called me a week before she died. Said she wanted to talk to me about something important. I wanted nothing more than to have a chance to sit down with her, because we all knew something was really messed up in her life. I thought I could help. She sounded very upset, almost hysterical. Her voice was shaky, and she sounded as if she were on the verge of crying.

"We agreed to meet at the breakwater. That way we could talk without others around. We met in the evening, before sunset."

Suddenly, he had Deidre's full attention, and she encouraged him to continue.

"Jill was really scared and jumpy. We took the trail by the lake around Light House Point, and the whole time we walked, she kept looking behind us.

"She started to cry and said she'd made some terrible mistakes over the last few months. Now she wanted to change, to get her old life back. She said she saw where she was headed but didn't know how to stop the train wreck looming in her future."

Peter paused for several seconds, still picking at his nails.

"Did she say what was so messed up in her life?" Deidre quietly asked.

"She was using drugs. She said it started last summer, well, not last summer, I guess. Last summer was only a couple of months ago. You know, a little over a year ago.

"She said she thought her life had become so humdrum she wanted a little excitement. That's when she began going out occasionally with another crowd."

"What other crowd did she mean?" Deidre wanted to know.

"You know, the rougher crowd, the ones who keep apart from the rest of us."

"The ones who carouse around?" She added, "Are they kids who dabble with drugs?"

Peter nodded while continuing to stare at the floor. After another long pause he looked at her. "They do a lot more than dabble. They smoke pot and drink beer, but they don't use hard drugs. They're sellers, pushers, and they sucked Jill into being one of their customers. I think they get kids to start using cocaine by giving them stuff that isn't too potent to begin with. More kids at school are hooked on the stuff than anyone imagines."

Deidre stopped him so she could ask a question. "Do you know where this stuff is coming from? Who's selling it?"

"Three guys at school sell to the other kids. One of them moved here two years ago when we were sophomores. He was different, talked differently than we do, acted differently. The word on him was he'd moved here from the Twin Cities and was staying with relatives up north of town, although we never did see his folks. The other two have been in our grade since kindergarten, but they always were outsiders, never really fitting in. As we got older, they hung together and did their own thing."

"Were they good students, any problem in class?" Deidre asked.

"That's the funny thing. They got Cs, and they never caused the teachers any problem. They didn't say much in class, but they didn't create any disturbances either. Outside of class the new guy was friendly. Soon he had a group of kids following him, mostly ones who had few friends. It wasn't long before they were the group some wanted to be with. I think that's what happened to Jill."

"How did you respond to Jill telling you her troubles?"

"I said she should get help to get clean, that if she was hooked on something she couldn't do it alone. I told her to tell her folks. I even said I'd go with her if she wanted, but she turned down my offer."

"What did she say to your suggestion about getting help?

"She agreed with me," Peter said. "She told me she had informed the kids she had been running with that she was through, that she wouldn't hang with them anymore.

"Then she said the next morning she was going to make an appointment at the Human Development Center. She thought that would be the best place to start. Two days later, I saw her in the hallway at school. We only had two weeks left before summer vacation. I asked her if she had made an appointment, and she said she had. She said she was scheduled to see a counselor on Monday of the next week. She died on Friday."

"How do you think she died?" Deidre asked.

"I think they killed her so she wouldn't talk. She never used meth, said it scared her to death. But from what I heard, she died of an overdose. I think they gave it to her without her consent."

Deidre audibly exhaled. "Do you have any idea where they get the cocaine from?"

"Just rumors. They said a guy named Skinny was their source, but now he's disappeared. Somebody else must have taken his place, but I haven't heard who."

He looked at Deidre, his face sincere. "Now do you understand why no one talks to you? Two people have been killed or gone missing because of what they were saying or doing. None of us wants to take a chance. I know you must have thought I was some nut case the way I approached you, but I'm afraid, really afraid."

Deidre waited a moment before she spoke. "I think you're incredibly brave for what you've done. But I'm curious, why did you wait so long to see me?"

"Guilt, I guess. Maybe I should have done more for Jill when she was alive. The more it pulled at my conscience, the more upset I became with myself. Finally, I had to tell someone."

"Thank you, Peter. You don't know how valuable this information is to me. But now you'd better get home. Please don't share our conversation, even with your friends." Then as an afterthought she asked, "Does the name Ed Beirmont mean anything to you?"

Peter shook his head.

"Do you have a cell phone in case I need to reach you?"

Peter nodded and dug it out of his pocket. "Hit 'Contacts' and 'My Phone.' My number will come up."

Deidre did as he said, then punched in his number to her phone's "new contact" listing.

They drove to Ninth Street in silence, but before Deidre opened the door she squeezed Peter's arm. "Thanks," was all she said, and stepped outside.

CHAPTER FIFTEEN

ON HER WAY HOME, DEIDRE realized her muscles were tensed into knots. She parked in her driveway and looked at the lights burning in her kitchen. A flood of relief swept over her. John had decided to stay another night, and she needed the comfort of his company and whatever else.

As she entered her kitchen she was almost overwhelmed with the aroma of spaghetti sauce and Italian spices. The table was set, and a goblet of red wine stood next to each plate. John had picked a bouquet of deep purple mums from her garden and placed them in a vase on the table. Their color almost matched that of the wine.

He came from the next room, an apron around his waist. "A long day," he said, rather than asked. He put his arms around her and started to massage her neck. Deidre buried her face in his chest.

As they shared the meal, Deidre couldn't keep her emotions bottled up, and she told him all that had transpired that day.

"I don't know what we'll find tomorrow, but I'm sure it's not going to be good. We know of the one body and the other six sites look too suspicious to not expect the worst. I feel sorry for those deputies out there tonight. They should be home with their families, not out in the woods trying to stay warm. I doubt they'll get any rest."

She finished about the time they had cleaned up the last of the pasta and meatballs.

"How are you going to proceed on this case?" John asked.

"As I said, the BCA's heading up tomorrow. They should be here by the afternoon. I have two calls to make in the morning, one to Mac at the Lake Superior Drug and Gang Task Force and the other to the FBI. I suspect we may have some interstate trafficking going on, but I'm waiting on a call from the Drug Enforcement Agency before I bring in any other departments. I'll see where we go from there."

"Sounds like you're ready to move on this thing, but enough shop talk for tonight," John said as he poured another glass of wine for each of them. "Why don't we go in the other room? I've got the fire going, and you look like you could use a backrub."

He escorted Deidre into the living room and made her comfortable in front of the fire with two large stuffed pillows for her to recline against.

"Relax while I clean up the kitchen. I'll be back in a few minutes. I've already cleaned the pots and pans, so the only thing left is to rinse the plates and stick them in the dishwasher."

Deidre was beginning to feel drowsy by the time he returned. He sat next to her, letting her use him as a support.

They had hardly settled onto the cushions John arranged on the floor when the phone rang.

"Hello," Deidre answered rather abruptly, "Sheriff Johnson speaking."

"This is Neil Jacobs of NBC News. Is it true you uncovered several graves north of Two Harbors?"

"I have no comment at this time," Deidre spoke the well-rehearsed words, and hung up. She turned her phone off.

DEIDRE KISSED JOHN GOOD MORNING and rolled out of bed before the clock radio automatically turned on. "We'd better get moving. You have to drive to Duluth this morning, and I've a full day-and-a-half ahead of me."

The two of them went to their separate bathrooms and did a quick version of a morning cleanup: combing the knots out of their hair, brushing their teeth, and applying fresh deodorant.

"I don't know if I'll be home tonight, but I'll call when I can," Deidre said after draining the last drop of her morning coffee. She stood on her tiptoes and kissed him goodbye before they stepped outside.

"Be careful," John said. "I love you."

Those three words stopped her for a second. He had never said them to her before. Deidre looked up at him. "I love you, too," she said.

On her way to work, she couldn't shake the strange feeling inside her being. It was the first time in her life a man had said he loved her, and she smiled a broad smile, actually feeling as though someone genuinely cared for her as more than as a friend.

Only two officers were in the office to greet her for their morning meeting. Three were camped up in the woods,three more were on their way to relieve them, and one was on vacation. The meeting was over almost before it began.

Deidre wasted no time making her phone calls.

"Hi, Mac. I think I uncovered something last night you have to know about." Deidre told about her meeting with Peter and the possible link to Skinny's disappearance. Then she told him of the grave they had unearthed and of the other suspicious depressions.

"I think I'd better come up right away so we can talk, if it's okay with you." He was careful not to sound too demanding.

"No can do today. The BCA is on their way as we speak, and we'll be heading to the site before you would get here. I promise to call you as soon as we get back, and then we can meet. By then we'll have a better idea of what we're facing, at least on that front. Right now, I have another call to make, so I'd better go."

She cut off their connection and dialed the FBI office in Duluth.

The receptionist answered, "This is Janice. How may I direct your call?"

Deidre explained why she was calling and heard the familiar response, "One moment please while I connect you to your party."

She heard the familiar buzz as her call was transferred, and a man answered. "This is Agent VanGotten."

"Ben! What a surprise. I didn't expect you to answer."

Ben seemed as pleasantly surprised as was Deidre. What had begun as a bitter relationship in high school had evolved into a friendship and quite a deep appreciation for each other. He had shown nothing but respect for her since the terrorist plot a year ago in Two Harbors and after she was gunned down at Gooseberry Park. In fact, when he left the Sheriff's Department to join the FBI, he had tears in his eyes when he said goodbye to her.

"What's happening up there?" Ben asked.

Deidre went through the whole story again while Ben listened intently.

"Right now, I don't think there is enough evidence to warrant the FBI coming in on the case, but it sounds like that might change," he responded after a moment of thought. "Between you, Mac, and the BCA, I'm confident you'll handle this well. I'm afraid it's out of our jurisdiction until you can link it to a gangland murder, a serial killer, or a kidnapping. Call me as soon as you can if the evidence points in that direction. My extension is 467. I'm going to relay your information to my boss, and he can decide where we'll go from there."

"Thanks, Ben. Take care," Deidre responded, truly meaning it.

A call came in before she could leave her desk.

"This is Melissa Sobranski from the BCA. Our crew is passing through Duluth right now. We'll be taking the expressway and should be in Two Harbors in no more that a half-hour. Besides me, there is a forensic pathologist and two field officers to assist you. We're bringing the equipment we'll need to perform the excavations. Do you have any questions I can handle while we're on the road?"

Deidre chuckled. "Do I have to serve you lunch?" She was joking, but it dawned on her that they would be spending a lot of time in the woods and would need to eat. After Melissa hung up, Deidre called one of the local restaurants that did carryout.

"Hi, Oscar. I've a pretty unusual request. Can you deliver meals up to the Whyte Road?" She listened to his response with a smile on her face. "Yep, that's the place, turn off about a mile past the Pines Picnic Area."

At first Oscar couldn't believe what Deidre was requesting, but when Deidre promised mileage and wages for the delivery person, he saw dollar signs.

"We'll need meals for six delivered three times a day until I tell you otherwise. We'll need eating utensils, plates, cups, everything for a picnic in the woods—understand? Keep the price under fifteen dollars a meal per head, okay? And we'll need you to start with supper tonight. Oh, and be sure to send plenty of coffee."

"Will you tip the driver? Remember, he'll be losing a lot of business with you being his only customer," Oscar demanded.

Deidre assured him his workers would be remembered.

Chapter Sixteen

A PARADE OF VEHICLES MARKED "BCA" pulled up in front of the Law Enforcement Center at ten-thirty. Deidre was there to meet it.

"Hi, I'm Melissa," the tall, dark-haired woman said as she exited her SUV. Deidre could see the back of the vehicle was piled high with equipment. She towed a long trailer loaded with four ATVs.

A three-quarter-ton pickup pulling a trailer laden with flood lights and standards on which they could be mounted, a generator, and various other needs for working in the dark parked next to Melissa's rig. Behind the pickup was an enclosed van.

When the group had assembled, there were four persons in all: Melissa Sobranski, Dan LaRosa, Jennifer Williams, and a middle-aged woman who introduced herself as Dr. Judith Coster.

Deidre suggested that they eat before they left town. She explained that meals would be provided for them at the work site, but they would be on their own as far as personal hygiene items.

"I hope you are prepared as though you are entering the Boundary Waters Canoe Area Wilderness. We'll be roughing it," she added with a grin.

That statement reminded Deidre that there were no restrooms out there, and they would need some sort of facilities. From her cell phone, she dialed her office and asked the receptionist to find a sanitary service that could deliver two portable outhouses to the Whyte Road.

"Have them dropped off where our trucks will be parked on the side of the road," she instructed.

The five law enforcement people opted for fast food, and they rode with Deidre to the nearest burger place. As they sat down at the one round table large enough to accommodate them and their trays of food, she said, "Enjoy the comfort now. I've got a feeling we are going to be in the sticks for at least a couple of days."

In a half-hour they were on their way up Highway 2, heading for the worksite. They had hardly left town when Deidre realized she had been too abrupt with Mac. She was still in an area where her cell phone worked, and his number was on her speed dial. She pressed "SEND."

"Hello, Mac McAlpine speaking."

"Mac, I cut you off too short this morning. I'm sorry. Do you want to come up and join the team, at least for as long as you feel you can spare the time."

"I knew you had a lot going on this morning, and I felt badly about putting you on the spot. Thanks for wanting to include me. Something has come up, and I won't be able to join you and the others. Sounds like it might have been fun, though. You have plenty of help with Melissa there. She's a good one, easy to work with. As soon as you are back in town, I'll be available, and the three of us can sit down and go over the findings. Good luck up there."

Deidre said goodbye and hit "END" on her phone. For a moment, sweat beaded up on her forehead. *Calm down, Deidre,* she tried to tell herself. *Things will fall into place, if you let them.*

As they approached a long, steep incline known to the locals as Five Mile Hill, they passed what looked like a large motor home lumbering up the grade. Viewed from behind, a collection of antennas folded onto the roof protruded like branches.

Deidre passed it and was shocked to see the logo on the side, ABC News. The others in her group followed, and soon they had left the bus far behind. When they neared their destination, Deidre turned off the highway onto the Whyte Road, which was beginning to be pounded down with all the traffic that had passed over it the last couple of days.

In a few minutes she stopped where they would enter the woods. The trail in was easily visible by this time. Melissa stopped behind her. "Deidre, you'd better call for some more help. That news team we passed is only the beginning of what is soon going to be a regular city in the wilderness."

She turned to Dan and Jennifer who were getting out of their pickup. "Quick, string out some BCA crime scene tape. Cordon off an area about fifty yards in radius from this entry point. Deidre, can you call in some deputies right away?"

Deidre was a little irked, not that Melissa was giving orders, but that she hadn't thought to secure this area better herself. She leaned into her Explorer and called dispatch on her radio. "I need two squads out here on the Whyte Road," she demanded. "Have them get here as soon as possible, if not sooner. Oh, and Jaredine, call the Downtown Cafe and make sure Oscar includes some of his apple pie with our meals. The others deserve something special for all they're going to be asked to do."

They all began unloading what Melissa and her crew had brought. The trailer loaded with much of their gear was unhooked from the pickup and its hitch placed over the towing ball on the rear of one of the ATVs. Jennifer started in, but before she could move far, Deidre flagged her down. "There are three deputies back there. Have two of them come out to the road. Tell them Jeff should stay at the site."

She turned to where Dan and Melissa were hooking the empty flatbed trailer behind an ATV. It was the same trailer that had hauled the ATVs from the Twin Cities.

"Deidre, could you help me with this stuff?" Dr. Coster called to her. "We'll pack as much on the trailer as we can, but we might have to make two trips. They hauled box after box to the trailer and were in the process of tying everything down when Deidre heard sirens in the distance.

Two squads arrived at about the same time. Deidre stationed one deputy a hundred yards up the road and the other the same distance back in the direction they had come. Her directions were to allow no one to pass. That taken care of, she and the others followed the trail to the burial site, Deidre riding on Melissa's four-wheeler. They met two deputies on their way out, and she flagged them down.

"I'll need one of your ATVs. You can ride out on the other. When you get there, Jed and Al will tell you what's up." Both of the deputies looked exhausted.

Deidre took the lead and was surprised at how the trail had smoothed out since her first trip. The repeated traffic had knocked down the rough spots, and someone had taken the time to remove the tree trunks they had been forced to crawl over with their machines.

They made the now familiar trip in half the time she had expected. Deidre was happy to see Jeff looking in better condition than the other two had been when she met them on their way out. Evidently, he was accustomed to camping out in the woods. She trusted him as much as anyone and had a better working relationship with him than with any of the others on her crew.

Deidre half expected that the BCA members would want to dive right in, but they didn't. Dr. Coster went over and looked in the open grave.

"Yep, he's dead all right," she said, stating the obvious.

Melissa began to give orders. "Let's get the trailers unloaded. Dan, you and Jennifer get the three tents set up. Judy, tell them where you'd like your work space, and they can set up that tent first. Then we'll help you unload your supplies and store them under cover. Jeff, is that your name? Would you give them a hand with the tent?" When Jeff started to move, Melissa tossed over her shoulder, "Thanks, Jeff."

She walked over to a rock and sat down. "Deidre, let's draw up some kind of plan for how to proceed."

Deidre sat beside her, wondering if she and her deputies were going to be marginalized for the rest of the time.

"What do you think our plan should be?" Melissa asked, catching Deidre off guard.

Deidre didn't want to answer too quickly. She thought for a moment. "I think the first thing we should do is screen all the dirt we removed from the grave when we uncovered the body. We weren't too careful as we dug and might have missed something when we scooped the dirt out. I think we should begin by sorting through the sand. Did you bring a screen with you?"

"Good idea," Melissa said, and then in one breath hollered to Dan, "When you get Doc's tent up, set up the sand screener over there. We'll begin by sifting the dirt that's been dug out." She turned back to Deidre and waited.

"I'd like Dr. Costa to look at what we've uncovered so far. I think she should determine how to continue. The body is quite decomposed, and I don't have the expertise to continue any further than we've gone." Melissa nodded. Deidre continued. "I think we could begin to dig into the other suspected graves. If Dan and Jennifer started on one, Jeff and I could work on another. That way, when you and Dr. Costa are finished with this fresh site, you could move to the next one without delay."

"That sounds okay to me, but do you suppose Jeff could work alone? I'd like you to work with Judy and me. Three pairs of eyes are better than two."

Deidre looked at her and smiled. *This might work out after all.*

By the time the two investigators had finished laying out a rough schedule of what they would do, the others had erected the tents. They were bigger than what Deidre had expected, and it was plain to see that Melissa had come prepared to stay at the site for a while. Deidre began to relax a bit.

Dr. Costa removed a camera from its case and started making a filmed document of each of the suspected grave sites. She turned to Deidre. "Did you photograph the open grave before you dug into it?"

Deidre's face flushed. "No, I didn't have a camera, and to be honest, I didn't think to do that at the time."

"That shouldn't be a problem," the doctor said. "I'll take some shots now. They'll show the location well enough, and the body's still not totally exposed, evidence enough that it wasn't dumped in after the grave was opened."

She continued to snap pictures.

Chapter Seventeen

DEIDRE LOOKED AT HER WATCH and was astonished to see it was already five-thirty. Their food was to be delivered by that time, and she had said she'd be at the road to pick it up.

"Time has slipped away from me!" she declared to the others. "Our meal delivery is waiting for us at the road, and I promised the caterer I'd be there to meet him. I'll be back as soon as I can."

Deidre jumped onto her ATV and sped as fast as she could up the trail to the road. She was stunned at the sight when she came out of the woods.

In a clearing outside the crime zone tape were parked a half-dozen news trucks like the one she had passed on Five Mile Hill. People milled about, and her deputies patrolled the line. As she swung off the vehicle, people came running to the edge of the restricted area, microphones in hand. Behind them were cameramen recording her every move.

"Sheriff, can you verify that you have found seven graves?"

"Have you dug them up yet?"

"Do you know who the victims are?"

"How long before you bring them out?"

They reminded her of a pack of wolves going after prey. "I'm sorry, but I can't comment at this time. Excuse me," was all she said.

The caterer's deliveryman looked like he wanted to leave as quickly as he could. He helped Deidre secure the boxes of food to her ATV and ran back to his car. Deidre returned to the woods, following the now well-traveled trail.

By the time she arrived, the camp was set up, and she noticed that spotlights had been rigged so light would flood the work area. She expected a long night.

Each person was given a dinner boxed up in Styrofoam containers. Under other circumstances it might have been fun, but this time they wolfed down the meal. The meatloaf sandwiches tasted like gourmet food to Deidre, and the way the others were devouring the sandwiches, they must have thought so, too. The hot coffee made them want to linger awhile longer, but the work ahead called.

Dr. Costa finished first and threw the remains of her meal into a black garbage bag hanging from the branch of a tree.

"Okay, time to get this over with. I probably shouldn't have eaten anything, but I was starved. Melissa, Deidre, let's suit up. For now, Jeff, Jennifer, and Dan, will you start screening this dirt? There are plenty of evidence bags in the supply tent. Have a few on hand and bag anything you think might be of significance."

Deidre followed her and Melissa to the tent where Dr. Costa pulled out three hazmat coveralls. Dr. Costa looked up at Deidre as they were struggling to get their feet through the legs.

"Don't forget to put on protective glasses. We don't want any of that gunk splashing in our eyes. By the way, I'd appreciate it if you'd call me Judy. I hate formalities."

Deidre smiled her gratitude.

The three of them moved to the open grave, the synthetic material of their blue suits swishing with each step. They climbed down into the hole. Above them, they could hear scraping as shovels full of dirt were dumped onto and then worked through the fine metal mesh of the dirt screen.

Deidre spoke first. "It looks to me like he was simply dumped into the grave. If you look at what we uncovered, you can see he is on his side, but his head is twisted back so his face is pointing up. What do you think, Doctor, ah, Judy?"

Judy reached down and gently pushed some dirt back away from the corpse's head. "I think you're right. There certainly was no respect shown for the body. Deidre, you start where you think the feet might be. Melissa, work where you might imagine his belt, and I'll work around the head. Take your time, and try not to disturb the body. Use the small trowels to work the dirt loose, and scoop it out with your hands. It'll be slow, but being careful will pay off in the long run."

Then she added, "It's a good thing you and Jeff made this hole as large as you did. Otherwise I'd be down here alone."

The three women worked in silence, every few seconds straightening up to gasp for a breath of fresh air. Deidre discovered why Judy said she wished she hadn't eaten so much of her own meal.

"I think you were right, Deidre. The more soil I remove, the more I see that this person's neck is twisted almost sideways. He wasn't laid in the grave, that's for sure."

Deidre was too nauseated to care, but she kept skimming back the gravel from where she thought the victim's feet should be. Finally, a foot came into view, and she continued to tease away the dirt until an entire foot was exposed. The sock on it was badly deteriorated, and she could see that the foot was shoeless.

A little more digging revealed the other foot. It had a brown loafer on it. Deidre stood up and looked down at her discovery. She knew where the lone shoe's mate could be found.

"I'm pretty sure I know who this is," she announced. "We've had an unsolved missing person case. I think we just found him. His pickup was abandoned in the ditch a few hundred yards back on the road where we came in. When I searched his truck, I found the mate to this shoe." She pointed to her find. "Say hello to Skinny Tomlinson."

By seven o'clock it was getting dark enough that they were having trouble seeing. Judy looked up over the edge of the dig.

"Jennifer, I think it's time to crank up the generator. Dan, can you focus the spotlights where we need the most light?"

Deidre heard the cough of a gas engine and then the smooth sound of a generator running. The whole scene lit up as the lights came alive. Dan adjusted them so the work area was as bright as day. Deidre wondered what was going on out by the road.

She wasn't the only one wondering. "Tomorrow one of us should meet with the press and act as spokesperson," Melissa said.

Deidre had to agree with her, but appearing on national news was the last thing she wanted to do.

"I'd just as soon keep our team together while we try to sort this mess out. Do you have any suggestions who we might call to do the dirty work out there?"

Judy kept digging, her head bent down so she wouldn't have to make eye contact. Finally, Melissa spoke up. "I've faced them before. I suppose I can do it again. I'll toss them a herring and see if they go for it. They won't give up, but I'll try to buy us some time before we all have to face the cameras."

Deidre and Judy each said a silent thank you, and kept at the messy job before them. By ten o'clock the form of a man lay exposed under the glare of the bright lights that penetrated to the bottom of the pit. One of his knees was bent so that his foot was drawn up beside his other knee. He was almost on his belly, and his neck was twisted around so he looked up at the sky. What they all found most disturbing were his hands. They were bound behind his back with a plastic tie.

"An execution," Deidre said, and the others nodded their assent. The three made their way up the bank, and everyone looked into the hole.

"I want to get him out of there tonight," Judy announced. "That way I can do a preliminary exam right here. Then we'll body bag him. Can you reach the morgue tonight?" she asked Deidre.

Deidre nodded as she looked down at what was left of Skinny. *He had never contributed much to the community, but he certainly didn't deserve to end up like this,* she thought.

"Why don't you get suited up, too," Judy said, motioning to those who had been working on top. "It's going to take a group effort just to get him on a stretcher."

Enough room had been cleared on one side of the corpse that five of them could stand side by side. Jennifer stood at Skinny's head, holding a stretcher. The others began to slide their hands under the body and tried to lift it high enough for her to slide the sling under it. The body was so deteriorated that it almost fell apart in their hands when they lifted. They held it just long enough for Jennifer to complete her task.

Dan turned his head and vomited what was left in his stomach from supper. His action was contagious.

"Okay, that's done with," Melissa said, her eyes watering and tears running down her cheeks. "Jeff and Dan, get up on top. Jennifer and Judy, you take one end. Deidre and I will lift the other. On three: one, two, three," and Skinny was lifted from his grave. Jeff grabbed one end of the stretcher and Dan the other. They carried his body to a table that had been set up under a light.

Deidre skinned off her hazmat suit and started up her ATV. Judy began her examination before Deidre was able to leave.

At the road she marched quickly to her Explorer and called into dispatch. "Notify the mortuary to come out to the Whyte Road site. We'll have a body for them to take back in an hour."

She turned to head back to the camp, but by that time the press had gathered again. One called out to her.

"Sheriff, have you found anything yet?"

Deidre faced the man. "No comment at the present time. Tomorrow, at eight o'clock, we'll have a statement for you."

"How many bodies do you expect to find?" Deidre heard shouted from behind her as she drove back into the woods.

By the time she saw the spotlights filling the night with brightness, Judy had all but finished her preliminary exam of the corpse. Deidre hurried over to the makeshift examination slab.

"Anything?" she asked.

"Death appears to have been caused by a single small caliber bullet to the back of the head. There are no other gross indications of injury before the fatal shot. However, because the body is so deteriorated, we won't know until more testing is done."

"Was there any ID on him?" Deidre wanted to know, although she was almost certain who the victim was.

"Not a thing." Judy shook her head as she spoke. "Dan, bring a body bag, and we'll get this one hauled out."

Chapter Eighteen

DAN AND JEFF CARRIED THE BAGGED BODY to one of the ATVs and strapped the stretcher across its front carrier rack. While they were doing that, Deidre approached Melissa. "When I was out the last time and saw the crowd, I decided it's not fair to place all of the public appearances on you. If you don't mind, I'll come with you when you meet the horde tomorrow. I don't want to shy away from what's probably my job in the first place."

Melissa smiled. "Thanks. I think it will be good if more than one of us shows up."

Deidre drove the ATV carrying the corpse, and Melissa followed on another. When they arrived at the road, the mortician had backed his hearse to where the body could be transferred, and Deidre pulled up behind it. Floodlights streamed from behind the many TV cameras, and Deidre could see the red eye of each glowing. They were going to be on national TV whether they wanted to or not. She couldn't help squinting into the glare of the piercing lights.

Fortunately, the crowd gathered behind the crime scene tapes were momentarily cowed by the solemnity of the moment, and a strange quiet enveloped the night.

Deidre took one end of the stretcher, and when she lifted it, she was shocked at how little it weighed. *There's not much left of Skinny,* she thought.

Melissa had the other end, and they set his body on the floor of the black Lincoln Navigator. The mortician closed the back door of the hearse.

"Store this one in a cooler," Deidre instructed him. "Be sure to secure it with a lock until we can do a full postmortem."

Without comment, he got in the black hearse and slowly drove away. The gang of reporters came alive.

"Do you know who he is?"

"How did he die?"

"Will there be others?"

Deidre turned to them. "Ms. Sobranski of the BCA and I will return to meet with you at 8:00 tomorrow morning. We'll answer as many questions as we can at that time. Thank you for your patience." She and Melissa hurried to their vehicles and sped off into the solitude of the black night.

By the time they made it back to the dig site, the others had finished screening the excavated dirt and were in the process of cleaning up. Deidre was surprised to discover that the loaded trailer they had hauled in contained a large tank of water with disinfectant for their use. She and Melissa joined them in removing the day's grime.

"Did your screening turn up anything?" Melissa asked Jeff and Dan, hoping for good news.

"That was a lot of dirt to process," Jeff said. "But we did find a few things: a chewing gum wrapper, three cigarette butts, and a scrap of light weight pasteboard, like from a box. It looks like it might have a phone number written on it, but the ink is too faded to tell."

"Well, that's something," Deidre said.

"Anything else?" Melissa questioned.

Jeff couldn't keep a straight face, and Dan answered. "Just a shell casing."

Both Deidre and Melissa straightened up with that announcement. "Let me see the bag," they said in unison as they both held out their hands. Jeff gave it to Deidre, and she and Melissa almost collided heads as they bent over it.

"Twenty-five caliber," Melissa said.

"Center fire," Deidre finished her statement.

"That's a common pocket pistol, the kind carried by people who think they need a gun for protection." Melissa turned the bag in her hand and held it up to the light. "The problem is, its projectile has no stopping power. The shooter would have more luck if he threw rocks."

"Yeah, unless the shooter is six inches away from his target. It stopped Skinny, if that's who we dug up," Deidre added. "Anyway, it's a significant piece of evidence for us to find. If we come across a suspect firearm and can match the casing marks to the gun, we have the murder weapon."

Judy came out from the third tent. "It's after eleven, and I think it's time to call it a day. Tomorrow we'll start on the next grave site while Deidre and Melissa go out to the road. We'll get in a full day's work tomorrow. One mystery we'll have to try to solve is the order of the burials, assuming there is a body found under each depression."

When Deidre entered the large tent, she was amazed to find that it contained a camping cot for each of them, and a sleeping bag. Melissa's team had come prepared.

It was a restless night for all of them.

NO ONE IN THE TENT COULD SLEEP past daybreak. For one thing, the temperature had dropped below freezing, and they were shivering in their sleeping bags. Also, when the first rays of the sun started to light up the woods, it had come alive with the sounds of squirrels scolding each other and woodpeckers pounding away on dead trees. Nuthatches chirped as they squabbled with each other over the treasures hidden for them in a rotten tree trunk. Ordinarily, these would have been soothing sounds to Deidre, but today was not ordinary.

She crawled out of her sleeping bag and stretched. She wondered what she looked like and tried to straighten the wrinkles in her uniform. *Time to face the music,* she thought.

Melissa pulled the sleeping bag down from around her face. "The glamour of working for the BCA," she said, and mimicked Deidre's actions.

They looked at each other and laughed. "Are you ready to face the cameras?" Melissa asked.

By the time the two department heads were ready to meet the press, the others were up and out of the tent. Judy was getting them organized to begin digging, and they were sorting through the tools they'd need. It looked to be a sunny autumn day. Deidre promised them breakfast when she and Melissa returned.

A full contingent of news people had gathered, anticipating a statement. As Deidre and Melissa dismounted their ATVs, flashes from digital cameras flickered, and the red lights of the TV cameras glowed, indicating they were recording. Reporters waited with microphones in hand and audio recorders were turned on. This was the first time Deidre had been in such a tension-packed situation, and she was glad Melissa was there to take the lead.

Melissa began. "Ladies, gentlemen, first I will provide you with a brief statement about this case. Then we will allow fifteen minutes for you to ask questions. After that, Sheriff Johnson and I must return to the site to supervise the excavations that are in progress."

"Does this mean you expect to find more bodies?" the reporter pressing against the crime scene tape blurted out.

Melissa fixed a withering stare of disgust on him and stood silently. The crowd became silent, and his face reddened at the lull. She had made her point that she was in charge and not they.

"Thank you," Melissa continued. "I am Melissa Sobranski of the BCA, and this is Sheriff Deidre Johnson of Lake County. Two days ago Sheriff Johnson and her deputies partially excavated a grave. After confirming the presence of a body, and after noting what may be six other graves in the same area, she called the Bureau of Criminal Apprehension for assistance. We arrived with a team yesterday and completed the disinterment of the body of a man. It appears that he met a violent death. As of now, his body is stored in the morgue in Two Harbors awaiting further examination. We have not uncovered any significant clues. Neither do we have any suspects. The case is in its earliest stages of investigation. Do you have any questions?"

Immediately, a woman who was buried in the crowd shouted, "How long will it take to unearth the other suspected graves?"

"We hope to have that phase of the investigation completed by the day after tomorrow. Tomorrow evening would even be better," Melissa answered, her voice sounding confident.

The same voice rang out before another question could be asked. "How long will it take before the victims are identified?"

Again Melissa had a quick answer. "We expect to have those answers within six weeks, maximum."

From there, others fired their questions.

"Do you have any idea who is behind these murders?"

"No, but keep in mind, only one murder has been confirmed at this time."

"Is this the work of a serial killer?"

"We don't know. So far we have only one body."

The back and forth went on for several minutes with Melissa providing succinct answers. Finally, a reporter directly in front of them lifted his hand and said, "This question is for Sheriff Johnson. Weren't you the sheriff involved in a shooting somewhat over a year ago?"

"Yes, that was me."

He continued. "Have your wounds fully healed?"

"Yes, totally. Thank you for your concern."

"Could there be any connection between these graves and the threat of terrorism that took place in your county a year ago?"

"No, there is absolutely no evidence of any linkage. That case has been closed."

The questioner would not give up. "But if I recall, one of the terrorists involved last summer escaped and has never been located. How can you say that case has been closed?"

Deidre was becoming irritated by his line of questioning, but she managed to keep her voice calm and matter of fact. "This appears to be a local issue. The victim we have unearthed is possibly a local man. We'll know shortly if that is the case.

"Other indications that it is a local problem are the remoteness of the grave and the fact that neither the FBI nor the Department of Homeland Security has received any indication of a terrorist threat.

"We must be careful not to allow this investigation to be led into areas beyond probability," she chided the questioner.

Melissa stepped forward. "We promised you fifteen minutes for questioning, and we're already five minutes over that limit. Thank you for your patience. We'll try to keep you updated as the story unfolds."

Melissa placed her hand on Deidre's shoulder as they walked towards their ATVs. "Well-handled," she said.

CHAPTER NINETEEN

WHEN THEY CAME OVER THE CREST of the ridge, they could see that the group had made considerable progress. There were piles of dirt marking where the screen had been used, and Judy paced between two grave sites, directing the workers.

Dan and Jeff were in one hole with only their torsos and heads showing. Jennifer was working by herself.

Judy greeted them. "Hope it went well out there. These graves aren't marked in the order they were made, so we started at random. I'm hoping they were made over a significant period of time so the differences in the condition of any bodies will be pronounced. Deidre, if you will, I'd like you to help Jennifer. Melissa, why don't you start on a third grave? Be sure to carefully scrape away the duff covering the third depression. We don't want to lose any evidence lying on top of the ground."

Deidre noticed that many roots had been cut by Jennifer's shovel when she penetrated the first two feet of soil.

"Judy, have you noticed how many roots are growing here compared to the relatively freshly dug grave of our first victim?" She looked over to where Jeff's and Dan's heads were visible above the dirt they had thrown out of the hole. "What's it like where you two are digging?" she asked as the two men labored with their shovels.

Jeff stood up and wiped his sleeve across his sweaty face. "Not many roots here at all, and the ones we went through were only a half-inch thick."

"What do you think?" Deidre asked Judy. "Could the roots be a means of aging the dig?"

Judy looked a little shocked. "You're right. The older the grave, the more roots we should be finding, and they should be larger, too. I don't know of any study that has quantified the rate of root growth, but we should be able to compare relative root diameters for each of these sites. Great thinking, Deidre."

Judy went to the first grave and recorded, in her ever-present notebook, the number and diameter of roots that had been cut through by the excavators. She did the same for the other two suspected graves being opened, measuring and recording quickly.

"Melissa, when you find a root, try to cut it off squarely if you can. It'll make measuring a lot easier."

The six investigators worked steadily for the next thirty minutes with little talking.

"We've got something here," Jeff called out excitedly. He was standing next to the dirt screen, and held a small object between his thumb and forefinger. "It's another casing, similar to the one we found last night, the same caliber and same make. Why do you think they're leaving this evidence behind?"

"Maybe they thought no one would find these graves, and it was the safest place to leave the evidence. Who knows," Judy added. "Maybe they thought leaving a calling card was a joke."

Before Jeff could get back into the hole, Dan hollered, "Judy, come here quick. I've uncovered what looks like a leg bone."

Judy rushed over and looked into the hole.

"We have to move more slowly now. You and Jeff can handle it, but use only the small tools, the trowels and brushes. When you're finished, I'd like to see the skeleton lying uncovered but complete."

"What about clothing?" Jeff asked. "It's so far gone it falls apart when we touch it."

"Bag what you can and try to keep the pieces as large as possible," Judy instructed. "Buttons, zippers, anything that's retrievable should be bagged as evidence. We never know what can be traced to a significant source."

Judy paced nervously, spending most of her time by the dig where Jeff and Dan labored on their hands and knees. Occasionally, she would move to the other sites and measure roots.

By noon a second set of remains had been totally uncovered. It lay face down in the dirt, its arms pulled behind its back, and its wrists cinched with a plastic tie.

Judy took photos of every step of the process, forming a chronological visual report. She was about to gather everyone to help extricate the bones from the hole when Melissa shouted. "We have another one here. I've uncovered what looks to be the top of a cranium."

Progress was more rapid than Judy had anticipated. The soil was soft, gravelly, and easy to scoop up with a shovel.

"Let's stop work on those other two sites and remove these bones before we go any further. What's the condition of the skeleton?" she wanted to know.

"The bones seem to be still articulated. I think enough ligaments remain that it isn't falling apart," Dan said as he gently moved a leg bone.

"Do we need suits for this one?" Jeff asked.

"I think we're okay," Judy ventured. "Everything's pretty dry. We should be okay if we wear elbow-length gloves."

Although a few bones fell from the skeleton, the five workers were able to bag it mostly intact, but not before Judy noted what looked like a small hole in the back of the skull.

"We're on a roll now," Judy said, "but I'm hungry and tired. I think we should stop for lunch, or else we are going to run out of gas before the job is finished. Is there any chance we have a meal ready?"

Deidre looked at her watch and saw that it was already after noon.

"The caterer will be waiting at the road, so I'd better get moving," she said. "Be back in a half hour. I'll make sure we have something good for supper tonight."

"Do that," Judy said. "In the meantime, I think the rest of us should sit in the shade until you return. It's been a long morning."

As Deidre approached the road, she could see that more reporters had joined the tent city. An immediate cry went up as she rode out of the woods.

"Sheriff, do you have anything to report?"

"Have you unearthed another grave?"

"How is your crew holding up?"

Deidre dismounted her ATV. "People, I can't comment at this time. Ms. Sobranski and I will spend a half-hour with you, recapping the day's findings, when we return for supper at six o'clock. Thank you." She turned her back on a wave of questions.

The delivery person, a young lady she knew from town, helped her secure the packages of food and drink to her machine, and Deidre followed the trail that was beginning to resemble a road into the woods.

During the ride back into the burial site, she realized how famished she was. The work and discoveries had been so exciting all other needs had been ignored, and she was thankful to see that the others had set up a table where they could have their "picnic."

"I have beef sandwiches, turkey sandwiches, and here is the Mediterranean veggie sandwich you requested, Judy. Smells good," she commented as she handed it over. "Oscar sent plenty of hot coffee, and we each get a piece of his famous apple pie to go with it."

The five investigators savored the meal and commented on how much fun this would be if there weren't so many bodies.

"Well, gang," Judy said as she stood up from the table. "I hate to break up this fun time, but we have an awful lot of work to do before we sleep tonight. Let's get at it."

The body bag was placed inside Judy's work tent, and they shifted their attention to the third set of remains, the one Melissa and Deidre had discovered before the lunch break. The complete uncovering of the bones took less time as the team became more proficient with practice.

This skeleton was almost completely disarticulated. Most connective tissue had decomposed and there was no way to lift it intact. The team resorted to bagging up a collection of loose bones that would be reassembled by Judy at the morgue. Her notes showed that there were a large number of roots with diameters ranging up to an inch in diameter that had to be cut through.

"This grave certainly appears to be older than the other two," Judy exclaimed. "It seems these murders were spread out over a period of several years. Melissa, why don't you, Deidre, and I work where you uncovered what you suspected was a cranium. Dan and Jeff, perhaps you would start opening a fifth depression. When we are ready to remove victim number four, we'll give a holler."

The skeleton the three women uncovered in the fourth grave was not totally articulated. The skull, vertebral column, and ribs were intact, but when they tried to lift it out, most of the arm and leg bones came loose.

"This is better than nothing," Judy groused. "At least I won't be starting from scratch."

By the end of the day, the team had unearthed a total of three skeletons in addition to the body they found in the first grave. Each bore the same disquieting signs: hands bound behind their backs and a single bullet hole to the back of the head. Each soil screening produced a single empty center fire shell casing bearing the markings ".25 CAL., WIN., ACP."

Deidre and Melissa made the trip out so they could bring in the evening meal. They knew a crowd would be waiting to hear of the day's progress but were surprised at how the city of reporters had grown, even since noon.

"Sheriff, will you be making a statement at this time?"

"Yes, Melissa and I are prepared to offer a report of our progress at this time." She gave Melissa a look that asked the question, "We are, aren't we?"

Melissa gave a slight nod and held out the palm of her hand to Deidre, a sign for her to continue.

Deidre took a deep breath. "In all, we have found three skeletons and one decaying corpse. They have been unearthed, the corpse has been taken to what serves as our county morgue, and the bones have been bagged for later study. We should have all seven sites explored by tomorrow evening if we are able to continue working at the present rate. Then the investigation will be moved into town."

There was a flood of questions. Deidre chose one to answer. "Have you found any evidence that might indicate how these murders were committed?"

"None of any significance," she said as she looked directly at the questioner. *No use tipping our hand when I don't have to,* she thought.

"I'll take one more question."

"Do you have any suspects in this case?"

"None."

As she and Melissa turned to leave, a reporter shouted out, "Ms. Sobranski, are your two agencies working well together?"

"Yes," Melissa called over her shoulder. "Thank you for asking."

After another "picnic" in the woods, work continued on graves five and six. By ten o'clock, they had dug down almost three feet. The soil of one of the graves had been infiltrated by a growth of thick roots, and the other had less than a dozen half-inch tendrils crossing through it. Judy decided they should call it a day, and everyone retreated to their cots for a second night of camping out.

In the dark, Judy commented, "We can be thankful for this sandy soil. It makes for one of the easiest digs I have ever worked. This would have taken us a week if we were in clay or rocks."

They fell asleep, physically and mentally exhausted.

The next day, everyone was eager to get on with the task, and they discussed the expectations of what they would find.

When the other bodies were unearthed, the only deviation they found from the day before was the condition of the bones. Most were not held together by residual tissue. One set of bones was darkened and more deteriorated than the rest. Otherwise everything coincided, right down to the single shell casing found in each grave. By four that afternoon all the excavating had been completed.

Deidre and Melissa made their way out to the road again and faced nearly the same questions they had the day before. They explained what the next step in the investigation would be. Deidre made a call to Search and Rescue, asking that they bring their large transport vehicle to the site. That way all of the remains could be taken away at once. Judy had requested that the skeletons, as well as the decomposed body, be taken to the Twin Cities, where there was room to work and where her staff would be on hand.

Afterward, the two women laughed together about how their appearance must have shocked the nation. Well, at any rate, they looked as if they had been working.

By the time they were back at the grave sites, the others had pretty much disassembled the camp. The body bags were loaded onto one of the trailers, and they began a solemn procession out. Not, however, before they scoured the area one more time for any clues.

"It'll be difficult to keep the reporters out of here much longer. We might as well let them have at it."

When they reached the road, Search and Rescue was waiting. Loading the bodies through the back door of the large orange-and-white van was a solemn event. Even the many journalists on hand paid their respect for the dead with their silence. The place became as quiet as the inside of a church.

After Search and Rescue had driven away, Deidre and Melissa stepped up to the crime scene tape behind which the reporters stood waiting.

"Melissa and I are prepared to answer as many questions as we can for you. All we ask is that you be courteous to each other and allow everyone to get answers to what you want to know. If you have a question, please indicate so, and we will call on you. We will stay with you as long as you have questions."

Immediately, several hands shot up. Deidre called on a balding man standing in the middle of the pack. "How many remains were discovered?"

"There were seven bodies found." She pointed at a young female reporter standing in the front. Her black hair was flyaway and bound up with a red bandana. "What were the conditions of the bodies?"

"They were in various states of decay. The first had flesh still clinging to the skeleton, although it was badly decomposed. One appeared to have been in the ground longer than the others as was evident from the decomposition of the bony tissue itself. The others were found to be in varying states of decay."

A gray-haired lady with her hair held back by combs and a pencil was called on next. "This evidence seems to indicate that the murders were spread out over a period of time. Am I correct in my thinking?"

"Yes." Deidre said and pointed to a younger man who stood off to the side. He seemed to be uncomfortable in the crowd, and his thin, pointed face was flushed with anxiety.

He stuttered, "Wo-wo-would this m-m-mean that w-w-w-we are d-d-d-dealing with a-a-a ser-ser-serial k-k-k-killer?"

Deidre knew what it felt like to be an outsider, so she answered more completely than she might have another person. "It is too soon to make any guess at that. One thing we must guard against is creating a mindset. Right now we are considering all options."

She pointed to a confident-appearing middle-aged, gray-haired man. "Why haven't you called in the FBI? It seems they have more expertise than your local force. Wouldn't the public be better served by outside experts than by your people?"

Deidre's eyes flashed, but before she could answer, Melissa spoke. "So you're not kept ignorant any longer, at the present time this is out of the FBI's jurisdiction. The Lake County Sheriff's Department has a sterling record, including thwarting a terrorist attack on the ore docks last year. Evidently you didn't read about that incident in your paper. Also, I represent the State Bureau of Criminal Apprehension, and we are recognized nationally as being in the forefront of forensic practices. You can rest assured that if our investigation turns up evidence that indicates this is a matter to be turned over to the FBI, we will. When and if that happens, you'll be the first person we'll call. Just give us your name and where you can be reached."

The man's face turned red, and he shook his head.

Questioning went on for another forty-five minutes. Sometimes the questions were repetitious, asked by persons who evidently wanted to hear themselves speak. Finally, it appeared as though everyone was talked out. Deidre was about to close the session when she noticed the tongue-tied young man timidly raise his hand.

"One last question," and she pointed at him.

He paused, took a deep breath, and then closed his eyes for a second before speaking. "Might there be a connection between the death of that young girl, J-J-J-Jill Moore?," he paused and took another deep breath before continuing "and these deaths?"

His question caught Deidre totally off guard. In the confusion of the past few days, Jill hadn't come to her mind once.

"That's an excellent question, but one I can't speculate on at this time. It is certainly something we will consider. Thank you."

Deidre and Melissa turned their backs and walked away from the crowd.

CHAPTER TWENTY

THE FIRST THING DEIDRE DID when she was nearing Two Harbors was to call John.

"Oh, it is so good to hear your voice," she said. "The last three days have been incredibly difficult, but we finished what we had to do. I need a hot shower, a warm meal served at a table, and you."

"In that order?" John teased her. "I heard you'd be done by this afternoon, and I'm way ahead of you. In fact, I'm at your place now. The steaks are ready to put on the grill when you're cleaned up. The wine is chilling in the bucket, and I'll have a fire going in the fireplace when you get here."

Deidre ended the call with a smile of expectation on her face. It took her over an hour to put things in order at her office, and she left for home as soon as she could. John was waiting for her at the door.

Deidre wrapped her arms around him and buried her face in his chest. She inhaled his scent and stood with his arms enveloping her for many seconds. Then she pushed back from his grasp and looked up into his face. She traced his nose with the tip of her finger and said, "I love you, John Erickson."

John smiled and hugged her close again.

A hot shower had never felt so good in her whole life, and fifteen minutes later she was still standing under the flow. A half-hour later she came down the stairs dressed in clean clothes, her hair swept back and held by a band, and the fragrance of Estée Lauder perfume drifting from her warmed body. She felt like a real person.

The night was one of relaxation and therapy. John sat silent most of the time as Deidre recounted what had transpired. He interrupted her once.

"You looked great on TV." Only then did it dawn on her that she had been seen by millions of people, including friends.

"Oh, Lord," she said. "I must have looked a mess."

"Well, put it this way. I'm not too worried about men saying 'Look at that babe of a sheriff.'" He laughed and drew her close to him.

Deidre told her story until well past midnight when they finally went to bed.

THE NEXT DAYS FLEW BY. Deidre was busy tying up loose ends and attempting to regain some sense of order in her department. Her deputies were exhausted from around-the-clock duty on the Whyte Road, and they needed rest. Schedules had to be altered, and a number of relatively minor incidents had to be investigated. The world had not rested while she was away.

Eventually, though, the hubbub died. Another tragedy occurred somewhere else, and the news reporters shifted their attention to the latest hot story. Deidre was left alone to do her work. A week later she had a meeting scheduled with Mac of the Lake Superior Drug and Gang Task Force. At 8:30 a.m. he knocked on her office door, and after he sat down, she offered him a cup of freshly brewed coffee.

"You've had quite the past two weeks," he said as a greeting. "I'm almost sorry to burden you with more work, but I have an urgent matter that can't wait."

Deidre sat down in the chair opposite where he was sitting, and Mac continued.

"We've been working with an undercover person in your county. He's discovered evidence of a group targeting mostly high school kids and recent graduates. Seems you have a cocaine problem up here. Best of all, he has names. I think it's time to make a sweep. If we move at one time, we can grab six people he's named before they can alert each other. That, however, takes manpower."

Deidre looked at Mac through eyes dark-ringed from too many hours of work. "What do you want from us?" she asked, her voice gone flat.

"Most of the arrests will be made in Two Harbors. For those we'll use the city police force. Unfortunately, they have only enough officers to cover three of the houses we'll be targeting. That leaves one more house in town and one in the country, which is in your jurisdiction anyway. We'll need four of your people. It should go smoothly and shouldn't be too stressful for your deputies. I know they've been through a lot lately, but nobody said this job would be easy."

Deidre sat back in her chair. "When will this happen?" she asked.

Mac looked at the floor. "Well, that's the tough part, this afternoon at six o'clock. Can you be ready by then?"

"We'll be ready, Mac, but I think you're going to find that things go a lot deeper than you expect. The partially decomposed body we found is almost certainly that of my missing person, Skinny Tomlinson. The night before the news of the graves broke I visited with a young man, a high school student. He was scared stiff, but he came forward with information you'll want to hear. He said that Skinny was rumored to have been pushing cocaine to kids, and he named Jill Moore, the girl who died of an overdose of meth, as one of his customers. He also implicated a student he thought was involved. It's like a spiderweb of people out there preying on teenagers. If we get to the bottom of your drug investigation, I think we may find ourselves taking the lid off the seven murder cases we found on the Whyte."

Mac let out a soft whistle. "You're right, Deidre. I didn't see that coming."

Deidre continued. "I'm calling Ben VanGotten of the FBI today. At the least, I think we have a serial killer at work. At most, we are in the middle of gang activity, a vicious gang."

Mac stood to leave. "We're going to move fast on this. You're in if the operation goes into effect this evening at six? I hope you don't mind if we meet here at five for final instructions."

FROM HER OFFICE, DEIDRE DIALED the number of the FBI in Duluth and entered the extension number 467. "Ben, how are you?"

"I'm great, Deidre. How about you?Have you showered yet?" He laughed.

"Okay," she shot back. "I know I wasn't at my best during those interviews. Seriously, Ben, the last time we talked you said we needed more evidence to have the FBI involved. I think we have it."

Deidre went on to explain all that had transpired and hadn't been divulged to the news. When she finished, Ben didn't hesitate.

"I think it best that I pay you a visit tomorrow. Is there any time that's best for you?"

"Right after morning report, if you can make it."

"I'll see you then."

She no sooner disconnected from that call when her phone rang. "Deidre, this is Judy from the BCA."

"Judy, it's good to hear your voice. I suppose you've been swamped since returning to the Cities."

"That's what I called about. We've been working around the clock, and we have a positive ID on the corpse we exhumed. You remember that we were able to dig up, no pun intended, the dental records for Mr. Tomlinson. It's lucky for us that the retired dentist, Doctor Steward, had saved all his records. Even though they were from when he was a teenager, I was able to make a definite determination. The body is that of your missing person, Skinny.

"The cause of death was a single gunshot to the back of the head. We found the slug in his cranium, and as we suspected, it is a .25 caliber. Its markings are in good condition, so if we find the gun from which it was fired, we will be able to match it to the murder weapon."

"That's great news, Judy, although I'm a long way from putting the pieces of this puzzle together. It's like they're scattered all over the place, with a few of them missing. I have to say that with seven murders, a possible drug connection, and a dead teenager, I feel like I'm rapidly getting buried."

Then Deidre asked, "Have you made any progress on the other remains?"

"We have most of them reconstructed. We'll be finished by next week. Is there any chance you can come down to my lab? There is so much evidence I'd like to spend a day going over it with you. Besides, it'd be good to see you again."

They settled on a tentative date, and Deidre rocked back in her chair. Her head throbbed, and she massaged her temples. *Mac's right. No one said this was going to be an easy job.*

She called dispatch. "Jaredine, would you get hold of Jeff? He's patrolling the south end of the county today. Have him come in at four o'clock. Call Dave and Jo. They are not scheduled to work today, but we need the extra bodies. Have them meet me here at the same time."

Her next call was to John. "Hi, my dear, how's your day going?"

"I'm bored out of my mind. I've been behind my desk all morning and need a break from this paperwork. How's yours?"

"Don't even ask," Deidre responded, the tension evident in her voice. "How about lunch at that little place where we held our first meeting? I'll be the one in the sheriff's uniform with the crazy look in her eyes."

John laughed. "Sounds like you could use a break more than I could. I'll be there at one. See you."

CHAPTER TWENTY-ONE

WHEN JOHN SAW DEIDRE WALKING toward him in the restaurant, his heart was torn. The wear of the past two weeks' happenings was evident on her face, and he couldn't remember ever seeing her look so drawn. There was no spring in her step.

"It's been pretty rough, hasn't it," he commiserated.

"One layer has been piling on another until I feel buried beneath the stack. Not only do I have seven murders to deal with, but now they may possibly be linked to a drug ring that has been operating under our radar for Lord knows how long. I miss being with you, but I don't know when this cycle's going to break. Again, tonight, another serious call has to be answered. When are we ever going to get some time together?"

John reached out and held her hand. "You can't go on like this without a break, or you are going to end up being broken yourself. If you don't take care of yourself, no one else is going to do it for you."

Tears welled up in Deidre's eyes. A little over a year ago, she would never have allowed herself to cry, let alone cry in front of anyone else.

John rubbed her fingers. "Today is Tuesday. What if you make a concerted effort to clear your desk of all but these two serious cases by the end of Friday? I'll make reservations for us at the Red Fin Trout. It's only forty miles up the shore from Two Harbors. I think it was built before the strict zoning laws were enacted so they could get away with building so close to the lake. It sits almost on the water's edge of Lake Superior. Anyway, it is the most secluded spot I've ever found: few units, great food, a real upscale atmosphere, and at night you can hear the waves wash upon the beach. I think it would be good for you. Besides, I want to be with you. There's something I think we should talk about."

Deidre didn't answer at first. Then, in a barely audible voice she said, "You're right."

During their meal, John tried to be positive. He talked about the good things happening with his job, how much he'd enjoyed the night she came home from the woods, how much he missed being with her, and how he wished that happened every night.

By the time they finished their dessert, Deidre's spirits had lifted, and she realized how much she needed John in her life.

BACK IN HER OFFICE, Deidre looked up at the clock and watched the minute hand click to 3:50. Any moment she expected the three deputies she had tagged for the drug raid that evening to walk into her office. Jeff was first, quickly followed by Dave and Jo. Jeff had been with her the longest. In fact, he had been on the force before she was hired.

He had a lovely family, two little girls and a wife who adored him. Deidre knew the past two weeks had been as hard on him as it had been on her. She knew he missed evenings with his family. But Jeff was a true professional, always willing to step up and do more than his share, always wanting to better his understanding of the legal system.

Jo was hired after Ben had taken his job with the FBI. She was not your ordinary woman. Deidre guessed she stood five-seven and didn't want to guess at her weight. Her eyes were a steel blue, and without trying, her stare was like ice. Deidre knew that wasn't her true nature, and she had seen a tender side to the woman that was seldom exposed.

Jo held both a sociology and a criminology degree and had worked as a probation officer for five years before joining the force. Deidre had hired her because of her experience and because of her academic preparation.

Dave had been hired three months after Jo and was the youngest member of the force. After a prolonged battle, the county board had given in to Deidre's request and expanded her force by one more person.

He was so ordinary-looking he could become invisible in a crowd of four. What impressed Deidre about Dave was that he knew how to handle people. Whenever he became involved in a dispute, he could usually talk the parties down and defuse the situation. Deidre knew these were the people she wanted on the job tonight.

"You all know Mac of the Lake Superior Drug and Task Force." She waited for a response, but no one spoke up. Deidre took that to mean "Yes."

"He'll be coming in at five o'clock today to give us a briefing on an operation we'll be assisting him with tonight. The Two Harbors police will be taking part, also. They'll have more people on this than we will."

"Why us?" Jeff asked, weariness evident in his voice.

"There are five houses involved, four in the city and one rural. The warrants must all be served at the same time so one party can't tip off the next. The city has enough personnel to cover three of them. Mac asked us to pick up the fourth in town. The rural site is ours anyway. I'm really sorry to have to ask you to put in more overtime, but I'm over the barrel on this one. At least you're storing up a lot of comp time. When we get a breather around here, use it. It's for your own good."

Members of the city department began to trickle in. Mac was five minutes early, and Deidre could see the strain in his eyes. He didn't smile, and his greeting was terse. As he waited he absentmindedly thrummed the table with his fingers and stared off into space.

Eventually, everyone arrived, the last officer walking in at exactly five o'clock. The group gathered around the conference table.

"We have good reason to believe we're going to nab some people with a significant amount of drugs tonight. The evidence is enough that we had no trouble securing search warrants from the judge yesterday, and we're confident that some arrests will be made. Be sure to read them their rights. I don't want anybody getting off because of a technicality."

Mac went on to outline how the raid would take place. They would begin leaving the Law Enforcement Center at five-thirty, but not in one group. Each team of two would drive away in a different direction, timing their movements so they would be able to enter their assigned house at exactly six.

"I talked to Jeff, Dan, and Jo before you got here, Mac. Is it okay if Jeff and I take the rural site and Dan and Jo the city?"

"That's exactly what I wanted," Mac affirmed. "Here are your assigned addresses and the names of people who should be there."

Mac went down the list. "Deidre and Jeff, your assignment is two miles out of town. The fire number is 131C. The person you will probably encounter is Ed Beirmont."

Deidre's eyes narrowed at the mention of his name. "I know where he lives, and it'll be my pleasure."

"Good. You and Jeff leave right now. That'll give you enough time to leave town in the opposite direction as a ruse and then swing back toward the lake. The rest of you leave at intervals as I said." He handed out the search warrants as Deidre and Jeff took theirs and walked out the door.

"I KNEW THAT SOONER OR LATER we'd get a crack at Ed," Deidre said to Jeff as they headed west out of town. "There's something not right with that guy. He does so little work, and yet he always has money. And the crowd he hangs with doesn't fit with his running a business either."

Deidre took a right turn onto County Road 21. It looped around town and back to the east, then connected with Highway 2. In ten minutes they were parked a quarter of a mile from Ed's driveway. At one minute before six she and Jeff drove up to his house.

Ed answered his door, part of his supper still in his mouth.

"Ed Beirmont, we're here to serve you with a warrant to search your home. Please move back into the house, and allow us in."

Ed said nothing, but stepped back as he had been told. "Please be seated at your table," Deidre instructed. Ed complied without a word after Jeff patted him down, looking for weapons.

The two officers began a systematic search of the premises. They started in the kitchen, going through all the drawers. Jeff took the unenviable job of checking the garbage can. Fortunately for him, it had hardly been used.

"Nothing here," he reported.

Deidre asked Ed to move to the bedroom, where they continued the search. As she went through his dresser drawers, she was surprised at the neatness of the folded clothes, not something she expected to find in a bachelor's place, especially one who spent most of his time hanging at bars and dives.

She lifted a stack of undershirts, and a plastic bag containing a green herb-like material was uncovered. *Marijuana,* the word flashed through Deidre's mind.

"Got something here," she called to Jeff. He came over to where she was standing. Ed looked up at the corner of the room, obviously ignoring what was going on.

Deidre fumbled a second in opening the bag. Her gloved hands didn't work as well than if her fingers were bare. Both of them sniffed the contents. There was no mistaking the pungent odor of the drug. She resealed the bag.

"How much do you think is in here?" she asked Jeff.

"I'd guess pretty close to one-and-a-half grams." They both knew that was an important amount. Anything less and all they had would be a petty misdemeanor, unless Ed had prior convictions.

Deidre bagged the evidence and labeled it. She continued going through the drawers while Jeff checked the closet. When she reached under a pile of neatly folded jeans in the bottom drawer, her hand contacted something steely. She pulled out a snub-nosed pistol.

"What's this?" she asked Ed. He didn't answer, only sat expressionless in his chair beside the bed. Jeff came to look while Deidre was checking if it was loaded. She removed the full clip from its magazine and ejected a live round from its barrel.

"What caliber is it?" he asked expectantly.

"It's a .380, not what we were expecting." She turned to Ed. "We're going to have to take you in, Ed." Then she read him his Miranda rights. "Stand up and place your hands behind your back."

Ed didn't object, didn't say one word while Jeff placed handcuffs around his thick wrists. They marched out to the Explorer Deidre drove and returned to the Law Enforcement Center.

Once seated in the interrogation room, Ed spoke for the first time. "I want to call my lawyer," was all he said.

By this time the rest of the sweep team began to arrive. None of them had apprehended a single person. Mac came in, his face red with exasperation, and he pounded his fist on the conference table.

"Not a thing. Not one damn thing," he sputtered. "At one house, the police heard the toilet flush just before they stepped in. A guy came out of the bathroom with a shit-eating grin on his face and said, 'Had some business to take care of. Can I get you a cup of coffee?' Every place we checked, we found nothing. Not one damn thing." he repeated to no one in particular. "Deidre, what did you find?"

She explained what had happened at Ed's. "We have a bag of marijuana, but it's borderline petty misdemeanor or misdemeanor. We'll have to weigh it to be sure. Then we'll have to check Ed's record. If he is a repeat offender, the charges can be elevated. Also, there is the issue of his gun. If it's not registered or if he has a felony conviction on his records, we have him. Otherwise, he'll be free to leave."

Mac continued to pace around the office.

Deidre had Jeff get on the computer and begin a thorough check of Ed's record. She took the bag of marijuana to the evidence room and weighed its contents. She left it locked in a screened cage where confiscated drugs were kept. The elevator ride to the top floor seemed to take forever.

"Well?" Mac wanted to know.

"It's almost as though Ed measured the quantity before we found it," she said, disappointment evident in her voice. "One point four-five ounces, five hundredths of an ounce below the limit. All we have is a petty misdemeanor."

She slumped in a chair. "Did you come up with anything, Jeff?"

Jeff shook his head. "The pistol is registered to him, and besides that he has a concealed carry permit. He has no prior history of drug use or dealing. Except for what we found tonight, he's squeaky clean, at least on paper."

"That's it, "Deidre declared. "All we can do is hand him a citation to appear in court. He'll end up paying a two hundred dollar fine. He'll even walk away with his handgun.

"Don't you just love this job?"

Chapter Twenty-Two

It was nine o'clock by the time Deidre left her office. Ed was on his way home, without his marijuana but with his gun and bullets in his jacket pocket. Deidre fumed as she drove home, almost forgetting to stop for the red light on Seventh Avenue.

The moon was in its new phase, reflecting no light to earth, and only the stars were visible. The alley behind Deidre's house was lit by only one streetlight high on a wooden pole, and as she swung into the spot next to her personal car, the SUV's headlights swept in an arc. For an instant, she saw a piece of paper being held in place by the wiper blade on her car's windshield.

Curious, she stepped out of her official vehicle and over to her car. She removed the paper from under the wiper, and walked up the sidewalk to where she could read it under her porch light. Her eyes opened wide, and her nostrils flared.

Printed with a black marker was: "Back off—or else."

Deidre's hands shook as she removed her revolver from its case. She tried her door. It was still locked. Hidden by the shadows, she quietly moved around the perimeter of her house.

She remembered the story told by a retired city police chief of his being in a similar situation. He had been chasing a suspect at night and had stuck his head around the corner of a building. He found himself looking directly into the bore of a pistol held by the man he was chasing. The chief heard "click" as the gun misfired. As Deidre forced herself to turn each corner, the thought of that incident lingered in her mind.

After several minutes of circumventing her home, Deidre was back to where she started. She unlocked the door, her pistol still ready. She searched every corner inside of what had been her safe place. Only when she was sure she was alone did she relax, but not completely. Not now.

Deidre flopped into her favorite recliner in the living room and dialed John. She had come to rely on his being there for her. She needed his support.

"John," she said with her voice full of tension and went on to tell him all that had happened.

"Do you want me to come be with you right now?" he wanted to know. Deidre could detect the concern in his voice.

"No. No, it's so late. I'll be okay. I just needed to hear your voice and be able to tell you about this."

They talked for a long time, until most of the tension had drained from her body. That left Deidre feeling completely wrung out by the time they hung up. She was ready for bed and climbed between the sheets without cleaning up.

THE NEXT MORNING, AFTER SLEEPING fitfully, Deidre showered and had a quick slice of toast and coffee for breakfast. Her mind on the morning's meeting with Ben, she had almost forgotten about last night's note. She hurried down her walkway to the Explorer and stopped in her tracks. Under its wiper blade was another note. Tentatively, she removed it. Scrawled in black marker were the words: "BANG! YOU'RE DEAD, UNLESS . . ."

Deidre's heart raced and her stomach knotted. For a moment she felt totally vulnerable.

Shaken, she got in her vehicle and drove to her office. She climbed the stairs slowly, thinking, *What do they expect, that I'll quit working? Working on what, the seven murder victims' case? Or the drug problem that seems to be surfacing? Or the death of Jill Moore? Maybe everything is one case. At any rate, do they think they'll scare me into quitting? What do they expect to accomplish by these threats?*

In her office she continued to mull over the notes. *Now what? I can't report this to the sheriff. I* am *the sheriff. Well, at least I can talk to Ben. He might have some advice. I wonder what it will take to get the FBI on our team?*

During morning report, Deidre shared what had happened, including the notes she had received. The others were upset, not only because of the messages, but also with how little they had to go on. With little else to discuss, she adjourned the meeting and waited for Ben.

He arrived shortly after Deidre's deputies left for their assignments. He looked good, somehow more confident, as he took her extended hand. She couldn't help but remember how his size had been so intimidating to her when they attended the police academy together. Now they were allies.

"Deidre, it's good to see you. You've had a tough run these last few weeks, and I sure hope I can help you. We think there is enough evidence of gangland involvement for the FBI to become involved." Both of them sat down.

"I've been briefed by Mac, so I know what happened on your raids last night. I've also been briefed by the BCA. Judy says next week she should be done with forensics on those remains you unearthed.

"How about you, has anything new happened?"

Deidre took a deep breath and related to Ben what had transpired, going back as far as the death of Jill Moore. She told him about her clandestine meeting with Peter Wilson.

"Last night when I got home from our sweep, I found this under my wiper blade." She showed him the first note.

"This morning when I came out to go to work, I found this." She handed him the second note.

Ben leaned back in his chair. "Deidre, this is serious. These notes are terroristic threats against you, a felony if we catch the individual responsible."

"Do you think these warnings are credible, or are they just a way of bluffing?" she asked, wanting Ben's opinion.

"If it were me, I'd take these warnings at face value. Someone doesn't want you around anymore."

For the rest of the morning, Deidre and Ben drew up flow charts delineating what would be each agency's operative mode. Ben suggested that they call in the BCA again, and that the four agencies, the FBI, the Sheriff's Department, the City Police, and the Lake Superior Drug and Gang Task Force join ranks. It seemed to him that each agency had a unique expertise they could share, and the crimes seemed to overlap everyone's jurisdiction.

She was heartened by the attitude of cooperation rather than the competition she'd anticipated. By the time Ben left, Deidre felt more on top of things than she had for a long time. They had a plan.

Ben was going to convene a meeting with Deidre, Mac, Melissa Sobranski, the Two Harbors Police Chief, and himself in his Duluth office. It was time to go to war, he said.

Later that afternoon, Ben called. "I cleared next Wednesday with the others. Can you spare that day to meet? I think this is necessary. What about you?"

Deidre responded without looking at her calendar. "If I have anything else scheduled, I'll cancel it. Thanks, Ben. It means a lot to me to be working with you again."

After the call, Deidre spent the remainder of the day doing what John had requested. She tied up a number of loose ends that had been ignored while she obsessed over the murders, the drugs, and the death of Jill. By late afternoon, she had made a significant dent in the paperwork on her desk and was ready to go home. She knew John would be waiting for her.

JOHN WAS THERE, A SMILE on his face and an apron around his waist. He laughed. "I'm starting to feel like Mr. Mom." He hugged her, the spatula still in his hand.

Deidre beat him to the question. "How was your day, dear?"

"I'm starting to think I've become nothing but a paper pusher. All I did today was read reports of what's happening in the Duluth Harbor. By the end of the day, I came to a conclusion: nothing." He shrugged in mock disgust. "How about yours?"

As John finished cooking dinner, they sipped sauvignon blanc. Deidre told him all that had transpired, including finding the second note.

"I'm so glad you're able to spend the night. I don't want to be alone anymore."

Just then the buzzer on the stove sounded an alarm.

"Damn," John cursed. "The chops are done. I forgot about them," and he jumped up to save the meat from overcooking.

Deidre laughed. "Good job, Mr. Mom."

Deidre made a point of not talking shop over dinner, other than to tell John that most of the day-to-day minutia was completed and she was free to leave for their weekend getaway.

After supper, as they lounged in front of a burning fire in the hearth, Deidre expressed her concerns.

"John, this is the first time I've felt like things are getting away from me. Everything seems to be like a tightly wound ball of string, and I can't find the loose end that will unravel it. I'm afraid. Afraid I'm losing control of the situation, afraid for my own safety."

John held her close. "Just remember," he said. "Nothing lasts forever. Furthermore, you have assembled a great team behind you, and you're not facing this alone. They're here to help you. Let them. As for your safety, I'm planning on moving in with you for the duration of this case. No way am I going to allow you to be in this house alone at night. Don't bother arguing, because I'm not taking no for an answer. That's final."

Deidre snuggled against his chest. "Who's arguing?"

Chapter Twenty-Three

In the morning the world looked brighter to Deidre. On the way to her car, she hummed a familiar tune and stopped to look at the colorful fall mums growing next to her walkway. She opened the back gate to her yard and stood motionless in her tracks. She could see another note on her windshield.

Hesitantly, she slid it from under the wiper blade. It read "This is for real—Stop."

As she stood trying to figure out what to do next, Mrs. Olson opened her back door.

"Deidre, Deidre dear," she called. "Would you come over here for a minute? I don't want to shout."

Slowly, Deidre walked over to her.

"I noticed that you have a man staying with you some nights," Mrs. Olson began. "Not that I try to snoop on what you're doing, but I do have trouble sleeping at night."

Here it comes, Deidre thought. *Just what I need on top of everything else, a morality lecture.*

"Mrs. Olson—" she began but was cut off.

"Oh, please. Call me Inga. Anyway, I wanted to tell you how happy I am for you. I used to watch you and wonder why such a pretty young lady didn't have a man in her life. And especially now, I feel better knowing you have someone with you most nights."

"Why, thank you, Inga," Deidre responded, shocked by what her neighbor said. "But what do you mean by 'especially now'?"

Inga looked at her as if she were about to tattle on someone. She looked over her shoulder before leaning closer to Deidre, and in a hushed voice said, "The night before last, you were late getting home from work. I happened to look out my kitchen window and saw the figure of a man by your car. He was fidgeting with something on your windshield. Then, the same night, I woke at about three in the morning—I'm a light sleeper, you know. I looked out my window and the same figure was by your truck, doing the same thing. I thought of calling the police, but I didn't want people to think I'm nosey or anything. But last night I saw the same man out there again, at least I think he was the same man. Anyway, I thought you'd like to know."

Deidre was stunned. "Could you see who it was?" she asked expectantly.

"No, it is just too shadowy where you park. All I could see was his figure."

"You keep calling this person a man. How do you know that, Inga?

"He's either a man or an awfully large woman. He stood taller than your sheriff's van. And his shoulders were so broad. He was a very large man. I thought he looked athletic, narrow waist, and he moved with ease."

"Mrs. Olson, Inga," she corrected herself. "Thank you so much. You've been a big help to me. And thank you for understanding about the man who visits me. It's such a comfort having him with me, especially since someone's been lurking around my home. I'll bring him over and introduce you soon."

"That would be nice, dear. I'd like to meet him. Have a good day, and be careful."

By the time Deidre arrived at work, she was beyond being frightened. She was enraged, and she stormed through her morning meeting. As soon as the deputies were dispatched to their assignments, she stomped down the stairs to her vehicle.

In minutes, she was wheeling out of town. She had a few things she wanted to tell Ed Beirmont. Her truck skidded to a stop in his driveway, and Deidre sprinted up the stairs to his deck. She pounded on his door.

Ed opened the inner door, but not the screen. "Can I come in?" Deidre demanded.

"Do you have a warrant?" Ed countered.

"No, I don't have a warrant."

"Then why are you here?" Ed asked in an emotionless voice.

"Someone's been messing around my vehicles at night. That person was seen on three occasions, and his description fits you."

Ed never raised his voice. "I'm only one of ten thousand people in this county. Do you have a reason for singling me out? Was there a witness able to ID me? If not, I'd like you to get off my property."

Reality began to set in for Deidre as she calmed down. "No, but he was your size and build."

"So your witness never saw the person's face? Why are you talking to me? I can name a half-dozen people in town my size. If that's all you have to go on, I'd like you to quit harassing me. I've done nothing to cause this visit." Ed looked her square in the eye, but he never so much as raised his voice.

"Before I leave," Deidre narrowed her eyes to mere slits, "I want you to know that your scare tactics aren't going to work. If you think you can intimidate me into backing off, you're wrong. I'm pissed, and when I get that way, I only work harder. If I were you, Ed, I'd watch your every move. I will be, you can be sure of that."

Deidre walked away without waiting for a response. As she drove back to town she thought, *That was a waste of time. Calm down, girl, and screw your head on straight. Nothing will get done if you don't.*

By the time she reached her office, she had stopped shaking and her heart rate was almost back to normal. *Time to straighten up my desk. The weekend's coming. By tomorrow night, John and I will be alone for forty-eight hours. I wonder what he wants to talk about. Not work, I hope.*

The rest of her day went smoothly. Deidre checked with Judy about meeting the next week and confirmed they would get together on Thursday. She still felt like she was treading water with the two cases, and she wondered if they'd ever find Skinny's killer or the person who injected Jill with meth.

Deidre was home at her normal time for a change, and she waved at Inga, who was looking out her kitchen window. She ate a microwave meal, missing John's home cooking but more so his banter. John planned to move in on Monday, and she wondered what it would be like to have him around so much of the time. Wonderful, she hoped.

She fell asleep in her recliner during the ten o'clock news, woke at eleven and dragged herself to bed. The next morning she was relieved to see that there was nothing stuck to her windshield.

The only thing of consequence that happened on Friday during work was that Ben called. He had contacted Mac and Melissa, and they had verified they would meet at his office in Duluth. Other than that, Friday seemed to last forever, and by three o'clock she was ready to knock off early. John was waiting for her when she walked in the back door of her home.

Chapter Twenty-Four

As John and Deidre drove out of town, she could feel the weight lift off her shoulders. The temperature on that wonderful autumn day held near sixty-five degrees, the yellowed leaves of the aspen trees were highlighted by the dark greens of the balsam and spruce trees, and the lake was more nurturing to her than Deidre could ever remember. John opened the sunroof, and the fresh air off the lake circulated inside the car, bringing with it the smell of crisp, newly fallen leaves. Deidre inhaled deeply.

They entered the first of two tunnels that had been drilled through solid basalt rock cliffs, and as they emerged from the other side, Deidre drank in the spectacular view of Lake Superior and its Maine-like shoreline. The blue of the sky was condensed by the water, creating an even deeper blue, and the white-capped waves swelled across its surface.

Deidre looked at John and wanted to wrap her arms around him but had to settle with placing her hand atop his. They rode in silence for several miles.

Deidre was the first to speak. "Thank you."

"For what?" John wanted to know.

"For rescuing me," Deidre said, and squeezed his hand.

It took forty-five minutes to reach the Red Fin Trout, and John eased the car down the long, winding driveway. Deidre had never been there, and the layout took her breath away.

The lodge had been constructed nearly three-quarters of a century ago from old-growth white pine logs, some as much as thirty inches in diameter. It was three stories tall, and Deidre wondered how the builders had hoisted such huge timbers to that height without the aid of hydraulic lifts.

Inside, everything was constructed of logs: the upright supports, the rafters, the ceiling joists. The massiveness of the structure overwhelmed her, and the smell of wood timbers time-polished to a golden sheen captured her senses. For a moment, she stood in awe of the monument to the past.

John checked in, and an employee carried their bags to the elevator and escorted them to their third floor room. It faced the lake, and Deidre was treated to a spectacular view. *Perfect,* she thought.

John gave the bellman a tip, and when he left, Deidre flung her arms around John.

"I love you, John Erickson," she said and held him as though her life depended on it.

They dressed for dinner, John in a suit coat and Deidre in a tightly fitted white wool dress that accentuated her lithe figure. As they entered the dining area, the maitre d' glanced up, and when he saw Deidre, he did a double take. Catching himself and clearing his throat in embarrassment, he ushered them to their table.

A vase with a half-dozen red roses arranged with a few sprigs of fern sat to one side of her plate. John ordered wine, and in minutes their waiter returned with their glasses.

John looked at Deidre as though it was the first time he had seen her. He raised his glass in a toast.

"To us."

Deidre replied, "To us."

At that moment John began to appear quite nervous, and Deidre saw beads of sweat form on his upper lip. His face seemed to have lost much of its color.

"John, are you feeling okay? We can go back to our room if you'd like to lie down for a while. I wouldn't mind."

John smiled a weak smile. "No, believe me, I'm not ill. It's just that suddenly it feels too warm in here. I wonder if their air conditioning isn't working."

Deidre was actually chilly, and she was sure something had to be wrong with John. "I'm practically freezing sitting under this air vent," she said as she wrapped her arms around herself, even shivering a little.

John changed the subject. "Look, there's something in the bouquet they left at our table."

Deidre's eyes fell upon a card attached to the roses, and she lifted it out from the bouquet, careful to not disturb the arrangement. She slid the message out of the small envelope and read it. "Deidre, will you marry me?"

For a moment she sat silently. John inhaled a deep breath, expecting the worst. The silence was so thick he was about to say that he understood and that it had been foolish, impulsive of him to take her yes for granted.

Before he could force his lips to form the words, Deidre's eyes filled with tears that rolled down her cheeks.

"Yes, yes times a thousand," she blurted out.

A look of relief broke out on John's face. He reached into his jacket pocket and pulled out a small leather-covered box. He lifted the lid on its hinges, held it in front of Deidre, and the light from the candle at their table danced off what was in the box.

Again, she sat stunned. "John, it's beautiful!" He took the ring out of its slot and gently slipped it on her finger.

Deidre stared at the diamond, one solitary stone set high in its setting. As she tilted it, first one way and then another, the light reflected off it in streams of blue sparkles.

"Oh, John, it's perfect. If I had chosen it myself, I would have chosen no other." Then she added, "And I feel the same way about you."

Deidre leaned across the table and kissed him, not on the cheek, but square on his lips. "I love you, John Erickson, love you, love you, love you" she repeated. Never before had she felt this way.

Their meal was served, and Deidre ate as though she were in a fog. She couldn't take her eyes off her future husband, and every time she looked at him, his eyes were on her.

After supper they walked the stairs to their room. After luxuriating in the room's hot tub, it was time for bed. John had turned down the covers and placed rose petals on her pillow. Deidre inhaled the attar and lay down on her bed of dreams.

The weekend sped by all too quickly, and before they were ready to leave, Deidre and John had to check out of the lodge. On the way home, Deidre rode silently for miles, her hand resting on his thigh.

"I don't know how much longer I can take this job, John," she finally said.

He looked at her with understanding eyes. "Nothing lasts forever . . . nothing," was all he said in return.

CHAPTER TWENTY-FIVE

THAT NIGHT DEIDRE SLEPT CURLED in John's arms, her job the farthest thing from her dreams.

In the morning, they had a quick breakfast of toast and strong coffee and were off to work, he to Duluth, she to downtown Two Harbors.

"Deidre!" her secretary, Anne, exclaimed, jumped up, took her hand, and stared at the ring. "Did you know this was coming?"

Deidre beamed. "It was a complete and wonderful surprise. I've never had a weekend like that before, or ever will again, I imagine. John's the most special person I've ever known."

Deidre filled her in on almost all that had happened over the weekend, uncharacteristically sharing her feelings with the woman who had been her secretary for years. The two carried on like teenagers, until Deidre realized that she had duties to fulfill.

"It was so difficult leaving him to come to work today, but I'm here. I suppose we better get at it. Do I have any messages?"

Anne picked up a memo from her desk. "Mac McAlpine called Friday after you left for the weekend. He wants you to call him as soon as you can this morning."

Deidre thanked Anne and closed her office door. At her desk, she admired the new addition to her finger, rotating the ring so the fluorescent light reflected off the diamond's facets. She forced the thoughts of the weekend from her mind and punched in Mac's number on her phone.

"Mac, here," she heard his voice. "How you doing, Deidre?"

It always caused her to pause a second when someone responded with her name without her having introduced herself. Sometimes caller ID was a scary thing.

"Wonderful, just wonderful," she heard herself say and then caught herself, hoping Mac wouldn't ask what was so wonderful. She didn't want to go through the whole story of the weekend with him.

"Well, that's a change from the last time we talked. Has something broken on one of your cases?"

"No, no, nothing like that," she answered. "It's Monday, and things haven't started to pile up yet. What have you got, Mac? I received a message you wanted me to call this morning. I assume it isn't that you want to know how I'm doing."

"I do care about that, too, but the reason I wanted you to call is that my informant has come up with three names I think you should check out. We did a background check on them, and they're bad actors. We traced them to Chicago, where they grew up. All three have extensive police records beginning when they were in their early teens. What started out as mostly bullying when they were in middle school escalated to car theft, property damage, and assault by the time they reached high school. One of them was convicted of possession of a firearm but never served time for that offense.

"I'm going to fax you their information and their pictures. Will you check around and find out if anyone has seen them? From what our informant told us, you might check the northern end of the county, maybe hit some of the taverns and dives up there. You'll understand when you see their pictures, but if they have surfaced up there, someone will remember seeing them. On the other hand, keep an eye out around town as well."

Deidre wanted to know if the men still had ties to Chicago.

"Glad you asked that," Mac responded. "I forgot to mention, none of them live in the Windy City anymore. Two of them moved to Minneapolis about eight years ago and have been in several scrapes since then but nothing serious that could be pinned on them. They always seem to be on the periphery of trouble. There were two drive-by shootings in Minneapolis, and they were the principle suspects, but law enforcement couldn't get anyone to roll over on them. It's as if they are so intimidating that everyone is afraid to talk."

"Does that ever sound familiar," Deidre remarked. "Do you have anything else?"

"No, but if anything comes up, I'll let you know. Take care now," Mac said and disconnected the call.

Five minutes later, the receptionist knocked on her office door, and Deidre looked up.

"The faxes from Mac just came through," and she placed them on Deidre's desk.

Deidre laid the pictures down side by side on her desk, and couldn't help but think the first two looked every bit as intimidating as Mac had said. Each had at least one scar on his face, and their rugged, unshaven faces scowled at her. The third picture was different. The man's boyish good looks hid the fact that he had been in trouble with the law since he was eleven years old, beginning with shoplifting and ending with having been involved in a fracas outside a tavern on Nicollet Mall in Minneapolis two years ago. She read the memo attached to the bottom of each picture:

Elias Howard	Joseph Durante	Jason Canton
Ht: 6'4"	Ht: 6'5"	Ht: 5'8"
Wt: 250 lb.	Wt: 295 lb.	Wt: 165 lb.
Race: Caucasian	Race: Caucasian	Race: Caucasian
Eyes: Blue	Eyes: Brown	Eyes: Blue
Hair: Black	Hair: Brown	Hair: Blond
Age: 32	Age: 35	Age: 21

Deidre studied the faxes. *Elias and Joseph would be too easy to spot in this small community,* she thought, *but hardly anyone would notice Jason. In fact, he looks young enough to be attending high school.*

She jumped out of her chair and rushed to the outer office. "Would you make enough copies of these so every deputy has one?" she said to the startled receptionist. "Make a copy of this one right away so I can take it with me."

With the copy of Jason's picture in hand, Deidre headed out the door. On her way to the high school, she glanced at the picture sitting on the seat beside her.

He could pass as a sophomore.

Deidre parked in the visitor's lot and walked into the school, fully aware that her uniform, handgun included, would draw stares. *That's okay,* she thought, *make my presence known.* She looked for the principal's office, entered in a hurry, and stepped up to the counter.

"Yes, may I help you?" the student assistant asked, a little cowed by Deidre's no-nonsense appearance.

Deidre held out the picture. "Can you tell me if this person is a student here?" she asked trying to control the agitation in her voice.

The color drained from the assistant's face. "I . . . I think you should speak with Mrs. Zemmler about this." She called over her shoulder, "Mrs. Zemmler, would you come here for a moment? The sheriff has a question for you." The assistant disappeared into the adjoining work room.

Mrs. Zemmler had been the school secretary long before Deidre was in high school, more than fifteen years ago. She slowly pushed herself up from her chair, where it looked as if she had been working on some kind of scheduling.

"Why, Deidre, it is so good to see you again. How are you doing?" she wanted to know.

Deidre extended her hand. "It's good to see you again, Mrs. Zemmler. I'm doing very well, but I do have a question you might be able to answer. Do you recognize this boy as a student here?"

Deidre had folded the paper so the printed information wasn't visible.

"Why, yes, of course. That's Aaron Sarstrom. He moved into this district midway through his sophomore year. I believe he lives with his parents someplace north of here. I understand it is a long way back in the woods, up near Isabella."

"Can you tell me anything about him, as a student I mean?"

"Of course I can't allow you to see his personal file without a court order, but in general, he's an average student. I don't think he's ever been in any trouble in school, at least he doesn't frequent this office the way some kids do. I'm telling you, sometimes I wonder what will happen to this generation, but that's not why you're here. Aaron has never taken part in school activities, although he seems to be popular with some students. Most of them are those on the fringe, you know, those who don't have many friends and seem to blend into the woodwork. Other than that, I really don't know much about him."

"One last thing, doesn't a student's scholastic record follow him from his last school?"

"That's true," Mrs. Zemmler agreed. "Sometimes it takes a while to receive the record, but it should be in the student's file."

"Would it be possible for you to look in Aaron's file to see if his transfer is on record? You don't have to divulge any personal information."

Mrs. Zemmler hobbled over to a file cabinet, obviously favoring her left knee, and pulled out a file from the top drawer. She opened it.

"He does have a transcript here along with a memo saying he delivered it himself when he enrolled. It's from Matthew James

High School, Elgin, Illinois. That's a suburb of Chicago, a tough place to grow up. I know that, because my daughter lives in West Dundee, which is across the Fox River from Elgin. They don't cross the river into Elgin unless they have to. It's best that Aaron got out of there—probably saved him from a lot of trouble."

Or he brought it with him, Deidre thought. "Thank you so much for your help, Mrs. Zemmler."

"I didn't ask, is Aaron in some kind of trouble?" Mrs. Zemmler wanted to know.

"Not that I know of," Deidre answered. *Not yet, anyway.*

BACK AT HER OFFICE, Deidre made a call. "Matthew James High School, Julianne speaking," the receptionist at the Elgin school answered. "How may I direct your call?"

"Good afternoon. This is Sheriff Deidre Johnson calling from Lake County, Minnesota. I would like information concerning a young man who might have attended your school three years ago. Is it possible for you to verify his attendance?"

"I'm sorry. We're not allowed to give out that information over the phone. The best way is for you to check with your local school. They would have a record of his transfer papers on file."

"Thank you," Deidre said politely, although she wanted to blurt out several other select words, and hung up.

She punched in another number. "Hello, Mrs. Zemmler? This is Deidre. I am sorry to bother you again, but I need your help. You told me that Aaron Sarstrom presented his transcript in person. Do you know if anyone called his former school to verify its authenticity?"

There was a period of silence on the phone, and Deidre could hear papers rustling.

"I don't see any mention of direct correspondence here," Mrs. Zemmler finally said. "I don't think anyone checked. The transcript looks official."

"It's important I find out for sure. Mrs. Zemmler, will you send an official inquiry to Aaron's former school to verify his transcript? I want to know for sure he is who we think he is." Deidre listened to her response. "Thank you so much," she said. "Call me when you receive an answer."

She stepped out of her office for a minute to pick up a sweet roll from the open box in the meeting room and to pour a cup of coffee into her tannin-stained mug. Before retreating to her office, Deidre looked out the third-floor window of the Law Enforcement Center. From there she could see the ore docks in the harbor and a large boat being loaded with iron-bearing taconite pellets. Everything looked peaceful, and she wished her job was that way right now.

She left the calmness of the panorama and sat at her desk, peeling off layers of the day-old pastry and washing them down with coffee that had sat in the pot too long. Deidre looked at her calendar, contemplating the trip to Minneapolis on the coming Thursday and wondering what the forensic anthropologist, Judy, would have to say. Before she finished the stale roll, her phone rang.

"Hello, Sheriff Johnson," she mumbled, her mouth full of a coffee-soaked bakery confection.

"Deidre?" It was Mrs. Zemmler. "I have some news I thought you should be aware of right away. I sent a fax to Matthew James High School in Elgin requesting information about Aaron. Someone must have been standing by the machine and picked up the fax as it came off the printer, because they got back to me right away. Aaron Sarstrom was murdered during his sophomore year two-and-a-half years ago. He would have been a senior this year. He had been a good student up to that time, although his grades had slipped the last semester. He was found shot to death, but the case was never solved. Whoever calls himself Aaron Sarstrom isn't he. I've told the principal, but he wanted to speak with you before he took any action."

Deidre almost choked trying to swallow the bite of pastry. "Please, Mrs. Zemmler, say nothing to anyone else about this. It's extremely important that you don't. Thank you so much for your help. Will you please transfer this call to the principal?"

"Of course," Mrs. Zemmler replied, and another phone rang.

"Good morning, this is Principal Davis speaking."

"Mr. Davis, this is Sheriff Johnson. I just got off the line with Mrs. Zimmler. She gave me the information about Aaron Sarstrom and said she had informed you as well."

"Yes, Sheriff, I expected your call. What do you suggest we do about this matter?"

"If at all possible, I'd like you to hold off for a day or so before taking any action. Don't let on to him what we've discovered, unless of course he's causing trouble in school. I have a couple of things I want to check out before we confront him."

"I'm not sure I can do that, Sheriff," he answered. "There are seven hundred-fifty students in this building, and I'm responsible for the safety of each one. If there were to be any violence in this building and word got out that I knew Aaron was possibly involved in a murder, I'd never hold another job again. Not only that, I wouldn't be able to live with myself. I think we must take immediate action."

"Please," Deidre insisted. "He's attended your school for over two years without causing the slightest bit of trouble. I don't think he's going to suddenly become violent. It's vital to a case, or cases, we're trying to solve."

"Nevertheless," Principal Davis argued, "This places me and the district in a tenuous situation. I'm sure you can appreciate what I'm saying, can't you?"

"All I'm asking is that we delay speaking to Aaron for a day or two until I can obtain a search warrant from the judge. I know it's a risk you'll be taking, but on the other hand, a small delay might make a difference down the road as far as future problems are concerned."

Finally, Principal Davis agreed to help in any way he could, but he made it clear that he couldn't allow the situation to go unresolved for too many days. Deidre assured him she'd be diligent, and the call ended.

She looked at her half-eaten roll, her appetite suddenly gone. Then she called Mac McAlpine in Duluth to fill him in on her find.

"Mac, I've got some info we need to act on right away. One of the suspects you told me to be on the lookout for has been tentatively identified. If I'm right, he's assumed the identity of a student from Elgin, Illinois, who was murdered a couple of years ago. The poster you sent had his name listed as Jason Canton. I believe he goes by Aaron Sarstrom and is posing as a high school student."

"We have an address where he seems to be spending most nights," Mac responded. "All we need is an excuse to search it. Will you do some further work and find out the circumstances behind the murder of this Aaron kid? Then get back to me. If there is a plausible link between Aaron and Jason, I'll talk to a judge right away and secure a warrant."

Deidre said a hurried goodbye to Mac, and called out to her secretary. "Will you connect me with the police department of Elgin, Illinois, please?"

In little more than a minute the phone on her desk rang, and she was greeted by a receptionist in Elgin.

"This is Sheriff Deidre Johnson calling from Lake County, Minnesota. Will you connect me to someone familiar with an unsolved case in your files? Over two years ago, a student named

Aaron Sarstrom was murdered in Elgin. I believe I have information related to that case."

Without hesitation the receptionist answered, "That would be detective James Anders. He handles cold cases for our city. Please hold for a second, and I'll connect you immediately."

Deidre heard a buzzing sound as her call was transferred.

"Yeah, Detective Anders here, how can I help you?"

Deidre introduced herself for a second time and then went on to explain why she was calling. Detective Anders asked her to hold for a minute while he retrieved the Sarstrom file. In the background she heard a metal drawer being opened and the rustle of papers being shuffled.

Deidre waited a few minutes. "I have it," she heard him say. "Aaron Sarstrom's body was found floating in the Fox River on October 3, 2009. He had been shot once in the back of the head, execution style. His hands were bound behind his back with a plastic tie."

Deidre's eyes widened and she felt her back stiffen. She involuntarily sucked in a breath of air, but keeping her voice under control, Deidre asked, "Do you know anything about the ballistics of the weapon used?"

"Yep, got it right here. The weapon was a twenty-five caliber. Naturally, we couldn't find a casing to provide an exact ID of the gun, but we assumed it would be a handgun. I don't know of many rifles made with that caliber. Remington Firearms made a hunting rifle of that size dating back to 1909, but it had a large casing and plenty of power. In fact, it was rated for deer and bear. If Aaron had been killed with that kind of weapon, it would have blown his head off. The weapon used to murder him was almost definitely a handgun.

"Is there anything else you want to know?"

"Do you have much information about Aaron, his family, school record, anything like that?"

"According to this, he came from a two-parent home. His transcript shows he was an excellent student, at least up until a few months before he was killed. His grades took quite a nosedive during the months before he died, and we suspected drugs. However, the autopsy showed no traces in his system. He must have done something to have gotten on the wrong side of some very dangerous people. We have a lot of gang problems in this city."

Deidre thanked him for the information, and promised to keep him informed about what they discovered as far as the Aaron Sarstrom she was following. Then she called Mac.

"Mac, me again," she said not waiting for him to speak. "Aaron Sarstrom was killed with a gun of the same caliber that Skinny Tomlinson and the others were. The Aaron Sarstrom we have in Two Harbors is an imposter, and the photo of Jason Canton I showed at the high school was identified by two people as a student using Aaron's name. Does that give you enough to go on?"

Mac thought for a second. "With what our informant's uncovered, and along with what you've discovered, I think we have enough to get the warrant. I'll get on it right away, and by tomorrow morning maybe we can move."

Deidre made another call to the high school and asked to speak to Principal Davis. She assured him that she was moving as fast as she could and that by tomorrow afternoon Aaron would not be his problem any longer. He thanked her before hanging up his phone.

By that time Deidre was exhausted, and she looked at the clock on her office wall. It was almost five, time to clear her desk and go home to John. She hoped he had made stroganoff for supper.

Chapter Twenty-Six

Deidre liked the new arrangement of John staying with her permanently, although they had been spending so much time together before that he had become a fixture in her home. She knew he'd be spending more time on the road, driving back and forth from Duluth, but she was comforted knowing this was turning into his permanent home. Deidre had just changed into her comfortable civvies when she heard him call, "Stroganoff's on the table. Get it while it's hot."

She laughed as she raced down the stairs. Life was good.

After supper they cleared the table together, stored the left-overs in the refrigerator and decided to take a walk. Hand-in-hand they strolled down the alley, turned right at the street, and soon were walking on the paved path along Lake Superior. Together, they shared their expectations for the future, when the wedding date should be set, who would be invited, and even what their children might be like. Deidre had never been this happy in her entire life.

Building a fire in the fireplace had become a habit for John, and that night was no exception. As they sat on cushions on the floor and enjoyed a glass of red wine, a flood of warmth swept over Deidre like she had never experienced. She loved the man she was with more than life itself, and for a moment she experienced a strange panic. She wondered if she could ever again survive without him.

That night, both slept undisturbed, and woke in the morning refreshed and ready to tackle the problems of the day, although at the moment they seemed far, far away. Deidre kissed him on the cheek before leaving.

"Bye, my love, I'll see you after work. What do you plan on making for supper tonight?" she giggled as the door shut behind her, and she almost skipped down the walkway to where her sheriff's SUV was parked.

IT WAS SEVEN O'CLOCK when she walked into her office, and the phone on her desk was already ringing.

"Hello, this is Sheriff Johnson."

"Deidre, glad you're in early." She recognized Mac's voice, and he sounded as if the call were urgent. "The judge granted us a warrant to search where we suspect Jason Canton's been hanging out. He frequents a place in town, not up in Isabella as we had been lead to believe. If I get to Two Harbors by eight, will you be able to go with me to execute it? We should be able to take him by surprise."

"No problem," Deidre answered excitedly. "I'd bet he'll be in school. From what they say, he's a fairly diligent student, at least on the surface. Whatever his masquerade, he's carrying it out pretty well."

Deidre ended the call as her deputies were filing in for morning report. The picture to the puzzle surrounding all that had happened the past several weeks hadn't begun to materialize, but at least Deidre thought she was finding the pieces. To put them together was going to be the challenge.

By seven-thirty her office was empty, and she had time to pour herself a cup of coffee and grab a scone from the box on the table. She had just sat down to relax a minute and had taken her first bite when Mac walked in, a large smile creasing his face.

"Hi, Deidre, catch you at a bad time?" he joked. Then he became serious. "Are you ready to roll?"

"Give me a second to finish this," she said. "Pour a cup for yourself. There's one last scone in the box. I won't wait on you."

Mac sat down opposite her at the table. "Here's the address we're going to search," he said, shoving a pad of paper across to her. "I'm not sure what we're going to find when we get there, but from what I hear, it won't be anything good."

They gulped down the hot coffee and left the office, deciding to take Mac's unmarked car.

"When we get there, I'm going to let you off at the alley. Then I'll give you enough time to get in position at the back door. When I knock on the front, someone might try to make it out the back. Stay there until I come through and let you in. Here we are. It's the fourth house over. You can't miss it. It's painted a pastel blue. The place is a wreck: peeling paint, shingles missing, and rotten trim. I can hardly wait to see what the inside looks like."

Deidre made her way down the alley, walking decisively but not racing. She cut through the yard of a neighboring house and approached the back door of the target from its blind side. She stood silently outside until she heard Mac knock.

There was a scuffling sound inside, and the door she was guarding burst open. Two teenagers, a boy and a girl, tried to push their way out. Deidre was blocking their way, her pistol drawn and pointed at the person in the lead. He stopped suddenly, and the girl rammed into his back, tripped, and fell.

"Stand still!" Deidre barked. "You, stand up," she demanded of the girl. "Both of you, place your hands above your heads."

The teens, surprised and scared, instantly complied.

Deidre had started to pat down the girl when Mac appeared at the door. "They're the only two here," he said, his voice still edgy. "I'll take this one," and he began to search the boy.

"This one is clean," Deidre declared.

"Same here. Both of you get back in the house," Mac ordered.

When they had ushered the two into the living room, he had them sit on the couch, facing him.

"What are you doing here?" he demanded.

"Nothing that's any of your business," the boy mumbled, his head hanging. The girl sat silently, looking at the floor.

"I think you've been doing more than nothing," Mac said. "Sheriff, check their eyes."

Deidre took out a small flashlight and bent over the girl first.

"Look at me," she said none too gently.

The girl looked up and Deidre flashed the light in her eyes. She repeated the action with the boy and then turned to Mac.

"Both have dilated pupils. What do you think of their physical condition, Mac?"

"Looks to me like they haven't eaten anything in a month." He turned to the kids. "Are you anorexic or anything?" Both shook their heads.

"You," he signaled to the girl. "Stand up and walk in a straight line across the room."

She did, and swayed as she tried to regain her balance, then tripped as she approached a chair. She collapsed into it.

"You next," Mac said to the boy. He had the same success as had the girl.

"Okay, what have you two been using?" Deidre asked, her voice softening. "You show signs of being high on something. Tell us what it is, and we'll go easy on you."

The girl said nothing, but the boy smarted back, "Go easy on us? We haven't done anything. You found nothing on us. We haven't done anything wrong that you can prove. What are you going to do, arrest us for skipping school?"

So much for bluffing, Deidre thought.

"What are you doing here," Mac wanted to know.

"Waiting for a friend," the belligerent young man shot back. "I suppose that's against the law too?" He sat with a smirk on his face.

Deidre broke in. "Well, I guess we'll wait with you, and we can all have a talk when your friend gets here. Where do you live?"

The girl spoke first. "Why?" she asked, panic in her voice.

"So we can take you home to your parents."

"No," the girl sobbed, "Not to them," and she buried her face in her hands.

The boy sneered. "Take me home and you'll get an earful. Do you know who my dad is? He'll sue the pants off you. By the time he's done, you won't have a dime left."

"How can I know your dad? I don't even know your name," Deidre responded.

"I'm Gerald Colter, III. My father's an attorney, and he'll have a thing or two to say about this. You haven't even read me my rights." Gerald sat smugly, staring at them through venomous eyes.

"Thank you for the lesson in law, young man," Deidre said with a smile, "Although we have no reason to read you your rights, because you are not under arrest. We're holding you though, just until your friend arrives. Then we'll take you home—for your own safety. What about you, young lady. What is your name?"

Deidre could see her slump. "Naomi, Naomi Jackson. My father is Pastor Jackson." She covered her face and wept.

"Who lives here?" Mac continued his questioning.

"We don't have to answer your questions," Gerald sneered.

Naomi looked up, her eyes red-rimmed, not totally from the effects of drugs. "Aaron Sarstrom. He's in school now, but he'll be here at eleven-thirty. That's when his lunch period begins."

"Shut your mouth!" Gerald shouted. "Remember what happened to Jill!"

"What happened to Jill?" Deidre asked in a soft voice.

"Nothing," he answered.

Deidre saw fear rise in Naomi's eyes, and she went silent again.

"Why don't you sit with these two while I begin our search?" Mac suggested.

He started in the kitchen where a pile of dirty dishes was stacked in the sink. Methodically, he moved from one cabinet to another, removing the few pots, pans and dishes he found on the shelves. A half-hour later he announced that he had found nothing. Then he moved to the single bedroom. Deidre could hear him rustling around, removing drawers from a dresser, and rearranging heavier items.

"Bingo," Mac called out. "I've found his stash."

Mac came out of the bedroom carrying a plastic bag. Deidre could see at least three, maybe four, smaller packets of white powder.

"We've got another thirty minutes before Aaron, or whatever his name is, returns. Hold this while I finish in there," and he handed the evidence to Deidre.

Mac returned to the bedroom, and Deidre could hear him continuing to search. After a while he stepped back into the living room. "That's all I could find. Still, it's enough to bring him in. Right now, I think the important thing is to have a reason to get him out of the school and away from kids like these two," and he motioned toward Naomi and Gerald.

Deidre looked at her watch. "It's twenty after." Looking at Naomi, she said, "You and Gerald move into the kitchen. Sit at the table with your backs to the door and don't make a sound. Right now we've got nothing on you except truancy, but if you try to warn Aaron, we'll be able to charge you with interfering with an investigation. This time I'm not bluffing." She looked directly at Gerald.

Minutes later, they heard footsteps on the back stairs. Deidre took a position behind the entry door, and Mac ducked around the corner in the living room. Aaron walked into the kitchen.

"Hey, you're still here," he spoke to the backs of the two at the table.

Deidre stepped from behind the door. "Sheriff! Put your hands in the air and turn around!"

Aaron bolted for the living room door, attempting to escape out the front. Mac stepped into his way and barred the exit. Aaron saw Mac's gun and lifted his hands above his head.

"What do you want?" he demanded. "I haven't done anything. Anyway, do you have a search warrant? If you don't, get out."

"Place your right hand behind your back," Deidre ordered. She placed a handcuff on his wrist. "Now the other."

With Aaron under their control, Mac began the familiar words . . . "You have the right to remain silent . . ."

DEIDRE CALLED THE CENTER AND REQUESTED a deputy come to the house to transport their prisoner to the county jail. She and Mac wanted to take the kids home and speak with their parents.

On the way, the teens sat quietly in the back of Mac's car. There was a heavy wire screen separating the back seat from the front, and the inside handles of the back doors had been removed. It was a mini prison.

Gerald wore a defiant sneer, but Naomi was extremely distressed. She looked out the side window, refusing to interact at all. Deidre's heart went out to her, but she had to maintain her distance.

When they arrived at Gerald's house, Mac escorted him up the walk to the front of the house, rang the bell, and a woman he assumed was Mrs. Colter answered the door.

"Mrs. Colter?" Mac inquired. "We're escorting your son home because we discovered him at a house we searched. In that house we found what we believe to be some form of illegal substance. We suspect he's been using some kind of drug, but we found nothing on him."

Before the woman could answer, Mr. Colter bellowed from inside. "Anna, what's going on out there?" He came to the door, his suit coat off and his tie loosened at the neck.

"Who are you and what are you doing with my son?" he demanded.

Mac identified himself and tried to explain the situation.

"My son's not a junkie. How dare you come here and make false accusations. Who's in the car?" He pointed to Deidre and Naomi.

"In front is Sheriff Johnson. The other person is none of your business."

"Sheriff Johnson. It's time we elected a real sheriff in this county. Is she involved in this slander, too?

He turned to his son. "Gerald, get in the house. As for you, mister, I'll be in touch with your superiors this afternoon."

The door slammed in Mac's face. Mac returned to his car shaking his head in disgust at the man's ignorance and audacity.

"How'd it go?" Deidre wanted to know.

"Well, now we know where Gerald gets his attitude from," was all Mac said.

When they stopped at the church manse where the Jacksons resided, Deidre opened the door to let Naomi out. As they walked up the sidewalk, Deidre slipped her arm inside the crook of Naomi's elbow. She could feel the girl's slender arm shaking. She rang the doorbell.

"Hello, Mrs. Jackson? I'm Sheriff Johnson, and I'd like to speak to you for a minute or two."

"Naomi, what is this about?" Mrs. Jackson asked. Her brow furrowed. Then she regained her composure. "Please come in. My husband's in his study. Please, have a seat while I get him."

While Naomi and Deidre waited for her parents to return, Naomi sat on the couch, quietly weeping. She picked at her fingers.

"Naomi, what's wrong?" Pastor Jackson gently asked as he placed his hand on his daughter's shoulder.

Naomi stood, wrapped her arms around her father, and buried her face on his stooped shoulder. "I'm sorry, Daddy, so sorry, so sorry," she repeated over and over.

The trio, Pastor and Mrs. Jackson, and Naomi sat down on the couch, Naomi between her parents. Deidre explained as diplomatically as she could why she was there and how she suspected Naomi was involved. The whole time Naomi's father held her hand and her mother had her arm around her daughter's shoulders.

When she had finished voicing her suspicions, Deidre sat quietly. The silence was palpable.

"Is what Sheriff Johnson saying the truth?" Pastor Jackson asked his daughter. She nodded in silent agreement.

Deidre said, "Naomi, what did Gerald mean when he said 'Remember what happened to Jill?' Is there anything you can tell me?"

Naomi looked up and straight into Deidre's eyes. "I'm afraid to talk about it. But now, I suppose it doesn't make much difference. With Aaron being arrested, Gerald and I are in serious trouble."

"What are you so afraid of?" Deidre pressed. "Did you know Jill Moore, even as an acquaintance?"

Naomi reached for a tissue from the box her mother had placed on the coffee table in front of them. She wiped her eyes, blew her nose, and then steeled herself. "I knew Jill very well. She was trapped in the same situation I am, but she wanted out. When she told Aaron she was through, he said she should think about the consequences. She told him she was going to get help from you, Sheriff. They killed her." Naomi wept uncontrollably.

"Who killed her?" Deidre needed to know.

"They killed her. I don't know their names or where they live, but they did it. I know they did. Aaron said for me to learn a lesson from it."

"Do you think it was Aaron who killed Jill?"

Naomi shook her head. "No. He keeps a clean profile. It's others, but I don't know who they are."

"Do you believe you're in danger?"

Naomi nodded and squeezed her father's hand. Deidre found she had been holding her breath while the girl spoke, and now she let the air escape as her mind whirled. She looked at the worried parents.

"Will you assume responsibility for Naomi?" They both nodded through their tears. "I believe her," Deidre declared, then added, "but I also believe she'll soon begin to go through withdrawal if she has been using. Naomi, what drugs have you been taking."

Naomi looked at the floor. "Cocaine."

"I'll go with you to the hospital and help you check into detox. The doctors will help you get through the next few days. Then I'd like to talk more, get your full story. Aaron will be booked as soon as I get back to the office. We'll be able to hold him for a while, but I'm guessing he'll make bail. You'll be safe in the hospital. After that, we'll make arrangements for your safety."

Deidre stood to leave. Pastor Jackson walked her to the door.

"Thank you so much for your help," he said. "Naomi's mother and I appreciate what you're doing. We'll help any way we can."

Deidre looked at his haggard face. "You're welcome, sir. I think your daughter will come out of this just fine, especially with what I've seen here today. I'll wait for you to get in your car, and my partner and I will follow you to the hospital."

She and Mac followed the Jacksons without speaking.

Chapter Twenty-Seven

It was after six when Deidre was finally able to leave her office and head home. She walked in the door to the aroma of another homecooked meal. John walked over to her, a towel wrapped around his waist serving as a makeshift apron. He engulfed her with his arms. "You look like you've been drug through a knothole," he commiserated. "Tough day?"

"The toughest. Pour me a glass of wine, and let me unwind for a few minutes." She went on to tell him all that had happened.

John sat patiently, listening to his wife-to-be vent her frustrations.

"Why do kids allow themselves to get in these kinds of situations?" she asked. Then she answered her own rhetorical question. "I suppose some of them are lonely, others probably want to escape. Maybe some are looking for excitement. I don't know."

"Let's sit at the table, my dear one," John stated softly. "I've got a hot meal ready to go. Maybe after some food and another glass of wine the world will look a little brighter."

John helped her up and guided her to the table. He had scented candles burning and had bought some flowers at the greenhouse on his way home.

"You spoil me, John Erickson," Deidre said, aware of what a special man she had fallen for.

After supper, they sat in front of the open fire burning in the hearth. John seemed to get as much enjoyment out of hauling in the wood and kindling the blaze as Deidre did watching the flames dance and the embers shimmer. The two lovers talked into the night until Deidre could hardly keep her eyes open. She yawned.

"I hate to ruin this evening, but I have a busy day tomorrow. After seeing the county attorney, I have a meeting in Duluth with Ben, Mac, and Melissa Sobranski of the BCA. We have to decide how to join forces to tackle this many-headed snake we're fighting."

John stooped and picked her up.

"What are you doing? You'll break your back, you nut!"

"Quiet, lady. This is the FBI here to rescue you," and John kissed her.

He carried her up the stairs and set her down. "You get ready for bed, and I'll tuck you in. I have some dishes to take care of downstairs, and then I'll be up to join you. Scoot now."

When Deidre came out of the bathroom, John had turned down the covers of the bed and fluffed the pillows. She climbed between the covers, and he pulled them up around her chin.

"What did I do to deserve you?" she asked.

When John climbed into bed ten minutes later, Deidre was sleeping soundly. She sensed his presence and backed up to his warm body. He placed one arm over her, and they both slept until they were awakened by the alarm clock's buzzing. Deidre rolled over and faced him. She wanted this to last forever.

WHEN SHE ARRIVED AT HER OFFICE, Deidre walked next door to the courthouse, climbed the one flight of stairs to the second floor and entered the office labeled "COUNTY ATTORNEY."

"Good morning, Deidre," the receptionist said. "Art is waiting for you."

She walked into Art's office, a file folder under her arm. He looked up from his work, his concentration interrupted. Art was a large man, tall, but also grossly overweight. He wheezed as he breathed, and Deidre wondered how long he was going to be around as county attorney.

"Deidre, it's good to see you this morning. I understand you have some more work for me. Let's see what you've put together."

Deidre spread out her data. First she showed him the documents from the arrest of Jason Canton.

"I'd like you to pursue charges against him and prosecute him to the ultimate extent of the law. He knows much more than he's telling us. I'd like as much leverage to use against him as I can."

"You know I'll do what I can, but first I have to look up any prior convictions he's had for drug involvement. That'll determine what level we charge him with. Then we'll have to see if he needs a public defender. Whether he does or not, we'll have to make full disclosure to his attorney concerning the evidence we possess."

Deidre went on to explain what she had learned from her conversation with the Elgin cold-case detective, and she filled him in on what had taken place the day before with the two teens caught at Jason's place, including the confrontation Mac had with Gerald Colter II.

"I'm going to review your paperwork, and I'll try to be done with it later today. It looks like you have a solid case against this Jason Canton. I see he was fingerprinted and that he was positively identified as not being Aaron Sarstrom. We'll have to charge him by Friday or release him. Either way, he'll probably make bail and be out by the weekend. But I'm sure at the minimum we can make the charge of fifth degree drug possession stick."

The district attorney continued. "Be careful of this Gerald Colter's father, though. I've seen him be vicious in his attacks on law enforcement. He won't go easy on you for having suggested his son is involved in any way.

"Thanks for all you do in this community. You are going to leave big shoes to fill when you decide to hang up your badge."

Deidre thanked him and returned to her office. There, she gathered up the files and papers that pertained to the graves, Skinny Tomlinson, and the bust she and Mac had worked on together. It was time to leave for Duluth to meet with Ben and the others, and she realized how good it was to have all these people ready to cover her back.

BEN WARMLY GREETED DEIDRE when she got to his office on the fourth floor of the Federal Building in Duluth.

"It's so good to see you again," he said as he clasped her hand with both of his. "The others will be here anytime, and we'll be able to get going, but in the meantime, I want to tell you how happy I am for you and John. I don't know if he's told you, but we have lunch together once in a while. He's not been too busy lately, mostly reading and piecing together reports of threats to the Duluth-Superior Harbor. I've been stuck in this office too many days in a row, so we have time on our hands. We complain to each other a lot. I wish the two of you the very best. You're both top notch people."

Deidre couldn't help but think how Ben had changed in the eleven years since they had graduated from the police academy. She realized how much she trusted him and needed his help. Just then Mac walked in and a few seconds later Melissa followed. Deidre was amazed at how being with her colleagues gave her a sense of security.

Ben had arranged chairs around a small table in his office, and he invited them to have a seat. "Coffee, anyone? It's freshly brewed and I've got a few day-old cookies to go with it."

They all accepted his offer, and after pouring a cup for everyone, he took a seat.

"I think we should begin by having Deidre lay out a chart for all of us to visualize. Do you mind?" he asked, looking at her. "I have a flip tablet over there you can use. Here's a marker."

Deidre stood, feeling too much like a lecturer. She made three headings and filled in the details under each column:

JILL/SKINNY INVOLVEMENT	SEVEN GRAVES
Murdered	Execution style murders
Involved with drugs	No evidence of drugs
Meth/.25 caliber	.25 caliber
Jill dumped/Skinny buried	Skinny
Jill/Jason involvement?	No apparent connection

DRUGS

Jason Canton (Aaron Sarstrom)
Suspicion of murder
Cocaine in Skinny's truck
Jason supplier?
Naomi/Gerald—Jason supplier

"That, folks, is about all we have to this date. Tomorrow, I'm heading down to the Cities to meet with Judy Coster, the forensic anthropologist working on the remains. She's asked me to look through our files for runaways in Two Harbors the past seven years.

"What do you make of it?" Deidre asked and looked at the others, hopeful someone would have an answer.

Ben spoke first. "Two things immediately come to mind. First, I think there is a good chance we are dealing with a gang or some other form of organized crime. Second, whatever it is, I think it's evident that drugs are involved. I know I'm stating the obvious, but I think it's a good to start with anything concrete."

"Yes," Mac chimed in, "but the degree of drug involvement we see, while disconcerting, is not enough to support any kind of large gang activity. If it is drugs, something more far-reaching than local involvement is going on."

Melissa doodled on her note pad, writing reminders to herself about the conversations.

"The gun used to kill the seven people in the graves was the same for each murder. That we have ascertained from ballistics. Was the slug ever recovered from Aaron Sarstrom's body? The real Aaron Sarstrom," she added.

"I think this job is getting away from me," Deidre said, looking a little sheepish. "I didn't even ask if they still had the slug from Aaron. I'm sure they do, but sometimes evidence gets misplaced.

"When I get back to my office, I'll call Elgin again and find out. Should I have a photo of the microscopic analysis sent to you, Melissa? Can you tell anything from that?"

"We can make a preliminary find, and if it looks like it could be a match, then we'll have to have the slug in our possession to make a definite decision."

"Anything else?" Deidre wanted to know.

"There's ample evidence to be able to bring in the Drug and Gang Task Force," Mac said without hesitation.

"That goes for us, too," Ben added.

Melissa reminded them that the BCA was already involved and wouldn't be pulling their support. Then she added, "Deidre, I'd like you to coordinate the case. You're closer to it than any of us and have the most to gain or lose. What do the rest of you think?" And so, Deidre found herself being the coordinator. She wasn't quite sure she wanted the distinction but didn't want to shirk her responsibilities.

"I've got some leads to check out this afternoon. Like I said, I'll be in the Twin Cities tomorrow. Let's have a conference call on Monday. Is ten in the morning okay?" They all nodded and the meeting adjourned for a quick lunch.

On the way home, Deidre mulled over how glad she was to have the support she was getting. It would be good to get home to John, but first she had a phone call to make and some checking to do about two forgotten runaway kids.

"ELGIN POLICE, HOW MAY I direct your call?"

"This is Sheriff Johnson calling from Lake County, Minnesota. Please connect me with Detective James Anders."

"His extension is 151. I'll transfer your call."

Deidre heard the phone ring. "Hello, this is Detective Anders."

"Good afternoon, detective. This is Sheriff Johnson again. We spoke two days ago about Aaron Sarstrom."

Before she could say more, he interrupted. "Yes, of course I remember. After we talked, and while I had his file out, I signed out the evidence box. In fact I have it in front of me as we speak."

"Detective, I have further information. We arrested a person on drug charges. He is using Aaron's name and scholastic record and was posing as a student at our local high school. His prints show that he is Jason Canton, and he has a prior record in Elgin. He is twenty-one years old. Here's something else. We unearthed seven graves in a heavily wooded area north of Two Harbors. Each victim was shot execution style with a twenty-five caliber bullet, the same caliber used to kill Aaron. By chance do you have the slug from his body?"

Deidre heard rustling. "Yeah, it's in a sealed bag, looks to be in good condition to my naked eye."

Deidre let out a sigh of relief. "We have microscopic photos of the slugs used on our seven victims. Could you by any chance have a photo taken of the one in your possession and fax it to me for comparison?"

"Don't have to," came back his response. "I've got photos taken at the time of the active investigation. They'll be to you by the end of your workday. Let me know right away if you find a match on the ballistics. In the meantime, I'll do some checking on Jason Canton."

Deidre smiled in relief. "Thanks, you've made my day."

She hung up and stretched as she walked to the outer office. "Will you please check the records for all runaways in Lake County since 2005? I need the names of any who have not been accounted for," she requested.

She returned to her office, trusting that Anne, her secretary, would not delay. In less than fifteen minutes, the report was on her desk, along with the fax from Detective Anders. She looked at the greatly enlarged photo of the bullet, and slid it into an envelope. Melissa would be able to help her tomorrow when she was in the Cities. She looked at the two folders Anne had given her. One was titled "Jean Dickerson" and the other "Tom Glise."

Deidre discovered that Jean had a troubled history, but nothing terribly serious. Once, when she was fourteen, she had run away and three days later was found at a friend's house in Duluth. She had been arrested for shoplifting once and had served a community service sentence.

Tom had been picked up for assault when he was sixteen and was placed on probation. He had one count of auto theft against him a year later, his father's car, and had been remanded to his parent's custody.

Other than that, the two, although they weren't angels, had done nothing that stood out. Tom had disappeared and had not been heard from since in 2007. Jean disappeared in 2010. Their home phone numbers were listed.

With each call she was confronted by parents still hoping to find their child, and in each case, Deidre had to tell them there was no additional news. She asked each of them to allow their child's dental records to be released so she could take them with her the next day. She hoped she would not bring back bad news.

At five-thirty she looked at the wall clock, already past quitting time.

Chapter Twenty-Eight

Thursday morning as Deidre was driving to the twin cities of Minneapolis and St. Paul, her mind wandered from one topic to another. She glanced at the two folders lying on the seat beside her. Inside were the dental records of Jean and Tom, along with other notes of skeletal anomalies that might help to identify their remains. Per had helped her obtain them from their medical files. She hoped there wouldn't be a match that would destroy the thin thread of hope held by their parents.

Her thoughts shifted to the report from Elgin, Illinois. Would the ballistic markings on the slug that killed Aaron Sarstrom match those in the skulls of her seven victims?

Then there was Jill. Had she been deliberately given a lethal dose of meth, and if she had, why, and by whom? And why Skinny? He was not what you'd call a productive citizen, but what had he done to get himself executed?

All these thoughts and a lot more hammered away as she drove the monotonous freeway. It was almost a three-hour drive.

However, her thoughts always returned to John, and when they did she couldn't stop thinking of how blessed she was. She could almost feel his warm body next to her, almost hear his voice, almost smell his aroma. She thought love was something more special than she had ever anticipated.

Eventually, her thoughts evolved to wondering if she wanted to maintain the pace her job required after they were married. Perhaps this would be her last major case.

The trip went smoothly and quickly with all the thinking she was doing, and soon she found herself in the heavy traffic of I-35E, heading to St. Paul. She exited the freeway, and a left turn off of Sixth brought her to the parking ramp across the street from the BCA offices. Deidre had left home early so she could arrive around nine o'clock. She looked at her watch—eight-fifty-five.

Gathering all of her paperwork together and tucking it under her arm, she headed for the room Judith Coster had said was the lab. It was hidden in the basement.

"WELL DEIDRE, HOW ARE YOU DOING?" Dr. Coster held out her hand in greeting. Not giving Deidre an opportunity to answer, she continued. "Come in, come in. I'm so excited to have you here. There is so much to go over. Let's get started."

This was not the same person Deidre remembered working with when they were onsite in the woods near Isabella. Today, Judy was almost giddy. Deidre thought she was like a person who had been on a treasure hunt and had found the hidden chest of gold.

"Before we go in, I'd like you to suit up. There are scrubs on the chair in that room." She motioned to a small room off the back of her office. "We'll wear gloves while we're in the exam room just to preserve the integrity of the evidence. No need to worry about contracting anything from the bones."

Deidre did as she was told, emerging from the closet-size space feeling like a medical person of some sort. Judy handed her a pair of blue vinyl gloves, and they both were ready to begin. Judy nonchalantly led the way, but Deidre was not quite prepared for what greeted her when they entered the exam room.

Lined up across the expanse of a large room were six stainless steel tables on wheels.

A skeleton was on each. The bones that had been disarticulated when dug from the ground had been reconstructed, and Deidre couldn't help but remember the words to the children's song. *The knee bone's connected to the shin bone. The shin bone's connected to the ankle bone. The ankle bone's connected to . . .*

"I've lined them up according to my best estimate of when they were killed, from the earliest to the latest," and Judy motioned which was which. "By the way, you were right in your hypothesis about the roots. With some data collecting, I think we may have discovered a new tool for determining the age of a grave. It'll be a simple matter of correlation."

Before Deidre could say a word, Judy continued. "This is the oldest, mortality wise. If you look at the deterioration of the ends of the bone, it is considerable. Also, the density is a clue. The longer the bone has been subjected to percolating water, the less dense it is. And too, these bones are totally devoid of soft tissue such as muscle, tendons, and ligaments.

"I would estimate the first victim was buried about eight years ago. The most recent, other than Skinny, maybe a year ago. Their deaths didn't take place at regular intervals. You can see that numbers three, four, and five are in about the same condition."

"What more do you know about these victims?" Deidre wanted to know.

"This first one, the oldest, was a male. Look at its rib cage. See how it's slightly flattened from front to back. And now look at where the pelvic bones meet. The angle they form is less than ninety degrees. These features are male characteristics. That, coupled with the size of the bones, makes me quite certain it was a man."

Judy moved to the next set of bones. "According to my evaluation this was the second person murdered. You can see from what I told you, this is also the skeleton of a male. I would guess his murder occurred about seven years ago, which would make it 2006."

Deidre looked at the lineup of bones. Judy's occupation must be like coming to work everyday to put together complicated jigsaw puzzles. And best of all, no one talked back.

By this time they were looking at the fourth set. "Look at the ribcage of this one. What do you notice?"

Deidre took a moment to look over the skeleton, and then she looked back at the previous set of remains.

"This one's rib cage is definitely more barrel-shaped than the first."

"Good. Now look at the pelvis. See the angle where the two major bones meet at the pubic symphysis? It's greater than ninety degrees. Also, look how the ilia, the hip bones, flare out. This is a female skeleton."

When they finished, Deidre asked the question, "When do you think numbers five and seven died?"

Judy checked her chart. "Number five, probably in 2007, same as two and three. Number seven, I would say 2009."

Deidre asked Judy to wait a minute, and she excused herself to the outer room. Judy smiled, figuring the scene had gotten to Deidre, but she was wrong. Deidre returned with two folders in her hand.

"Can we cross-check these right now? I'm interested in the 2007 male and the 2009 female. I've got their medical and dental records here."

Judy took the folders from her and moved down the line to skeleton number five. Deidre stood by while Judy nodded and from time to time made a clicking sound with her tongue behind her teeth. She shifted to skeleton seven and repeated the procedure. Then she returned to number five once more. Finally she looked up.

"We will need to make a more thorough exam before we can write up a report, but I am reasonably certain that number five was Tom Glise and number seven is the skeleton of Jean Dickerson. The record of fillings in their teeth match perfectly, and each had a broken bone, he a femur which is very unusual, and she the olecranon process, what you would call the 'funny bone,' of her left elbow. Both are pretty serious breaks and are not at all common."

Deidre could hardly contain her feelings of excitement coupled with pangs of regret. She made a note on the file of each runaway, now victim.

"Are you sure enough that I can inform their parents?" Judy nodded. "And what about ballistics," Deidre pressed. Do you have the records of the slugs you found in their crania?"

"That would be Melissa. I was about to suggest we go up to her office and discuss what our next move should be."

After removing their protective garb, the two ladies rode the elevator from Judy's basement office to the tenth and top floor of the BCA building. Melissa was waiting. Evidently Judy's secretary had called ahead.

"Deidre, it's so nice to see you again. Can I get you a cup of coffee?" Deidre thanked her and took a sip of the hot brew.

"Yesterday, when we met at Ben's office, you said you'd try to get a copy of ballistics from Elgin. Did you have any luck?"

Deidre smiled and without saying anything produced the print. It was a picture taken through a stereoscope of a slug fired from a weapon. The marks left from the riflings, spiral grooves found inside a gun barrel, were clearly evident as etched parallel lines. She felt somewhat vindicated for not having thought of getting them from the Elgin police in the first place.

Melissa dug through the folder that lay open on her desk. She produced a copy of the ballistics photo taken of one of the slugs retrieved from the remains of the six victims they had exhumed and laid them side-by-side on her desk. She studied them for a time under a large magnifying lens.

"Look at this."

Judy and Deidre came around behind Melissa's chair and looked over her shoulder. Deidre inhaled sharply, and Judy let out a whistle.

"They sure look like they match," Deidre inferred.

"I can't be sure from only photos, but I'm willing to bet that if we get the two under a comparison microscope we'll find they came from the same gun. If that's the case we have evidence that will stand up in any court of law.

"Deidre, this is where we at BCA can be of help. I think you'd have a difficult time getting Elgin to release their evidence to you, but we can take ours to them, make the determination, and have the results for you in a few days. Is that good with you?"

Deidre was all too willing to accept Melissa's offer. Another piece of the puzzle had been put into place, but unfortunately, Deidre thought, the puzzle just kept getting bigger and more complex. The women talked for a few more minutes until Judy looked at the wall clock.

"The day is slipping away. How about the three of us going to lunch together? Maybe we can find something else to talk about other than murder and skeletons. Okay?"

They spent the next forty-five minutes becoming better friends, but finally Deidre had to excuse herself. It was a long ride home, and she wanted to be there to have supper with John. She wondered what he would be preparing.

CHAPTER TWENTY-NINE

IT WAS FRIDAY, AND DEIDRE was exhausted from the week's accomplishments, failures, and surprises. She woke when the alarm sounded, and turned to look at John in bed beside her. He still slept, oblivious to the buzzer. Deidre had quickly reached for the snooze button, and now she lay in the silence, studying the man she loved. She reached over and brushed back a disheveled lock of hair from his forehead, and was rewarded by the flutter of his eyelids.

"Good morning, you," she whispered. "Time to go to work."

John groaned, and wrapped his arms around her. "But I don't want to," he complained with a half-laugh. "Tell me I don't have to."

"Oh, come on, be a good boy. Today's Friday, and we have tomorrow off. Make you a deal. Be a good boy and go to work today without complaining, and I promise you we'll sleep in tomorrow. Then I'd like to make you a big breakfast and take a ride into Duluth. We could take a walk near the lighthouse and the lift bridge.

"I hear there is a wonderful play at the Playhouse, one that is a real comedy. *Charley's Aunt* is playing. It's a farce, English I think. Maybe we can laugh ourselves silly for a couple of hours.

"I'll take you to your favorite English pub before the play. They have a bluegrass jam session going on over the supper hour. Deal?"

"Deal," he answered and rolled out of bed.

On the way to work, Deidre planned out her day. First, conduct the routine morning meeting with her deputies. Second, check with Art, the county attorney, on the status of Jason Canton. Third, visit with the parents of Jean Dickerson and Tom Glise. Fourth, drive up to Isabella and visit Terry at his bait store/tavern. Fifth, beat John home and fix him a special supper.

CALLS TO EACH SET OF PARENTS of the runaway kids resulted in meetings set up that same morning. Deidre didn't want to give them her news over the phone, but she could tell by their voices that they expected the worst. She phoned Art, and he told her to come to his office as soon as she could.

Five minutes later she tapped on his open door and walked in before he could respond.

"Well, Art, what do you have for me?"

"I charged Jason Canton with felony fifth degree possession of a schedule II drug yesterday morning. Bail was set at fifty-thousand dollars, but as we suspected he would, Jason posted bail by afternoon and was released. I argued that he is a flight risk, but his attorney, some shyster from the Cities, argued that he had no prior record, he had lived in the area for three years, and he wanted to face the charges to prove his innocence. The judge bought the argument, and he was released into the custody of his lawyer. I don't know who's paying the retainer, but I guarantee it's not Jason."

"When does the case go to trial?" Deidre asked calmly, even though she felt let down.

"Not for another month, that is if there are no delays. I didn't care for his attorney at all. He looked like a big city boy who thought he was dealing with hicks from the sticks. He might be surprised when this goes to a jury."

"Thanks, Art, I know you'll do a good job, but I've got two visits to make that I'd rather not. Have a better day than I think I'm going to."

On the way to her vehicle, Deidre rehearsed in her head the words she would use when she spoke to the parents. She knew they wouldn't come out exactly as planned, but it was better to have some idea of what she would say than to go in cold. By the time she arrived at Mr. and Mrs. Glise's home, she had mentally recited her speech several times. There would be no easy way to break the sad news. She rang the doorbell, and Mr. Glise answered it.

"Hello, Mr. Glise? I'm Sheriff Johnson. May I come in?"

"By all means. My wife called me at work and said you wanted to speak with us. I came home immediately. Please, come in."

Deidre entered the rambler, wiping her boots on the mat inside the entry. The floor was immaculate, and Deidre detected the odor of floor cleaner.

"Don't worry about your shoes. What you have to say is more important to us than a little dirt. Please, come in," and he motioned for her to go into the living room.

Mrs. Glise sat on the couch, a kitchen towel in her hands. She had wrung it into a knot, and she sat with it in her lap. Deidre's heart broke when she saw the haunting plea behind her red-rimmed eyes. She sat down opposite the couple without being invited and cleared her throat.

"I know this is difficult for you, but I have news concerning your son, Tom." Mrs. Glise gasped, and Deidre continued. "Over a week ago, we exhumed human remains from graves in the woods near Isabella. I am so sorry to have to inform you that one of them has been identified as those of Tom."

"No, it can't be!" Mrs. Glise cried. "Can what you say be a mistake?"

"The anthropologist with the Bureau of Criminal Apprehension is almost one hundred percent certain. She said the final report is only a formality. The dental records you authorized to be released to us matched the structure of the remains perfectly, as did the callus left on his broken femur. I'm afraid there is virtually no doubt. I'm sorry. If I may, and I know this will be difficult, I'd like to ask you and your husband some questions concerning Tom's behavior leading up to his disappearance. Is that all right?"

Both nodded, their lips quivering with emotion.

"The investigation revealed that Tom was nineteen when he . . ." Deidre stumbled and almost said "was killed" but caught herself. "When he disappeared? Is that about right?"

Through pursed lips Mr. Glise managed to answer. "Yes, he had just celebrated his birthday, although it wasn't much of a celebration."

"What do you mean by that?" Deidre gently prodded.

Again, Mr. Glise struggled to answer. "Growing up, Tom had been what you might call passive aggressive. He never sassed back, was always loving and caring to us." He had to stop and swallow hard and then he continued. "He had a way of agreeing to our rules, and then going out and doing pretty much what he wanted. It wasn't that he did anything really bad. Stuff like driving the car where we said not to drive, pushing his curfew as far as he could, not going where he said he would be, stuff like that. He always wanted to push the envelope.

"Tom was a good student, not straight-A, but a good student. He was very musically inclined, played the piano and sang in the choir. But his senior year he began to change, subtly at first, then the changes became more pronounced. The fall after he graduated from high school he enrolled at North Woods Community College in Duluth. By the second semester he was on probation, and by spring he was informed he would not be allowed back in the fall. The last semester he didn't pass any class, and we found out he had not attended any for the entire second half.

"His birthday was a week after the school year ended, and under the guise of having a party, we arranged an intervention. We were certain he was using drugs or alcohol. When he realized what was happening, he stormed out of the house. That was the last time we saw him. We heard he had been seen up at Friendly Jane's later in the summer, but when we tried to talk to her, she said he was an adult and that what he did was none of our business. That was the last time we heard anything about him." Mr. Glise's body trembled as he stifled his sobs.

"I'm truly sorry," Deidre said. "Thank you for sharing with me about your son. I can find my way out. No need for you to get up." She looked at the couple who were holding each other.

As Deidre approached the doorway, Mr. Glise spoke up. "Wait! How can we get Tom's remains? When can we get them?"

"How thoughtless of me," she answered. "The BCA will release them to you as soon as their work is done. That should be in a week or so. I wish I could be more definite. I'll leave word for them to contact the mortuary when they are ready to be brought back to Two Harbors. The people at the funeral home will notify you when they arrive. In the meantime you might want to begin making arrangements for his burial, or to have the remains cremated."

"Thank you for all you've done, Sheriff," Mr. Glise said as he looked up at Deidre. He stood and took her hand and didn't let go for several seconds. Then he burst into tears and returned to his wife.

It was only a ten-block drive to the home of Jean Dickerson's parents, and Deidre didn't rush. She needed a breather after the gut-wrenching experience she had just endured. It wasn't the first time she had delivered heartbreaking news to relatives, but she never got used to it. Too soon she pulled up in front of their house, a two-storey white clapboard with dormers. She walked up the sidewalk with her head down as though studying the lines in the concrete. She rang the doorbell, and was greeted by a trim, neatly dressed Mrs. Dickerson.

"Come in, Sheriff, we have been expecting you."

"I'm sorry I'm late. I had a previous appointment that ran longer than I expected." Deidre didn't say what that appointment had been."

"I hope you don't mind. We asked our pastor to be with us this morning. He was gracious enough to stop by. Please come in."

Deidre hesitated a moment when Pastor Jackson, Naomi's father, stood to shake her hand.

"Good morning, Sheriff Johnson. It's good to see you again," he said, his eyes searching hers. Deidre knew he had to be thinking of his own daughter and what could have happened to her, still could if they weren't careful.

"Have a seat," Mr. Dickerson said, motioning to a wooden rocker in front of a well stocked bookcase. "What news do you have for us?" Deidre couldn't miss the quaver in his voice.

Deidre was met with the same silent plea for help and hopefulness, and she began the same way she had at her visit to the Glises.

"I've returned from the Bureau of Criminal Apprehension in St. Paul. As you are probably aware, the remains of several bodies were unearthed awhile ago in the Isabella area. I'm very sorry to have to inform you that the BCA's forensic anthropologist has identified one of them as being your missing daughter."

Mrs. Dickerson let out a gasp. "Oh, no! No! No! Tell me it's not so!" she wailed.

"Is there any chance that you could be mistaken?" Mr. Dickers asked, and he covered his mouth with his hand.

"No I'm afraid not. I wish it weren't so, but all of the signs: dental records, medical records, age of the decedent, sex, size, all of them point to the remains being those of your daughter. One arm bone even has scar tissue that indicates her elbow was broken when she was a child. That matches her medical records. I'm so sorry to have to deliver this news to you."

Deidre sat silently, letting her news sink in and allowing the parents time to gather their emotions. Pastor Jackson asked for a time of prayer, and said a few words of comfort. Deidre wondered how anyone could survive such a loss, especially the loss of someone they loved so deeply. Eventually, the couple seemed to have regained enough composure that Deidre believed she could approach them.

"I know this might be difficult, but do you think you're able to answer some questions at this time?"

There was a period of silence, and finally Mr. Dickerson mumbled, "Yes, I suppose we can."

"I noticed in your daughter's record that when she was in middle school she had some difficulty, but it seems that she had no trouble after that. Can you fill me in with what happened that she seemed to have straightened out her life?"

Mrs. Dickerson spoke first. "We were so terribly concerned for her when she was in her early teens. She got in with the wrong crowd, and unfortunately, we discovered she was a follower, eager to do whatever it took to make friends.

"When she was fourteen she began to get into more serious trouble. Twice, she was arrested for shoplifting. One time she said she was going to visit her friend who lived three blocks from here. At nine o'clock that evening, I . . . we received a call from the police saying that they had picked her up at the bowling alley. She was drunk, and they wanted me to come and get her.

"We tried grounding her. That didn't work. She just sneaked out through her bedroom window. We tried the Human Development Center, but she refused to continue seeing the psychologist. We were at a loss as to how to help her. One day a girl she hardly knew invited her to a youth group led by Pastor Jackson. Something clicked, and he had a profound influence on her. We thought she had abandoned her destructive behavior. For three years, life was as we had always hoped it would be. We laughed, took trips together, played games together, and totally enjoyed each other's company."

"Yes," Mr. Dickerson broke in. "Her grades went to straight As, and she became involved in church activities. We weren't only happy, but immensely relieved. She became an ideal daughter, and then her grades began to slip. She quit going to church."

"Did you ever confront her about her attitude change?" Deidre asked.

Mr. Dickerson tried to clear his throat but couldn't speak. Mrs. Dickerson continued. "Yes, we had a long talk the night before she disappeared. Jean confessed she had been using drugs, mostly cocaine, for about six months. She was so pathetic, crying and telling us how sorry she was.

"We didn't berate her or make any accusations. Instead, we asked her if she truly wanted help, and she wept even harder. She could hardly get the words out. She wanted treatment more than anything. We promised her that first thing in the morning we would contact a rehab center.

"We would have done anything to get our daughter back.

"Her father wanted to know how she had become involved, and she said there were some kids who had introduced her to the drug at a party after a football game. Little by little she had abandoned her real friends so she could get high."

"Who were these people?" Deidre needed to know.

"Most of them moved away after their class graduated. She mentioned one underclassman. Someone named Aaron."

"Aaron Sarstrom?" Deidre questioned.

"Yes, I think that was the name she mentioned. It's been a while since I've thought about that, but I'm sure that was what she called him, Aaron Sarstrom. Do you know who he is?"

Deidre lied. "Not really. I've come across that name recently in my investigation of another incident. Do you have any idea who was supplying the cocaine to them?"

"Jean only knew his nickname, someone called Skinny." Deidre became ramrod-straight.

"Are you sure that's the name Jean said?" Both parents nodded. "Is there anything else you can tell me?" Deidre asked, but she had already heard more than she could process at the moment.

"Jean said she had had enough." Mr. Dickerson was able to say. "She wanted it to stop and go away, but she said she didn't know how to get out of the group she was running with. We agreed to take her to a doctor the next morning and get some advice as to what we should do next. That night we heard her on her cell phone in her room. It sounded like she was arguing with someone. Afterward, I went into her room, and she was shaking and crying. She told me she had to talk with somebody in the morning before we went to the clinic, and I agreed that would be all right.

"When we got up the next day, she was gone, and we've not seen or heard from her since. We reported it to the police, and they conducted an investigation. After no sign of her for three weeks, they told us they were considering her disappearance a runaway.

"We've heard nothing else until today."

A wave of nausea rolled over Deidre. She remembered three years ago when an alert of a missing teenage girl had come across her desk. It was at a time when her department was stressed with funding cuts and layoffs. There had been a backlog of work piled up on her desk, and she had set it aside. The report had been buried under a heap of folders until one day as she was sorting things out, she found it. By the time she looked into the matter, two weeks had passed, and neither hers nor the city police department had any leads to go on. The thought went through her mind, *What responsibility do I have in this tragedy? Would two weeks have made a difference in the life of this girl and these grieving parents?*

Deidre raised her head. "Thank you for your help. I hope that what you've told me will help us find an answer so we can make sure this doesn't happen to any others."

In her SUV, she hung her head and sobbed.

Chapter Thirty

Deidre turned left onto the State Road and headed north, all the while wondering if this would be her last term as sheriff. On the way to Terry's bar in Isabella, Deidre's mind wandered to what she could do besides this job. She had been in law enforcement for over twelve years and wondered if she could last another eight to retirement age. She wondered how much longer she could stand the sorrow and inhumanity the job required her to face on an almost daily basis.

She understood why so many officers had drinking problems, why so many of their marriages ended in divorce. She understood why so many became cynical and callous by the time they were fifty.

Deidre had been so preoccupied with her dilemma that she was surprised how soon she was at the intersection of State Aid County Highway 2 and Highway 1, and she realized she was only five miles from Terry's. Deidre had been so deep in thought she didn't remember going past Friendly Jane's or the Whyte Road where all this had started. She turned into the parking lot and spotted Terry standing in the doorway, a bottle of beer in one hand and a bag of peanuts in the other.

"Well look who's here!" he exclaimed. "Is this a social visit or is it business? I haven't seen you for so long, I wondered if you were still with the force." He grinned. "It's good to see you again, Deidre. Come in and have a soda on the house."

Deidre always appreciated Terry's banter. Today she needed it more than ever, and she was glad to sit down and talk to a friend.

"I'll take you up on the soda, Diet Coke, please. But as usual, we'll have to mix a visit with business. I had to drive up and ask if you've heard anything since I talked to you last."

"Only what I read in the paper and that isn't much." Terry's eyes twinkled. "You looked good on TV, Deidre. Could've used a shower, though," and he laughed at her reaction.

"No, really, Terry. Have you heard or seen anything? I'm particularly interested in knowing if Ed Beirmont has been around."

Before Terry could answer, two fishermen came in the door, their minnow bucket in hand. Terry got up from where he and Deidre were sitting. "Can I help you fellas?"

The two men asked for three dozen minnows, fat head chubs. Terry scooped into the live well where a thin jet of cool water continually replaced what was draining from the tank. A mass of minnows lay squirming in the net. He poured water into a plastic bag, dumped in the minnows, and added a shot of oxygen from a tank. The fishermen watched, making sure they got their full count, but Terry was always generous in what he dished out.

The duo inquired where the fish had been biting. Terry put his hooked finger in his mouth and stretched out his cheek. "Right about here," he said, and laughed at his own joke. Then he named some lakes further up in the woods.

"There's Surprise Lake. It's about five miles back in on Forest Service Road 219. A guy came in yesterday with a fifteen-pound northern he said he caught there. I'd try McDugald though. It's just off the blacktop and only two miles east from here. They say the crappies are hitting in the late afternoon off the first point to the left. But, if you want my opinion, nothing beats Dunigan Lake for big walleyes. Just go back to Highway 2, and it will be the first lake on your right."

The men thanked him for the advice and left with their bait. Terry returned to Deidre.

"You're so full of it," Deidre said. "You have no idea where the fish are biting."

Terry put his finger to his lips. "Shhh. I don't want the word to get out. Anyway, I want to save the best lakes for the locals. We got to stick together, you know." He grinned broadly.

"Getting back to what we were talking about. No, Ed hasn't been around for at least three weeks. In fact, things have been real quiet. It's hardly worth being open during the day. Something new must be coming in, though. Pete Eliot stopped in the other day. He said that he saw somebody hauling a five-hundred-gallon LP tank into April Lake last week. I don't know how they expected to get it in on that old road, or why they'd want to. That lake is nothing but a bog, no usable shoreline at all. Pete said it looked like it was on a four-wheeled trailer like the kind farmers down south use to haul their fertilizer tanks."

Deidre had a flash of an idea go through her mind. "Did Pete get a good look at it?"

Her insistence surprised Terry. "No, it was nighttime and he just got a glimpse of it as they pulled off the road and headed into the woods. Why?"

"Could it have been a fertilizer tank? They look just like LP tanks, but farmers use them to haul ammonia fertilizer from storage tanks to their fields."

"Who'd try to grow anything up here?" Terry's face screwed up. "It makes more sense that it was an LP tank. Probably some deer hunters from the Cities building a deer shack back in the brush. I know a few are squatters on federal land. It's pretty easy to put something up in the woods and not have it discovered for several years. Every winter the Fed Foresters find one or two. They torch them, but usually the hunters don't have much invested in the shack. They just find another spot and rebuild. But it was Pete who saw it. It'd be better if you talked to Pete about this yourself. Do you know where he lives?"

Deidre shook her head. Terry grabbed a notepad from the bar and drew a crude map as he gave directions. "Take U.S. Forest Service Road 7 to Dumbbell Lake. It's a ways in, I'd say close to twelve miles. Beyond there is a T in the road. Turn left, I can't remember the name of the road, doesn't matter, you can only turn right or left. Anyway, continue on that road for another five miles or so, and you'll see a driveway on the right. That goes into Pete's place. He has a pile of rocks stacked about five high where you turn in. Can't miss it if you're looking."

He shoved the map across the counter toward Deidre.

"Thanks Terry, what you've told me might be the big break I've been searching for. Things are finally beginning to come together a little bit."

Deidre had no problem following Terry's hand-drawn map. In this part of the north woods there were few roads and many lakes to serve as markers. She turned left off Highway 1 and drove ten miles toward Dumbbell Lake, finally coming to a Forest Service sign marked "BOAT LANDING." Three miles past that she came to the T in the road Terry had said would be there. Following his directions she veered left and eventually came to the cairn he had described.

Several hundred yards off the road, she came to Pete's cabin. An arthritic black Labrador walked out to meet her. His muzzle was grayed and one eye was cloudy because of a cataract.

"Hi, boy," Deidre said as she extended her hand and let the old dog test her scent. Then she ruffled his ears, and his tail gave a feeble wag of appreciation. The cabin door opened and Pete stepped out, looking as ancient as his dog.

"Can I help you?" he asked, looking at Deidre suspiciously.

"Hi, I'm Sheriff Johnson. Are you Pete?"

"Might be," the fragile looking old man answered. "Depends on what you're sellin'."

"I'd just like some information if you can help me. It isn't about you, Pete," Deidre added reassuringly. "I was just talking with Terry. He said you saw someone pulling a large LP tank into the woods a couple of days ago, said it was on some kind of trailer."

"Yeah, I seen that all right." Pete was very guarded with his answers.

"Well, Pete, if it's okay, I'd like to ask you a couple of questions about that. I know it was dark and you only caught a glimpse, but it would sure help me with something if you could remember any details about it."

"No, that's about it. Just seen it being pulled onto the logging road down toward April Lake. That's all."

"Do you know that logging road at all?" Deidre wanted to get Pete talking if she could.

"I should. I built that road when I logged off a half-dozen forties around April Lake in 1975. Back then we could cut right down to the lake, took out almost ten thousand cords of the nicest black spruce and pine you ever saw. I guess I know every twist and turn in that old road."

"That must have been great cutting," Deidre urged him to talk more. "Those old black spruce must have run about eight inches on the stump, didn't they?"

"Yup, five sticks tall and no limbs to speak of for the first four. We really made time in that swamp." Pete grinned a nearly toothless smile. Deidre knew she was making progress.

"Knowing the country the way you do, are there any good building sites down by April Lake?"

"Not a one. Any fool who'd try to live down there is out of his mind, nothin' but mosquitoes and black flies in the summer.

Winter'd not be too bad I suppose, but there's no reason to be there that time of year, not even any fish in that bog lake. It was good deer hunting for a while after I cut it off, but now the trees are grown up so tall, the deer have moved out. Not much food for them after the brush is choked out."

Deidre decided she'd bring up the subject of the tank again. "Do you know what company name was on that propane tank you saw being towed to the lake?"

"Not the usual. The only company I know to deliver up here is North Way Oil and Propane, but this wasn't one of theirs. The company letters were SDFU."

"Can you remember any markings on the tank?"

"I had only a short look, but I thought one of the words started 'AM,' but I don't remember the rest. There was another word starting with 'A', but I don't remember that either. They didn't mean nothin' to me."

Deidre tried to refresh Pete's memory. "Could it have been Anhydrous Ammonia?"

"By golly, I think that was it," he said, and spit the tobacco juice that had been building up in his mouth onto the ground. He wiped his chin with his shirt sleeve. "What is that stuff, anyway?"

"Fertilizer, Pete, fertilizer," Deidre answered as nonchalantly as she could. "Pete, I thank you for taking the time to talk to me. Believe me, you've helped a lot." *More than you know,* she thought.

"Stop back anytime, Sheriff. It's been real nice talking to you. Not many folks care much about what us old-time loggers did. If you'd like, next time I can take you down to April Lake and show you where I cut."

Deidre told Pete she just might do that, gave the old lab another scratch behind his ears, and stepped up into her SUV. On the way home, an idea began to form in her mind. It was ridiculous to imagine anyone needing ammonia fertilizer back by April Lake. The high ground was nothing but rock rubble deposited during the last ice age, and the low ground was nothing but muskeg bog. There was only one other use for anhydrous ammonia she could think of, and if she was right, the gangland style murders, the drugs, and the messages on her windshield all started to make some sense. The puzzle pieces were beginning to match up. She just had to put them together.

Back at her office, Deidre made a computer search. The company logo Pete had described as being on the side of the tank stood for South Dakota Farmers' Union. It didn't take long for her to check on the business. It sold ammonia fertilizer to farmers, and a little more checking revealed that one of their tanks had been stolen two weeks ago.

CHAPTER THIRTY-ONE

JOHN, ARE YOU HOME, HONEY?" she called out. There was no answer, and in a way Deidre was glad. She wanted to be the one to put together a nice meal for them. On the way back from Isabella, she had decided that, when the mysterious murders were solved, she would like to resign from office. She was worn to a frazzle.

After dinner she wanted to relax in front of an open fire and discuss the idea with him. But first, she thought, a romantic meal might be best.

Deidre had stopped at the grocery store and bought two steaks, filet mignon. She planned to serve twice-baked potatoes, cheese-coated cauliflower, and cheesecake for dessert. She had picked out an expensive red wine.

It was unusually warm for October, perfect weather to fire up the gas grill and prepare the steaks. She'd wait for that until John walked in the door.

Deidre had just finished the potatoes and the cauliflower was steamed when she heard his familiar footsteps come across the deck. She met him at the door and threw her arms around his neck.

John straightened up, lifted her off the floor and walked into the kitchen. He gave her a kiss on the lips and held her tight.

"What have I done to deserve this?" he asked.

"That's just because you are you. But you better put me down. I've got steaks to put on the grill," and she pointed to the two pieces of meat on the counter.

It took twenty minutes to finish cooking the meal, and when it was done, Deidre had to admit it was a masterpiece. She turned the lights down low and lit two scented candles that sat on the table. "Welcome home, my dear," she crooned as she lifted her goblet in a toast.

They took their time eating, never once mentioning work. Deidre felt her tension fade in John's presence. She was contented, loved, peaceful, and safe.

"Let's leave the dishes for now," she bargained. "I'll do them later. I've got something I'd like to talk over with you."

"This sounds serious," John said, but his face showed he wasn't concerned. He grabbed Deidre from behind, gave her a hug, and kissed the back of her neck. They took their goblets and the bottle of wine into the living room and adjusted some floor cushions to recline against.

"So," John began. "What's this important thing you want to talk about?"

Deidre took a sip of wine, but before she could begin, John got up and went to the fireplace. He picked up the poker, rearranged the dying embers, and added two billets of split birch. The bark immediately flared up, and the flames produced a warm glow in the room. John began to sit down next to Deidre, moving carefully so as not to spill his wine.

Without warning, the living room window crashed inward, sending shards of glass scattering to all corners of the room. At the same time, a series of gunshots shattered the joy of what had so far been a magical evening. She heard the squeal of tires on the pavement as a vehicle sped away into the night.

At the same time, before Deidre could react, she felt John push her to the floor, covering her body with his. She felt his arms tighten around her, felt the muscles of his chest tighten, heard his breath expel from his lungs as he came to rest. Then all was quiet, not a normal quiet but an eerie silence that could only be described as a total absence of sound.

"What was that?" Deidre asked, dazed.

John didn't say anything.

"You're so heavy on me. I can hardly breathe," she gasped. "I'm okay. Just roll off."

John didn't move. He didn't answer. Deidre gave him a shove, and his lifeless body flopped off hers.

"John, John, please John, look at me!" she shrieked. Deidre cradled John's head in her hands. Then she saw the puddle of blood growing under his thorax. "No!" she screamed. "It can't be." She sat holding him, rocking back and forth in her misery. She made no move to call 911. John was dead.

Time became meaningless to her. It may have been a minute or an hour, but the wail of sirens broke into her consciousness. She heard fierce pounding on the outer door, but she was too stunned to move. After a few seconds, she saw the unlocked door swing open, and two uniformed police officers rushed in. One took John from Deidre's arms, and the other knelt in front of her.

"Deidre," the woman yelled. "Are you hit?" Deidre looked at her blankly. The officer shook Deidre. "Deidre, say something to me." She tried to get up from the floor. The officer helped her. She looked at the other officer bent over John, and collapsed again.

Deidre was aware when the EMTs arrived, but their presence barely registered.

"What do we have?" one of the men asked.

Deidre heard the officer's response as if through a fog. "I'm afraid there's nothing you can do here, guys."

The two officers moved Deidre to a chair in another room, and she sat, nearly catatonic. Finally, she became somewhat cognizant of what was going on around her. "He's dead, isn't he?" she asked with no expression.

The officer who was attending to her answered with a barely audible, "Yes."

Deidre heard a recognizable voice.

"She can't stay here tonight. Why don't we get her over to my house? I've called her doctor. He's a good man, one of the few who will make house calls. He said he'd be here in fifteen minutes."

Deidre recognized the voice and looked up to see Mrs. Olson, Inga, standing in front of her. Mrs. Olson knelt down.

"Oh, my dear child, how dreadful. Will you come over to my house, at least for a while? It's best if we give these people space so they can do their jobs. Come, dear, let me help you."

Inga steadied Deidre with one arm while she gently placed her other arm around her shoulders. In that fashion, she steered Deidre out the back door and over to her home. She led Deidre to the sofa, and Deidre flopped down and curled up in the fetal position. Inga sat on the floor by her head and stroked her hair. She began to pray for Deidre, something Deidre could never remember anyone having done for her before.

By that time members of her department had arrived, and Jeff knocked on Inga's door.

"Come in," Inga said, raising her voice to be heard.

Jeff came over to where Deidre was lying on the couch, and he knelt down by her side.

"Deidre, I'm so sorry. Forgive me for interfering at a time like this, but you know how important it is to gather as much information as soon as we can."

Deidre sat up, her nose puffy red and her eyes swollen from tears. She nodded.

"Did you hear anything before the shots came through your window?" Deidre shook her head.

"How about after, did you hear a car leaving? Could you see anything?" Again Deidre shook her head.

"Thanks, Deidre," Jeff said and stood up. "I'll come back tomorrow. Maybe things will be clearer then," and he turned to leave.

"They were after me," Deidre said, her voice flat, muted.

Jeff turned back. "Yes, I know."

"All John was doing was stoking the fire. They had no reason to target him."

"I don't think they did. He was in the wrong place at the wrong time. From what we can tell, the gunmen sprayed the living room, hoping to hit you. I doubt they cared who else they took down."

"How many were there?"

"We don't know. We'll find as many slugs as we can. I'm sure some will be found imbedded in the walls and furniture. We found two different kinds of casings ejected onto the street from their guns. They are medium-sized. I would guess about thirty caliber.

"Whoever it was left the scene in a hurry. The tires of their car left rubber marks ten yards long when they sped away."

There was another knock at the door, and Inga gave the same invite she had to Jeff. This time it was Dr. Jonas. He spoke briefly to Deidre, tried to assess her mental state and seemed relieved that she would be staying with her neighbor during the night. Before he left he gave her samples he had brought with him.

"This is something to help you sleep. If you want more in the days ahead, call my office, and I'll write out a prescription. Please stop by anytime if there is anything I can do to help you. I'll leave a note for the receptionist to make time for you. You won't have to wait for an appointment."

Jeff and Dr. Jonas left Deidre sitting on the couch with Inga sitting beside her, holding her hand. "Can I fix you a cup of tea, dear?" Inga asked. Deidre nodded. "Would you like me to call anyone, a relative, a friend?"

"My mother died four years ago. I had a brother, but he was killed in a rollover when he was nineteen. He was drunk at the time. My sister was last seen on the streets of Birmingham. She hung out at a place called Five Corners, but she was pretty much a junkie. How's that for a dysfunctional family?" she asked rhetorically.

Inga patted her hand and went to the kitchen. Soon she returned with two steaming cups of mint tea. The two women, one in her seventies, the other in her thirties, sat in silence, each holding their hot cups as though the warmth could permeate their souls.

"You're very kind, Inga," Deidre finally said. "Will you stay by me tonight?" Deidre seldom allowed herself to reveal any vulnerability, so this statement surprised even herself.

"Certainly, my dear. I'll be here for you. My home is yours for as long as you need. I can't imagine you going back . . . You're welcome to stay with me as long as you want."

Deidre looked at Inga with a mixture of pleading and thankfulness. She put her cup on the table by the couch and lay down. She closed her eyes and drifted into a fitful, troubled sleep.

Sometime during the night—Deidre was unaware of the time—she awoke, clearly hearing John's voice and feeling his hand on her shoulder. He gently shook her, saying, "Deidre, Deidre."

She sat up with a start. Her heart raced and she answered, "What? What is it?" It took a moment, but she realized it had only been a dream. Inga had gone to bed. Deidre sat alone in the dark, feeling vulnerable, lost. Eventually, she lay down and fell asleep. She had no more dreams.

The sun came up around seven o'clock, and Deidre jerked awake at the first sign of daylight. She sat up, panicked for a moment, and then realized where she was. Inga was sitting in a recliner across the room, looking at her.

"You're awake. I was hoping you'd sleep a little longer, but I suppose that would be difficult. Why don't you use my bathroom, freshen up a bit, and I'll fix us a light breakfast."

Deidre looked at herself in the mirror. She was a mess. Her face was swollen, and her eyelids drooped in a way she had never experienced. Her blond hair was twisted in swirls that stood up from her scalp, and there were streaks of mascara marking her face.

"Can I take a shower, please?" she called down the hall. Deidre heard Inga put down a bowl in the kitchen, and the older woman came into the bathroom, laid out a fresh towel and washcloth, then turned on the shower. She hugged Deidre tightly and returned to the kitchen without saying a word. Deidre appreciated her silence.

She stood in the shower, letting the steamy water wash over her, raised her face into the spray, and wept. Eventually, she cried herself out. After toweling off, Deidre dressed, combed her hair, and resolutely faced the day.

Chapter Thirty-Two

INGA AND DEIDRE HAD BARELY FINISHED breakfast when Jeff rang the doorbell. Inga answered it, and Deidre could hear the two talking. She recognized Jeff's voice but couldn't make out what they were saying. Inga escorted him into the kitchen.

"Would you like a cup of coffee, Deputy?" she asked in her ever-proper manner.

Jeff sat down at the table across from Deidre. "Yes, please." To Deidre, he said, "I'm so sorry this happened. I've talked to the commissioners, and they asked me to tell you that you can take as much time off as you need. They've given the okay for me to act as sheriff until you're able to work again. Take your time. We'll be okay."

Deidre sat silently for several seconds, rotating her nearly empty cup in her hands. "Thanks, Jeff, I know you'll take care of things. Do you have anything to go on, any clues who did this? Is Jason Canton at all responsible?"

Jeff looked at the ceiling. "No, I'm afraid not, but that doesn't mean that we won't get a break. Too much has been going on around here lately. Somebody's going to slip up. They always do. As for Jason, I don't know. It's possible, I suppose, but there were at least two weapons used last night. If it was him, he wasn't alone."

Deidre nodded.

"We've notified the FBI about John. Ben will be here later today. He wants to see you. We called the BCA, and Melissa was heartbroken, said to tell you how devastated she is for you.

Jeff sipped his coffee. "John's mother's been notified. She said his father died fifteen years ago. Do you know her well?"

Deidre shook her head. "John took me to see her once. She seemed to be a lovely lady."

"That was my impression, too. She asked me to tell you that she'd like you to meet with her at the Archer Funeral Home in Duluth to help plan John's funeral. She wondered if you could meet with the director and her at three this afternoon. She knows it will be extremely difficult, but arrangements must be made, and she doesn't want to be alone. Do you have her phone number, or should I let her know your wishes?"

Deidre hadn't given any thought to John's funeral, and suddenly the realization set in that John was actually dead and would not be coming back to her. She buried her face in her hands. Inga stood behind her, gently rubbing her back and shoulders. Finally, Deidre gathered her emotions enough to answer. "Would you please call? Tell Mrs. Erickson that I'll be there to help."

INGA AND DEIDRE SPENT THE REMAINDER of the morning talking. Inga reminded her of last night's offer and assured Deidre that she could stay as long as she needed. Deidre told and retold her story until she didn't want to talk about it anymore. Her older companion said little, only nodded her head and encouraged Deidre to talk.

When noon had come and gone, Inga suggested that the two of them go to Deidre's house so she could pick up what toiletries she needed and whatever clothes she wanted to transfer next door.

They entered through the back door, and Deidre realized the odor of her home had changed. It wasn't hers anymore. She sensed that the rooms were darker, then realized the picture window through which the shots had been fired had been boarded up with a full sheet of plywood securely nailed to the framing. She walked up the stairway to the second floor and concentrated on not looking into the living room. The place was quiet, lifeless. There was the stale smell of dead ashes in the fireplace, burned out, cold.

Inga helped Deidre fill a small suitcase, and together, they left the house, locking the door behind them. Deidre was numb.

They carried her things to the room where Inga said she could stay. Deidre combed her hair, put on makeup for the first time in almost eighteen hours, and dressed in clean slacks and a beige blouse. She wondered what was appropriate for a funeral home meeting.

"Do you want me to ride along with you, dear?" Inga asked, concern apparent in her voice.

"No," Deidre answered. "Thanks, but I think I need to be alone for a little while. Thank you for all of your kindness. I don't know what I'd do without you, Inga."

It took her the better part of an hour to reach the funeral home. Deidre parked her car and slowly walked up the ramp to the entrance. Nothing seemed real to her. She straightened her shoulders, lifted her chin, and walked in. The place was too quiet.

"Good afternoon, may I help you?" a solemn-looking man inquired. He was a tall, thin-faced man, although his sad eyes gave Deidre the feeling that he cared for the people he served.

"I'm supposed to meet Mrs. Erickson, John Erickson's mother, here at three. Has she arrived yet?"

"You must be Deidre. Please, step into my office. Jeanette is waiting." Hearing someone use John's mother's first name seemed strange. She didn't feel she knew her well enough for that kind of informality.

When Deidre entered the office, Mrs. Erickson, a frail little lady, stood to greet her. No words came to her mouth, and she wrapped her arms around Deidre and wept. The director waited until both women were ready and invited them to have a seat.

He was a kind and gentle man. For the next hour, he led them through the service of burial, where it would be and who would officiate. When it came to naming pallbearers, Deidre realized she hardly knew who John's friends were.

His mother suggested two college buddies. She also thought it would be good if his working colleagues were asked. Deidre said she thought Ben and Jeff would be honored. The director suggested relatives, and Mrs. Erickson named two cousins with whom he had been close when they were growing up. That made six.

The funeral would be held at eleven o'clock the following Tuesday at St. Mark's Lutheran Church, the one John had been confirmed in, and its pastor would be asked to officiate.

The funeral director said he would take care of calling the minister, contacting the organist, and arranging for a reception after the funeral. There would be a visitation at the funeral home from five o'clock to seven the night before.

A soloist hired by the funeral home would sing "Amazing Grace," and the church women would serve a luncheon afterward. It all seemed so cut and dried to Deidre. What could be done to let the world know what she had lost?

Her thoughts were interrupted by John's mother. "Deidre, will you come to the flower shop with me? I don't think I can face this alone. Please?"

Deidre looked into the woman's pain-filled eyes and placed her arm around her shoulder. Together, they walked to Deidre's car and rode in silence to the greenhouse on Fifth Avenue.

It took another forty-five minutes to select a casket spray. They chose something masculine with pine boughs, cones, and woodland flowers. Deidre thought it would go well with the oak casket they had selected.

Mrs. Erickson wept when she picked out a banner to be placed on the bouquet she ordered. It said "Son."

Deidre had no idea what she should do. She knew she wanted more than a few stems of roses stuck in a vase.

Eventually, she settled on an evergreen wreath studded with wisps of forget-me-nots intermingled with roses and fall flowers. The florist suggested a banner that read "Until We Meet Again," but Deidre couldn't bring herself to use that. She didn't believe there would ever be an "Again."

As they were leaving the flower shop, Mrs. Erickson turned to Deidre. "Will you come home with me—just for a while? I can fix us a little something to eat, and we can keep each other company. I'm sorry, but I don't feel very strong right now."

Deidre was grateful for the opportunity to be with Mrs. Erickson. Somehow, it made her feel like John was coming back at any minute. John's mother had taken a cab to the mortuary, so they rode to her home together. Mrs. Erickson lived on the tenth floor of what had once been a luxury hotel on Superior Street in Duluth. Deidre was surprised by the grandness of her apartment.

Neither of the women were hungry, and they decided to pick at whatever fell out of the refrigerator. Mrs. Erickson poured wine for them, the same kind that had been John's favorite. She wondered how often he had shared a meal at this same table with his mother. Deidre wasn't the only one who would be lost without him.

"I have some old photo albums I thought you might like to see. Do you mind?"

"Oh, please. John never really shared much with me. I know we are . . ." Deidre rephrased what she was going to say. "We were engaged, but he didn't have much to say about his childhood."

Mrs. Erickson fumbled in a closet and returned with three large albums. "Come, sit over here," she said, motioning to a sofa in the other room.

For the next two hours they looked at pictures, turning each heavy page carefully so as not to dislodge the photos.

"This is John in seventh grade. He always was a handsome boy. That was the year his father was injured in an industrial accident. He could never work after that, although he did get a nice settlement from the insurance company. Because he was hurt on the job, he was able to collect workman's compensation, and the company was wonderful. They never forgot him."

John's mother wiped her nose. "John loved his father. He nursed him for so long and with such devotion, I thought his chosen occupation might be medicine. His father died the year John graduated from high school. That fall he started college. He announced he wanted to go into criminology. I tried to talk him out of that choice, but he was adamant. I quit trying to get him to change his mind and accepted his choice for what it was. But every day I worried that he would be injured. I prayed things would never end up like this."

At ten o'clock, Deidre announced she would have to be going back to Two Harbors. She hoped Inga would still be awake when she got there.

Chapter Thirty-Three

The ride back to Two Harbors was lonely. She wanted to reach over to the passenger seat, place her hand on John's knee the way she did whenever they were riding together. She looked at her cell phone and had the urge to dial his number, to say, "Hi, honey. You'll never guess what. I had dinner with your mother."

Then she realized the futility of such thoughts and burst into tears. Partway home, another emotion grabbed hold of Deidre: anger, pure raging anger, and she wished she could somehow inflict terrible harm on those who had taken part in such a cowardly act. She told herself that given the opportunity she would show no mercy. Deidre thought gruesome thoughts, shooting kneecaps off, slow strangulation, horrible things to their private parts, but then she controlled her thoughts and dwelt on justice being served, even for those who didn't deserve it.

By the time she reached Inga's, her rage had subsided to a burning desire and ambition to see John's killers in a court of law, and she imagined Art at his best, pacing before the jury and making point after point.

The lights were on. Deidre walked up to the door, trying her best to ignore the building next door. Should she walk right in, ring the door bell, open the door and call out, "Hello?" Nothing felt right.

As if sensing her arrival, Inga opened the door. "Come in, my dear Deidre. I was beginning to worry about you. This must feel strange," she said as though reading Deidre's mind. "From now on, consider this your home. Just walk in."

Deidre hugged Inga and murmured her thanks. She smelled coffee brewing, and Inga had baked fresh cinnamon rolls. Suddenly, she was very hungry.

They sat up talking until after midnight. Deidre had a chance to tell her story over again, and the entire time Inga listened attentively as though it were the first time. Each time she talked about John's death, a new twist was added, but it was essentially the same story. Finally, Inga suggested they get some sleep.

Deidre put on her pajamas, brushed her hair, and cleaned up at the sink. She took two of the sleeping pills the doctor had left for her, washing them down with water from the tap. The label on the bottle said to take two before bedtime. Deidre wondered what it would feel like if she took the entire bottleful. She immediately forced that idea from her mind. *Let's not even go there,* she thought.

Deidre opened her eyes to bright sunlight shining behind the window shade, and for a moment she forgot where she was. She struggled to focus her eyes on the clock, eventually making sense of the digital readout, nine o'clock. She jumped out of bed in a panic. She was late for work. Then she remembered, and the tears flowed freely once more. She lay on the bed, sobbing with deep, aching spasms for a half-hour until she could weep no more.

After dousing her face with cold water and drying it with a rough towel, she combed her hair, brushed her teeth, and dressed.

Inga was waiting in the kitchen, and when Deidre sat down at the table, she smiled at her. "I hope I didn't wake you with my puttering in the kitchen. Sleep is good. Your body and mind both need it during difficult times. I believe our mind processes while we sleep and is capable of healing itself while we do."

Deidre was impressed with the older woman's intuitive take on life.

"I've got something light for breakfast. Would you like a cup of hot tea and a bagel with cream cheese? Or would you like more?"

Deidre thanked her and said tea and a bagel would be just fine. Over breakfast, Inga brought up the subject of John's funeral, and Deidre filled her in on what few details she knew.

"You ate that bagel as though you're hungry. Would you like some yogurt? I have some fresh berries I can mix in, make a fruit parfait like they do at that bagel place downtown." Inga smiled at Deidre and touched her hand.

"That would be nice," Deidre replied, finding it unbelievable that she was actually hungry. Inga turned on a CD player, and the gentle sound of classical music filled the background. Deidre cleaned the bottom of the bowl with her spoon. Food actually tasted good.

The rest of the day was spent visiting with friends and people she hardly knew who stopped to offer their condolences and their help. Some dropped off food: bars, a pasta salad, sandwiches, even a frozen hot dish. Deidre was moved by the caring and generosity of people.

Even though she was not a member his church, Pastor Jackson called, asking if it would be possible to visit her in the afternoon after conducting his Sunday morning services. In fact, she had not attended any church in her life, except for weddings and funerals. Soon there would be a funeral, and tears began to form across her eyes. She pushed the thought to the back of her mind.

By the time he arrived, three other people had stopped to offer their condolences. The pastor conversed with everyone, adding an air of calm to the room, and Deidre was happy he had come. He did much of the talking, so she could sit quietly. Pastor Jackson stayed until the others left, and then he confided with Deidre.

"I'm so afraid for my daughter. If they came after you, what's to prevent them from killing her? They know she talked with you, and they have to assume she told you all she knew. Will you be done with the case now, or is there any way you can continue working? I know this sounds crass and selfish, but right now I think you're the only person Naomi trusts. Please help us if you can find the strength."

Deidre was dumbfounded. She had no feeling of anger toward Pastor Jackson, but instead she saw pain in his eyes and realized he not only hurt for her, but was in deep sorrow for his daughter. She could find no words to answer and sat in a stupor, looking past him.

"I'm sorry. That was so very insensitive of me. Forgive me please. If I can help you carry your burden in any way, please call. I'll not make such a request again."

After repeating his regrets, the reverend excused himself. Deidre heard him talking to Inga in the kitchen, but they spoke so quietly she couldn't make out their words. Deidre heard the door open and then close. She heard the rattle of dishes being loaded into the dishwasher, and then silence.

That evening, Inga prepared a light supper for the two of them, some kind of pasta that looked like rice grains in a butternut squash sauce. Deidre ate her serving without talking, but afterward put her arm around the cook.

"That was delicious, Inga. You know just what to say, what to do, even what to cook to make me feel better. How do you do it?"

Inga looked at her and smiled a caring smile. "Experience, my dear, experience," she answered.

MONDAY CAME FAR TOO SOON. Deidre woke in a sweat, her heart pounding from fear, remembering what the evening would bring, and she feared what would be expected of her.

After a breakfast prepared by Inga, the day passed too quickly, and by mid-afternoon, the fear she had experienced when she had awakened became an overwhelming case of panic. Inga sensed it in her eyes.

"Can I ride with you to the funeral home? I don't like driving after dark, and I know the wake will last until seven."

Deidre looked at her in appreciation. Inga had never balked at driving in the dark before, and she suspected it was her gentle way of saying she didn't think Deidre should be alone.

Deidre burst into tears. "Of course you can. I think I'll need you more than ever tonight."

The drive to Duluth was made in silence. Deidre wanted to just keep driving through the town, through the state, through the country to someplace where memories didn't exist. Instead, she parked in the lot outside Archer Funeral Home and resolutely got out of her car. Arm-in-arm she and Inga made their way to the entrance.

John's mother was already there, and Deidre was ushered into one of the viewing rooms. It was filled with bouquets of flowers and soft music, and the few people who were gathered stood in clusters of three or four. Deidre's eyes immediately went to the front, fearing what she would see.

Mrs. Erickson stood by the coffin, obstructing Deidre's view. She was hunched over, her shoulders moving convulsively as she wept. Deidre's knees lost their capacity to support her, and she felt herself slide into a chair. Inga was there to steady her, and she whispered into Deidre's ear. An employee of the funeral home brought a cold glass of water and a box of facial tissues. Deidre thanked her and regained her composure. She forced herself to walk up to where John's mother still lingered.

Her first look at John was like an electrical shock. She hadn't known what to expect, but as he lay in his coffin, he looked as though he would open his eyes, sit up, and greet her with a kiss. Deidre placed her arm around Jeanette Erickson, and they wept together.

Eventually they stood in full embrace, and their tears fell on each other. Deidre could not endure the pain any longer, and she moved away from the casket. She felt lost, alone among other people, totally disoriented. Then she saw Ben and Jeff with their wives walk in the door. Deidre hadn't expected the flood of relief she felt, knowing that her friends were coming to be with her. She almost ran to meet them, first throwing her arms around Ben. He held her in his firm grip, his frame towering over her.

Deidre turned to Jeff and hugged him. "You have no idea what a difference you two have made. Just seeing you walk in made me feel as though I can make it through the evening. Come with me, I'd like you to meet John's mother."

She led them to where Jeanette was standing, but not alone. Inga was beside her, holding her hands and talking softly to her. They were about the same age, but it was apparent that Inga was much more alive.

"Ben, Jeff, I'd like you to meet John's mother, Jeanette. Ben is also with the FBI and worked in the same building as John. Jeff and I have been with the sheriff's department for years. Not only is he a great officer, he has been a great friend."

The two men offered their condolences and murmured words of encouragement. Deidre introduced Ben to Inga. Tears welled up when she told them what a pillar of support Inga was.

The evening sped by faster than Deidre could have imagined, and there was a constant stream of visitors offering words of encouragement and sharing memories. The atmosphere fluctuated between periods of deep despair and almost manic joy, and Deidre was exhausted by the time the last visitor left. She, Jeanette, and Inga were alone again.

Deidre was the last to walk up to the casket. "Goodnight, my love," she whispered, and touched his folded hands. They were cold.

IN THE MORNING, INGA GENTLY KNOCKED on Deidre's bedroom door. "Deidre, you'd better wake up, dear. It's seven o'clock, and you have to be at the church by ten-thirty. I have breakfast ready whenever you are. Is there anything I can help you with?"

Deidre tried to rid her mind of the cobwebs. "No, no thank you. I'll be down in a few minutes," and she slid out of bed. She had not needed to take sleeping pills the night before, and she knew a hot shower would rejuvenate her.

After toast, tea, and a bowl of Inga's yogurt and fruit, Deidre went upstairs to dress for the day, basic black to match the occasion. She and Inga would be driving separately today. She wanted to get to the church well ahead of the other mourners.

When she started her vehicle, she discovered the radio had been left on, and she turned it off. The ride to Duluth was made in silence, with only random thoughts speeding through her mind. When she pulled into the parking lot, she realized she remembered nothing of the ride. A few people were beginning to arrive and gather in small clusters outside the church. They hushed their voices as Deidre walked past, and she felt as though she were on display.

From the back of the church she could see that everything was in place. John's open casket was flanked by rows of flowers, candles were lit, and the eternal flame flickered inside its red glass lamp.

Deidre had said her goodbye last night, and she moved to the lounge where the family would be meeting with the pastor before the service. As she waited for others to arrive, she thought about what she would do in the days to come.

Jeanette Erickson entered the lounge and headed straight toward her. "Deidre, I'm so glad you are here already." Deidre could tell she had been crying. Her mascara was smudged from her having dabbed her tears. "I want you to sit next to me during the service. I really have no one else." Deidre hugged the woman who would have been her mother-in-law.

Singly or in pairs, people began to straggle into the room. Deidre recognized cousins and an aunt from out of town. John's uncle from Bemidji arrived. He hadn't been at the wake. They were a small group, and it was evident no more would be attending. The pastor started in his accustomed manner to the grieving family.

"A reading from the third chapter of Ecclesiastes. 'There is a time for everything, a time to live and a time to die . . .'" The pastor continued his reading, but Deidre's mind wandered elsewhere until she was jolted by the words, "'a time to love and a time to hate, a time for war and a time for peace.'"

She became instantly more alert. *This is definitely not the time for love,* she thought, *and most certainly it is a time for war.*

He concluded the reading with "'A time to dance and a time to weep.'" Deidre was still thinking, *A time for war, and a time for peace.*

The pastor asked them to follow him, and he led them to the sanctuary. As they entered, the congregation stood, and Deidre was amazed at the packed pews. She looked in the direction of the casket and was relieved to see that the lid had been closed and the spray of flowers and pine boughs was laid in place on top of it. The pastor invited everyone to be seated.

He stood before the congregation, his white robe and vestments a reminder of the solemnity of what was to come. He opened a small green book and began.

"Blessed be the God and Father of our Lord Jesus Christ, the source of all mercy, and the God of all consolation."

Right, Deidre thought. *Where was he last Friday night, on a coffee break, out with the boys?* She knew her thoughts were sacrilegious, but she had never been religious in the first place. Her mind went to other places for the rest of the service. She stood when the others stood and sat when they sat. She was content to allow her anger to fester, even in church.

Jeanette reached over and took Deidre's hand, looked at her and smiled a weak smile, and then it was time to file out of the church. As they walked up the aisle, Deidre's eyes met those of person after person, and she sensed the pain they felt for her. She wondered if this is what life was about, helping each other through the tough times.

They rode in silence to the cemetery, following the hearse and the black Lincoln Town Car in which the pallbearers were being chauffeured. Deidre was shocked to see the green mats covering the open grave. The casket stand had been readied to support its load. Those who had followed them to the cemetery walked slowly to the gravesite, and the pallbearers carried the polished oak casket, set it in place, and respectfully stepped back.

Deidre had a difficult time concentrating, and all too soon she heard the words, "Earth to earth, ashes to ashes, dust to dust."

The brief graveside service ended with the pastor inviting anyone who wished to take a flower from the casket spray as a reminder of John. Deidre removed the one long-stemmed red rose, clutched it close to her breast, and whispered. "Goodbye, my love. Goodbye."

She stepped back and thought, *And there is a time to act and a time to mourn. I'll do my mourning later.*

Tears rolled down her face, not so much tears of grief but hot tears of anger.

Chapter Thirty-Four

INGA HAD LEFT IMMEDIATELY after the interment and was waiting when Deidre walked into her kitchen. It was four o'clock in the afternoon, and Deidre was exhausted. Inga took her hand and looked into her eyes.

"I won't ask how you are doing. I know the answer. You're exhausted, numb, and wanting to change into some comfortable clothes. Go change, and I'll have a cup of tea ready for you."

Slowly, Deidre pulled herself up the stairs and slipped out of her black dress. She put on a sweatsuit and pulled her hair back with a headband. The last thing she did was to slide the ring off her finger, the ring John had given her only weeks ago. She placed it in the small jewelry box she had brought with her and closed the lid. Deidre looked at her bare finger and clenched her fist until her knuckles turned white. No tears formed.

Inga had made tea, and they sat on her couch, sipping the hot brew. "Did I ever tell you about my husband, Eric?" she asked.

A pang of guilt flooded Deidre for a second. She had lived next to Inga for over ten years, and not once had she asked about her personal life. It hadn't dawned on her that Inga would have had someone before the two of them had met.

"I'm so sorry. I just never thought to ask," Deidre apologized. "I've been so wrapped up in myself all these years I haven't been a very good neighbor."

"Goodness, don't say that. You've brought me a great deal of joy. Your flower gardens and the birds they attract, watching you and John fall in love, knowing the success you've made of your life, all of these things have brightened my days. I owe you so much."

"Tell me about your husband," Deidre invited.

"Your John reminded me so much of my Eric. He was tall—and handsome, and that isn't just me talking. I think other women were envious. And he treated me with such love and kindness. We were as much in love as were you and John. He proposed to me on Valentine's Day. I know that's cliché, but that's what happened. We were married in June of 1965. Eric was twenty-two, and I was only nineteen, but we were deliriously happy.

"We talked of having a family but decided to put that off until we could afford it. At that time the railroad was hiring again. The ore docks were going full swing, and Eric was fortunate to be hired. He worked in maintenance, doing welding and repair work on those huge chutes you see on the sides of the docks.

"It was late October of 1968. Eric was working the afternoon shift, the one from three to eleven. He kissed me goodbye and said to not wait up for him. He thought he might have to work overtime, because something had to be fixed by morning. Around midnight I received a call from the foreman of his crew. The poor man could hardly speak he was so upset. He told me Eric had been getting ready to lower his equipment over the side of the dock, when they heard a whistle frantically sound. The airbrakes on one of the ore cars had let go, and the full car was hurtling down the track. It rammed one of the empties sitting on the dock, and even though the empty weighed many tons, it was hurled into the air. Eric was crushed by its massive weight. I thought my life would end with his that day. So I know what you are going through, believe me, I know."

Deidre sat silently, not quite knowing how to respond. Finally, she asked, "How did you survive?"

"First, don't be fooled into thinking you'll get over it. Oh, I know people will tell you that, but those words are spoken by people who haven't been there. You'll never get over it. The sharp pains will subside, but you are going to be forever changed, accept that. Second, don't curl up in your own little world. Force yourself to get out every day and be with people. It'll be difficult, and there'll be times when you think you won't make it, but you will, and you will be stronger for it. Third, follow your instinct as to what's best for you. No one else has a magic formula. When people tell you that you're not yourself, tell them, 'No, I'm not, and I'll never be again. I'm a new me. Get used to it.'" Inga chuckled a little at that thought, remembering the first time she had said that to a critic.

Deidre sat in silence, thinking. She finally said, "Thank you, Inga, for all that you've done. If it is okay, I'd like to go to my room. I want to think about what you just said."

DEIDRE SLEPT IN THE NEXT MORNING, something she seldom did. It was nearly nine when she jerked awake, and a moment of panic swept over her. She broke out in a sweat, until she was able to clear her head. She buried her face in her pillow, cursed into it, sobbed into it. Eventually, she could cry no more, and she went into the bathroom to clean up.

Each new day felt unbelievably strange to her. How should she be acting? What should she be feeling? She decided she would travel to Duluth and take a walk at Canal Park, maybe have lunch at the little Vietnamese restaurant close to the canal.

Inga had been up for hours and had eaten breakfast earlier. She was already contemplating what she would fix for lunch.

"Good morning, Inga," Deidre said, trying to sound less burdened. "If you don't mind, I'd like to drive into Duluth. I haven't been down to Canal Park for ages, and I'd like to spend some time by the lake. I'll catch lunch down there, so don't fix anything for me. I'll try to be home by early evening, unless you need me for anything."

Inga looked at her and smiled. "Do what you have to do for yourself. If you try to please others right now, even me, it'll only prolong your recovery, so go, have a peaceful day."

On the way to Duluth, Deidre thought of the advice Inga had given her the night before. She mulled over the thoughts she had been having the last two or three days, and she was almost certain she knew what she had to do.

Traffic in Duluth was light, and she reached the park sooner than she had expected. Parking was no problem. It was the middle of the week. Students were in school, and few tourists visited the area in October.

It was one of those rare perfect days in Duluth. Lake Superior was as flat as glass, and the temperature was nearly sixty-five degrees. When Deidre stepped out of her car, she inhaled deeply and let the fresh lake air fill her lungs. Then she walked out on the breakwater and stood by the waist-high concrete sidewall.

Her thoughts were interrupted by the loud blast of an air horn and a bell clanging its warning. The steel-girder frame of the lift bridge spanning the canal began to rise. Deidre wondered what it must be like to be the operator sitting in his tiny control booth on the bridge itself. Every time the bridge traveled to its apogee, he went with it. *The view must be spectacular from up there,* she thought.

A half-mile out in the lake an ore boat was approaching, and Deidre leaned on the concrete abutment, waiting for it to come through the narrow entry to the Duluth-Superior harbor. The boat captain and the bridge operator communicated with each other with a series of horn blasts. Deidre thought they made a lonely duet.

The boat came directly at her, and then slipped past, its blunt prow peeling back the water and creating a white, frothy wake. It was the *Edgar Speere*, one of the Great Lakes' thousand-footers. Deidre had watched it dock in Two Harbors many times.

The massive hull took more than a minute to slide past, and as she watched the stern disappear, the captain made his turn into the far reaches of the harbor. She watched the bridge return to ground level and saw traffic begin to move steadily across its deck.

For the next hour, Deidre sat on a bench, watching herring gulls swoop over the water, and she wondered what it would be like to be so oblivious to the cares of the world, to be free. They were carefree, wheeling into steep dives and the next minute catching the wind off the lake and effortlessly soaring into the sky. She watched as one skimmed the surface of the lake and came up with a small fish crosswise in its beak.

What would it be like to be oblivious to mortality? she wondered.

Deidre thought of her plan. She thought about John's killer or killers.

By three-thirty, when she started to feel hungry, it dawned on her that she hadn't eaten since yesterday evening. It took her ten minutes to walk to the restaurant she planned on visiting, and by the time she was seated, it was too late for most people to be having lunch, too early for supper. She was the only customer.

An elderly Vietnamese lady came to her table. "Can I get you tea?" she asked, her voice sing-song with an Asian accent.

Deidre smiled. "Yes, please." The owner of the restaurant disappeared and returned with a small teapot.

"It is jasmine. Good." Her face broke into an infectious, broad grin. She handed Deidre a menu.

"That's all right. I know what I want. I'd like an order of your shrimp egg foo young and two Vietnamese egg rolls."

The lady explained that their egg foo young was different than most, that it was steamed rather than fried.

"I know, John and I . . ." She caught herself. "I've eaten here often. You serve the best Asian food." The waitress beamed.

When the woman left with the order, Deidre put her face in her hands, feeling the pain of what she had almost said. As she sat waiting for her food, she couldn't stop the emotion of knowing how differently it felt to be sitting there, alone. She saw people walking by the window, talking, laughing, and she wanted to rush out and scream, "What are you doing? Don't you know John's dead?"

In minutes, her food arrived. Deidre was surprised at how hungry she was, and she had almost finished her serving before she realized how rapidly she was stuffing the food into her mouth. She was finishing her last egg roll when the waitress brought her the bill along with a fortune cookie. She opened it and read. "Answers belong to those who act." Deidre nodded in agreement and took the bill to the cash register. "Thank you, and come again," the Asian lady said.

Deidre stopped at John's mother's apartment, but no one answered the door when she knocked. She hoped Jeanette was with friends, visiting, being comforted as Inga had done and would continue to do for her.

She drove home slowly, taking Old Highway 61 that followed closely by the lake. She passed the small cafe where she and John had enjoyed so many gourmet meals together, and a wave of despair swept over her. She knew she would never be able to dine there again. The rest of the ride was filled with memories triggered by each bend in the road.

It was after suppertime when she arrived home at Inga's. The two women sat up late into the night, talking. Eventually, Deidre told Inga what she intended to do, what she thought she must do.

"I've decided I can't just sit around. What will I do? If I try to be active, all I can do is walk around town or in the country. I have no desire to work in my flower garden. Otherwise, I suppose I could stay inside and read, but that won't be healthy for me either. And anyway, I can't concentrate enough these days to absorb what I read.

"I've decided the best thing I can do is go back to work. I'll be with friends there, and my duties will take my mind off my troubles." She saw Inga begin to say something and cut her off. "I know it sounds foolish, but I've made up my mind."

"My dear," Inga said, "It isn't foolish at all. Everyone grieves in their own way and at their own pace. Listen to your inner voice and obey what it tells you. The time for grief will come, perhaps when you least expect it, but it will come. Whenever that is, you will become sharply aware of your loss, but until then, you must keep living. Just be aware that grief will rear its vicious head sooner or later, and when it does, let it out."

Deidre was silent for a while and then excused herself. That night she cried herself to sleep, wondering if she was making a mistake, but the next morning she put on her uniform and headed for her office.

Chapter Thirty-Five

Deidre, you shouldn't be here." Those were the first words she heard from her secretary. "We'll manage for a while without you. At least take a few more days off to rest." Anne looked at her over her glasses, and Deidre could see tears in the woman's eyes.

Deidre wanted to snap back, but she controlled her emotions. "No, I've decided this is what I have to do. Otherwise I fear I'll become even more crazy than I feel right now. I have to do something positive or I'll die."

She went into her office and closed out the world by shutting her door. Then she phoned Mac at the Gang Task Force, Ben at his office, and finally, Melissa at the BCA. Each of them expressed their surprise at her decision, but no one tried to sway her resolve. Mac asked if they could meet in her office the next day. He said he had someone important he wanted her to meet.

It took most of the morning for Deidre to catch up on what had happened in the county during the week she was away, and she was grateful nothing but a few traffic stops and petty misdemeanors had taken place. By noon she had decided to drive north. She wanted to talk to the retired logger, Pete, in Isabella.

The drive gave her time to organize her mind. She really had no plan, and she struggled to begin working on the puzzle again. Deidre realized she had completely blown through a stop sign. She looked in her rearview mirror, hoping no one had witnessed what she had done. She wondered if she would be able to concentrate on anything ever again.

It took longer to get to Pete's cabin in the woods than she remembered, and it was a relief to find that she recalled the twists and turns in the road. Pete's old dog hobbled out to meet her, with Pete not far behind.

"Hello, Sheriff. I was hoping you'd come back. Care for some coffee?" Deidre could tell by his attitude he hadn't heard her news. She decided to let it stay that way.

"That'd be good. While we do that, I've got something I want to talk to you about."

A little apprehensively, Pete looked at her, but led the way up the steps that still needed repair. He poured each of them coffee, served in chipped mugs permanently stained by the residue of grounds that had been left in them too long.

"I just made a fresh apple pie," he said as he dealt two saucers onto the table and tossed the forks after them. Pete cut two large slices of pie and shoveled them onto the plates. Deidre didn't have time to object. Whenever you visited Pete you had pie.

"Well, Sheriff, I was hoping this was a social call, but I guess you want to know something. What is it?" Pete didn't believe in beating around the bush.

Deidre took a bite of the pie and was surprised how good it tasted. "Pete, this pie's great. How'd you learn to make pie this good?"

Pete just shrugged, but his smile showed how much he appreciated the compliment.

Deidre continued. "The last time I was here you told me you had seen what looked like a propane tank being towed into April Lake. I'm curious, is there any other road into that lake?

Pete grinned. "None that anybody else knows about."

"What do you mean 'that anybody else knows about'?"

Pete grinned again. "Remember, I told you I logged that area back in the seventies. I built that road they went in on. We used it as our main haul road back then. Took out almost ten thousand cord over a couple of years" he bragged, repeating what he had said during their last visit.

"That's a lot of truck loads to haul over one road, pounds it down pretty good.

"Our main landing was down by the lake, but it takes more than one road to clear an area that big. So of course there were other roads, mostly grown over by now. I know every one of them, know every rock and knob and swale. When you work a timber sale every day of the year it all becomes second nature to you. I think I'd even recognize some of the stumps we left."

Deidre looked Pete square in his eyes. "Do you think you could guide me into the lake on one of those forgotten skid roads? Could we get there without anyone knowing we were there?"

Pete's eyes sparkled. "I could get you in there in the dark if I had to. But why?" he asked.

"Pete, I can't tell you why right now. But I will say it might not be safe for you, especially if anyone found out you'd taken me in. And you say you could do it in the dark. What about at dusk? Would you do it, knowing it might be dangerous?"

He drummed the table with his fingertips and looked at Deidre. "Do you have any idea how boring life is for me? I'm too old and broken down to work. All I do is sit around all day, talking to my dog and waiting for bedtime. You're giving me a chance to feel useful again. Did you think I'd pass that up? When do you want to go?"

They talked about how long it would take to get to the lake, and Pete decided they'd have to leave in a half-hour if they were to get there with enough daylight left to see anything. When it was time to go, they rode in Pete's old pickup, but to Deidre's surprise he turned away from the direction of the lake. "The timber sale loops around three sides of April Lake," he explained. "If we take this forest service road west and then turn north we can come in from the opposite side of the cutting area from where the other road runs. Then we can turn east on a logging road that's mainly kept open by grouse hunters with their ATVs. Lazy buggers can't walk anymore, and they call that hunting," he complained.

His pickup bounced over rocks nearly the size of boulders as he complained about wannabe woodsmen. Deidre was afraid they would be heard, and as though he read her mind Pete expounded, "We're making a lot of noise, but the main landing I was telling you about is over a mile away. There are a few hills between us and the landing, and with all of these pine trees grown up, they'll never hear us. Look at them. I bet they're over thirty feet tall. Ten years from now this'll have to be thinned. Oh, Lord, I wish I could do that again. I miss the sounds and the feel of a chainsaw in my hands, the sounds a tree makes as it falls." Pete imitated the whoosh of wind through tree branches.

"Most of all I miss the smells. Do you know that when you cut into a jack pine you can smell turpentine just as plain as if you had opened a can of the stuff?"

Pete became silent as he battled to keep the pickup on the rustic trail he called a logging road.

After what seemed to Deidre like miles of bumping over the so-called road, they reached the point where they could go no further. Pete opened his door, but before getting out he said to shut her door quietly, and he suggested that from then on they shouldn't talk loudly. He said they were still far enough away, but just in case, it would be best to act as though they might be heard.

Deidre was amazed at the way Pete maneuvered through the woods. He was as nimble on his feet as a cat slinking through tall grass, ducking under overhanging branches, stepping over fallen trunks, and gliding over the rough ground. What really impressed her was that he hardly made a sound. She had a difficult time keeping up. Pete was definitely a man of the forest.

After a half-hour walk, Pete held up his hand. He leaned over and whispered in Deidre's ear. "The lake is just over that rise," he said, pointing straight ahead. "To our right is a rock outcrop. We can climb the backside, and if we lie on our bellies, we'll be able to look down at the old landing without being seen. We'll be about two hundred yards away. I brought these." From inside his shirt, he pulled out a pair of compact binoculars. "Thought we might be able to use them," he said without looking at Deidre.

She had begun to admire this old lumberjack's talents. She followed him more easily now, because Pete was moving slower and more deliberately. The rock outcrop slanted upward, and it made for easy climbing. Pete got down on his belly and began wiggling his way to its crest. When Deidre reached his side, she was awestruck with the view. They were looking out over hundreds of acres of pine forest. Here and there a deciduous tree, devoid of its leaves, thrust its barren branches above the green of the conifers.

She shifted her gaze to a clearing that had been Pete's primary log landing. It was approximately the size of a city block, circular, but with an island of stunted brush growing in its center. Two newer model pickups were parked at the end of the loop. Pete had his binocs out and was scanning the area.

He whispered, "I don't see anybody here, but if you look past the pickups into the brush, you'll make out the tank I told you about. It's pretty well-hidden, but if you look close, you can see it."

Deidre took the glasses and scanned where Pete had said to look. There, hidden behind some trees and covered with several pine boughs sat the tank. She could barely make out some of the letters on its side. "AN Y ROUS AMM IA." She swung the glasses so she could get a better view of the pickups, and to her surprise saw five small propane cylinders lined up beside one of them. They looked to be the size commonly used in barbeque grills or tent campers.

She inhaled sharply at the sight of blue corrosion caking the brass fittings on their tops. Pete looked at her, wondering what she had seen. He motioned that he wanted the binoculars, and Deidre handed them over.

For several seconds Pete seemed to peer at the edge of the woods. Then he put the glasses down and whispered again. "Look through the woods, not at the edge where it meets the clearing. Look into it. You'll make out a path, and deeper into the trees you'll see the outline of a shack. Somebody's standing in front of it."

Deidre did as she was told, and it took a few seconds to understand what Pete meant. Finally she was able to ignore the foreground and concentrate on the deep forest. The outline of the shack became visible, and just as she was beginning to be able to focus her attention on it, a man stepped from the shadows. His face was visible for only a second. She went rigid. It was Jason Canton, the man who had been released on bail only last week, the one who had been impersonating Aaron Sarstrom and was arrested when they found cocaine in his house.

Deidre was getting nervous. It was late in the afternoon, and they had a mile walk back to Pete's pickup. She nodded to him, and began to retreat down the back side of the rocky outcrop. Pete led the way back to the pickup, homing in on landmarks invisible to Deidre. It was almost dark when Deidre spotted the outline of the old truck, and they quietly opened their doors, slid into the seat, and just as quietly closed the doors. Pete eased the pickup back the way they had come in. The reflection of the headlights off the needles made the pine trees shimmer as though they were covered with frost.

"Pete, do you know what we found?" she asked.

Pete shrugged. "Some crazies that want to get away from the big city? We've got a lot of them up here in the backwoods."

"That's a drug manufacturing camp, the worst kind. They're cooking meth down there. Did you see those small propane tanks lined up by the pickup? They all had blue corrosion on the brass fittings. They're being used to transfer ammonia from the big tank on wheels. They stole that large tank from a farm operation and pulled it up here. The letters you saw on the side, SDFU, stand for South Dakota Farmers' Union. They are missing one of their tanks.

"Pete, I hate to tell you this, but I've gotten you involved in something pretty dangerous."

Pete looked at her and smiled. "I ain't had this much excitement in a long time," and he laughed out loud and slapped the pickup's steering wheel.

On the way back to his place, Deidre filled him in on all that had happened the last month or more. Pete became somber when Deidre explained how important it was for him to not tell a soul, not even Terry, what they had discovered.

"There's no one much around for me to tell, but even if there was, I'd know enough to keep my mouth shut. Mother didn't raise no fool, you know."

It was after ten o'clock when Deidre finally got home to Inga's, and she was relieved to see the kitchen light still on. Inga had saved some supper for her, and they talked while Deidre ate. She was glad she didn't have to be alone.

Chapter Thirty-Six

THE DAY DAWNED CRYSTAL CLEAR and cold. Frost covered the grass when Deidre left for work, and she bundled her collar around her neck to ward off the October chill. She was at her desk, working, before anyone else arrived.

Mac had said he'd be there at ten o'clock, and she wondered who he would be bringing to meet her. She was anxious to talk to Mac. What she had seen yesterday could result in the break they had been searching for all these months.

As usual, Mac was right on time, and she looked up from her desk as he cleared the security door. Her mouth gaped open. Standing beside him, almost a foot taller than he, was Ed Beirmont. Deidre was befuddled. Why was this man, one she considered a lowlife, coming in with the head of the Drug and Gang Task Force? She left her office and met them before they reached her secretary's desk.

"Morning, Deidre," Mac said with a grin. "I think you know Ed?"

The look of puzzlement on Deidre's face gave her away, and before she could say anything, Mac suggested they go into her office and talk where they wouldn't be interrupted.

Deidre moved the chairs so they could converse easily without her desk between them.

"Well, it seems as though I have some catching up to do," she said, not altogether friendly. "What's this about?"

"Ed has been working this area for almost a year now. Tomorrow, he'll be leaving, although he can't tell even me where he's off to next. Ed is a contract worker hired by drug task forces to go undercover. That's what he has been doing in Lake County. I suppose you could say he's a modern day bounty hunter.

"I've brought a copy of his reports. If we need him to testify about anything, we can contact him, and he'll return for a day or two. He'd rather not have to appear in that function, however. The more he can keep his face out of the news, the better. It'll be up to us to put together a case and prosecute it. Ed, why don't you go over what you've discovered?"

Ed cleared his throat. "I know how you must have felt about me, Sheriff. That's good, because it means I was giving the impression I intended. But now, I apologize for how I acted and how I must have caused you some consternation. I'm sorry to have forced you to spend your valuable time chasing down dead end leads.

"That invoice with my company's name on it you found by Skinny's pickup was not my doing, though. Skinny must have picked it up when he was riding around town with me, and it fell out of his cab when he was dragged out. Again, I apologize for causing you to waste time checking me out."

Deidre's face flushed. It was she who needed to apologize, but Ed continued before she could speak. "Let's get right down to what I know, or at least suspect. Skinny Tomlinson was near the bottom rung of the organization. He was mostly a gofer for the big three. They supplied him with enough coke to keep him happy, and he delivered messages, brought groceries and beer up to them, pretty mundane stuff. Skinny thought he was on his way up the ladder to the Big Time. The problem was, he couldn't keep his mouth shut. It was Skinny who got my foot in the door so I even knew where to begin. Eventually, his mouth got in the way, and he was taken out of the picture. The last time I saw him I tried to intervene, but the way he was acting I couldn't do much without blowing my cover. That was the night they caught up with him on the Whyte Road."

Deidre interrupted. "Do you know what happened to him that night? We found him buried a long ways back in the woods, along with six other victims."

"I can only guess, but I'd say they followed him until they had the opportunity to force him off the road. Skinny never carried a weapon, and I think the people I'll tell you about would have easily overpowered him. It's only a guess, but I wouldn't be surprised if whoever did Skinny in also executed the others. They use people until they begin to become a liability, and then they snuff them."

"Who are these people?" Deidre wanted to know.

Mac interrupted. "Do you remember a while back, maybe a month or more ago, I faxed you some images?" Deidre nodded. "We're quite certain those are the people: Elias Howard, Joseph Duarnte, and the third, whom you've met, Jason Canton."

Ed broke in. "I'm almost positive those three are the ring leaders. The first two have managed to stay out of sight, but as you know, Jason has been a part of the community. He was able to blend in and keep a low profile. If you hadn't had the idea to check on his enrollment status, we might still be ignoring his role in the scheme. In my opinion, the other two are the most dangerous of the trio. Jason stuck his neck out further than they did by allowing himself to be seen, but I don't think he's as ruthless as Elias and Joseph. Those two are a couple of scary animals."

Ed took a deep breath and said, "A number of meth labs have been set up in the woods. They're scattered along the southern border of the Superior National Forest. They're squatting on federal land and have built these shacks in dense stands of conifers where they can't be seen very easily, not even from the air. I don't know where they're located, but from everything I've learned they were built in very inaccessible sites—bogs and swamp-bound places. From what I have gathered, they get kids hooked on coke, and then blackmail them into acting as drug 'mules.'"

"So, how does Skinny's death mesh with those of the other six? We have sound evidence that they're linked." Deidre looked at Ed expectantly, hoping his answer would help wrap up the case.

"I can't be sure, because the other deaths happened before I came to town. My best guess is that some of the victims got too loose with their mouths or started using the product themselves. When that happened they became useless to the organization. Like I said, this is a ruthless gang. Some of the mules saw where they were headed and wanted out, but there was no way they'd be let go. They knew too much and had to be dealt with. This is second-hand or even third-hand information, but I heard that's what happened to Jill Moore. She was refusing to carry their goods anymore and had told friends she wanted to go into rehab. Word is she was shot up with a lethal dose of meth."

Mac took over the narrative. "This gang's violent and uncompromising. They've such a fearful reputation that people clam up. That's why they're so tough to track down. The straight kids are fearful of their fate if they talk about what's going on. The gang wants word to get out among their mules when something like Jill's death occurs. They rule by fear and intimidation."

He shrugged. "That's about where we stand at the present time. Ed believes he's penetrated their system as far as he can without them becoming suspicious. They're a closed group and aren't going to allow others into their inner circle. That's why almost everything we've said comes with a great deal of conjecture, but we believe we're pretty close to the truth."

Deidre sat for a second or two, digesting what they'd said. Then, with a bit of pride she said, "I know where their main camp is, and I suspect they have satellite factories. In fact, I saw their main camp yesterday. They have a large tank of anhydrous ammonia hidden in the woods, the kind farmers use to transport the stuff to their fields. There were several smaller propane cylinders lined up by a pickup. They were either ready to be loaded into the trucks or had just been unloaded, I couldn't tell. The brass fitting on the top of each tank was corroded and a blue material was caked around the valve, a sure sign they were being used to transport the ammonia in smaller quantities. I think it is time we pay the judge a visit and apply for a search warrant, but from what you tell me about this bunch, I'd like to do a little more scouting of the situation with my own informant." She smiled at the two men.

"How did you manage that," they both asked at once, incredulous that she had made such a discovery without their help.

"Hard work, gentlemen, hard work," she verbally jabbed at them. "But let's go see about our warrant."

Ed went his own way, preparing to become lost in the world of surveillance in some other community, while Deidre and Mac walked across the street to the courthouse.

Chapter Thirty-Seven

AFTER FILING THEIR REQUEST for a warrant, Deidre and Mac left the courthouse together.

"How about some lunch?" Mac asked, but she turned him down.

"No, I've got some things to do right away. I want to find out more about the shack I saw yesterday. We can't just go barging in on them, or I'm afraid we'll find ourselves in a dangerous situation. It sounds like this bunch isn't going to roll over for us."

Mac looked at her weary face. "Deidre, it might have been good for you to come back to work. That I understand, but you've got to give yourself some slack. You won't be good to anyone if you run yourself into the ground."

"Let me be the judge of that," she snapped back. "I'll call you tonight. Is it okay if I catch you at home? I'll be late getting back from up north, and you'll be off duty by then."

Mac shrugged. "Sure, any time, any time." He got in his car and waved to her before backing out of his parking spot.

Deidre checked in with her secretary and told her she was going up to the Isabella area. Then she went to Inga's and changed out of her uniform into the clothes she normally wore when she was hiking in the woods. She left her official SUV in its place and drove her own car.

On the way north, she allowed herself to begin thinking about John. Suddenly, almost unexpectedly, tears welled up in her eyes, and she began to sob. Deidre pulled over to the side of the road and wept, her forehead resting on the steering wheel. After about five minutes, she finally cried herself out, and blew her nose on a tissue and tried to wipe the stringy snot from her face. After several minutes she was able to take a deep breath and compose herself. It was as though something had broken and released her pent-up emotions, and she felt better, at least for the time being.

She forced the memory of John from her mind, concentrated on the task ahead, and drove in a mental fog for the next forty miles. Before she realized it, she was at the fork in the road beyond Dumbbell Lake. In minutes she was at Pete's cabin and was being greeted by his ancient black lab.

Pete hobbled down the stairs, hardly looking like the man who had guided her through the woods the day before. "Hi, there, Sheriff, come back for another slice of pie?"

"No, Pete, something not quite as much fun. It might not look like it, but I'm here on business. I've looked at a map of the April Lake area, and there's another lake just to the north of it."

"That'd be June Lake. The two are only about two hundred yards apart."

"Well, is there any way to get from one to the other, a creek or a portage?"

Pete nodded, and spit what Deidre thought must be tobacco juice at the base of a tree. "There's a creek all right, but it's pretty rock-filled, especially this time of year when the water's down. You can make it through though, if you know where the channel runs. What's on your mind, Sheriff?"

"I don't like getting you any more involved than what you are, Pete, but you know the area better than anyone I could ever find. I'd like to go fishing on April Lake this afternoon."

"You've got to be kidding! There ain't any fish worth catching in April Lake, just a few hammer-handle northern pike. You'd be lucky to even get a hit in there. Let me take you to a lake where we can catch something worth bringing home. I know all the good places up here, even more than Terry, that old BSer."

Deidre laughed. "No, Pete, I really don't want to catch any fish, believe me. I'd like to get a look from the lake side at that shack we saw yesterday. It looked to me as though it must be pretty close to the water."

Pete shook his head. "I should have known you were smarter than to expect to catch anything in that muskeg hole. And don't worry about getting me involved. This is the most fun I've had since I quit logging. I got a little stiff after yesterday's walk, but taking a little paddle in a canoe will be good for me, loosen me up some."

He walked over to an old beat up and faded green fiberglass canoe leaning on its side next to his cabin.

"Let me help you with that, Pete. It looks pretty heavy for one person to carry."

Before she could stoop to grab the end of the canoe, Pete spat out orders.

"It goes easier if one person does this. Just keep your hands off it when I put it up. You'll throw off the balance, and then I will end up hurting myself."

Deidre was shocked when he flipped the canoe over onto its bottom, and then by placing one hand on the gunwale nearest him and the other hand on the forward thwart, Pete swung it up over his head in one motion and lowered its yoke onto his shoulders. She watched as he walked with it over to his pickup and set it on the carrying rack fastened to the truck's box.

He returned for the paddles, threw them in the back, and proceeded to tie down the canoe.

The whole operation took five minutes, and he said, "That's it. Grab your fishing rod and let's go."

Deidre reached into the backseat of her car and took out an antiquated rod and reel. It didn't matter. All she planned to do was cast a lure near shore as Pete paddled in the stern of the canoe. Deidre even contemplated removing the hooks from the lure to guarantee she didn't land anything. She made sure she had her sunglasses and hat and jumped in beside him. They rattled away down the washboard dirt road.

"We have to backtrack to the Tomahawk Trail and come in that way. Then we can paddle across June Lake. The creek flows north from April Lake into the south end of June. Good thing we have a fiberglass canoe, it'll be a lot quieter than one of those aluminum models."

Pete rambled on about the countryside through which they drove, pointing out the many places he had cut stands of timber when he was still working. Deidre couldn't help but be impressed how he remembered the places and dates.

It took forty-five minutes for them to reach June Lake, and when they did, Pete unloaded the canoe as quickly as he had put it up.

"Jump in, Sheriff, and grab a paddle. I'm not going to ferry you like you were Cleopatra or something." He laughed, and Deidre could tell by the sparkle in his eyes that he was thoroughly enjoying himself.

They paddled across the lake in silence, and every few strokes she could feel Pete make some sort of adjustment as he kept the canoe moving in a straight line. Soon her arms began to feel the strain of the pull-lift-swing forward-pull-lift-swing motion. Pete continued to stroke at an even pace, as rhythmically as a metronome. The canoe surged ahead, its prow slicing through the water, peeling back the lake's surface and forming a slight wake.

"Let's talk real quiet," Pete said as they approached the mouth of the creek. "Sound carries a long way over water." He eased the canoe between two rocks. "Let me paddle us through here. You just hold your paddle and be ready to point out any submerged rocks you see that it looks like we are going to scrape."

Deidre watched as he threaded the canoe around a sunken log and turned to avoid a rock that was barely showing above water. They made it through the congested waterway without touching any obstacle.

"All right, Sheriff. Start fishing. I'll keep us out about twenty yards, and you cast into shore. Reel in fast or you'll get hung up on the bottom. If you have a floating lure, use that. It'll save us a lot of trouble."

Deidre began casting, and Pete continued paddling very slowly. At the rate they moved, it took over a half-hour to travel part way around the lake. Deidre had seen the outline of the shack when they first came through the narrows, but now she could see it quite clearly through the trees. It had been built near the water's edge in a dense spruce swamp, and she wondered how they had ever been able to put in a foundation. She guessed they had driven posts into the boggy muskeg substrate until they hit solid footing. She thought that should be the least of her worries.

As they passed the building, she could see smoke rising from the makeshift chimney, really only a few sections of stovepipe shoved together. As they slowly glided by, Deidre took a mental snapshot of the lay of the land, areas where the building might be approached undetected, and any back door escape routes. There were none, and only two small windows, high up on the wall, broke the continuity of the backside.

She prayed that a fish wouldn't hit and cause a disturbance so near the cabin, and she mentally kicked herself for not having removed the hooks from the lure she was casting. Fortunately, the lake held few fish, and they weren't biting.

Deidre and Pete moved down the shore another quarter mile. Deidre turned and said, "It looks like they're not biting today. How about we go home?"

She reeled in her lure and set down her rod. They paddled in silence back to June Lake and Pete's truck. On the way home, Deidre talked with Pete about what was most likely going on in the shack, but she didn't let on about the murders or John's death.

"Pete, we're going to be executing a search warrant for that shack the day after tomorrow. There'll be quite a crew, and I know I can't get them in from the back way you know. It's asking a lot of you, but would you be willing to serve as our guide, to take us in the way you took me to the cabin through the woods?"

Pete's eyes lit up as he looked at her. "Sheriff, it'd be my pleasure."

"I thought you'd agree," and Deidre reached over and playfully punched the old lumberjack on the arm. She could feel his sinewy muscles contract under her hand. *I think you're not as fragile as you look,* she thought.

"Be ready sometime after noon. I don't know the exact time, but I'm sure we'll be at your place close to then."

It was almost dark when Deidre left Pete's place, and she kept her bright lights on the whole way back to Two Harbors, at any time expecting a deer to leap from the woods onto the road. Too often when they did, the bright lights blinded them, and they stopped, frozen with fear. She saw several sets of glowing green eyes beside the road, but none ran in front of her car.

Inga was up when she arrived. She had saved leftovers from supper, and Deidre was thankful to be able to sit down to hot food.

Inga watched Deidre as she devoured the warmed up meal, and her eyes teared up. "My dear, are you running away from your pain with such resolve you're harming your health? You'll not be able to run forever, you know."

Deidre swallowed and didn't take another bite. "Sometimes my grief swallows me up. Today, I had to pull off the road, and I cried harder than I've cried since John was killed. I cry myself to sleep every night, and there isn't an hour goes by during the day that I don't think of him. I'm grieving. But I also have a job to finish, a job that's crucial to Lord knows how many people, and I intend to finish that job. If John were alive, I'd still be working these long hours, because I think everything will soon come to a head. John's murderers are tied up in the whole mess, making it more important to me than ever. I'll be okay."

After she ate, Deidre called Mac at his home and told him all that had happened since she saw him last. They discussed what should be done next, and Mac suggested his SWAT team should pair up with her and her deputies to execute the warrant. They decided that, for the time being at least, the FBI wouldn't be needed. When it came time to work on the links to Minneapolis and Chicago gangs, then the case would be handed over to them.

Before going to sleep, Deidre made a list of what she would do the next day. First, she would pick up the warrant from the courthouse. Then she intended to visit with Pastor Jackson, his wife, and Naomi. She also wanted to sit down with Mac and draw up plans for their action the next day. She had to put together her team of deputies, too. She figured there should be three others besides herself.

Chapter
Thirty-Eight

THE OFFICE WAS STILL EMPTY when Deidre arrived. She hadn't been able to sleep that night and decided to come in early. She made a pot of coffee and took out the photos of Elias Howard and Joseph Durante. They had such sinister looks to them, each having a deep scar on his face and scowling eyes. In each photo the man was unshaven.

Neither of them had the expression of a person using meth, and this made Deidre all the more angry. She was sure they were manufacturing the stuff and selling it to those who were addicted, many of them kids and young adults whose lives would be ruined beyond repair. They weren't ruining their own lives but were destroying countless others, all for the sake of money and power.

At ten minutes to seven, she phoned Mac. He had just walked into his office and hadn't had a chance to take off his jacket. They set a meeting in his office for two that afternoon.

Deidre could see her deputies begin to filter in, and they were picking through the box of pastries, pretending to argue over who got the best of the treats. *What a great bunch,* she thought. *I just hope no one gets hurt tomorrow.*

They had a quick meeting. Nothing of any consequence had happened the night before.

It was a short walk across the street to the courthouse. The warrant was in the judge's hand when she came into the judge's chambers, and she gave it to Deidre. "The date of execution is tomorrow. I set the time for two in the afternoon. Is that all right?"

Deidre nodded.

The two of them discussed the parameters of the warrant. When Deidre turned to leave, the judge reminded her, "Be careful, Deidre. These are some bad actors you're dealing with."

Deidre tried to smile.

By nine o'clock her desk was cleared of the paperwork that seemed to grow overnight, and she made a call to Pastor Jackson and his family. He invited her to come over as soon as she could. It took ten minutes to drive the few blocks to the Jackson's home, and Deidre climbed the steps to their front door. Pastor Jackson was waiting for her, and he pushed it open.

"Good morning, Sheriff Johnson," he greeted her with his steady, quiet voice. "Do come in. Can I get you cup of coffee or something?"

Deidre declined the offer and sat with them. As before, the Jacksons sat on the couch, one parent on either side of Naomi.

"How are you feeling?" Deidre asked her.

"Well, thank you," Naomi answered. Deidre couldn't help but notice how clear her eyes were and how crisply she enunciated her words. Naomi smiled at her.

"The last time I saw you, I asked if we could talk after you were released from the hospital. Are you still willing to speak with me?"

Naomi glanced from one parent to the other. Mrs. Jackson took her hand and the pastor placed his arm around his daughter's shoulder. She nodded her assent.

"I'd like to know how you became involved with this person who called himself Aaron Sarstrom. Did he approach you, or was it the other way around?"

Naomi cleared her throat and took a deep breath. "Aaron was a very friendly person in school. He was easy to talk with and was a lot of fun, always laughing, always joking around.

"He didn't seem to have anyone you'd call a close friend, though. One day I was eating alone in the cafeteria, and he sat down at the table with me. He asked if it was okay, and I said yes.

"The next day I sat where he was sitting. No one else shared our table, and we were able to talk easily. He asked if I'd like to go for a walk with him after school, and we did, down by the breakwater. We talked about his life in Chicago, how his parents had both died and how he was living with an aunt up by Whyte. He seemed so nice. One thing led to another, and he asked me out on a date. He was fun and introduced me to some of his friends. They were fun, too."

Naomi paused considering what to say next. "One evening, I was feeling really low, and he told me he had something that would make my world a little brighter. He gave me a capsule, and I took it without questioning. I know that was stupid of me, but I never gave a thought to the possibility he'd give me anything dangerous or illegal. In about thirty minutes, I felt like everything was good, and my senses were heightened. I guess that was the start of it. Perhaps I'm weak or something, but it took only a few times of trying it, and I needed more. Then Aaron said it was getting too expensive for him to continue giving me the pills, and I'd have to do a favor for some of his friends if I wanted more."

This was hard for her. Tears slowly dripped. "To make a long story short, soon I needed the stuff so badly, I'd do anything for it. By that time, Aaron had shown me how to inhale it. I realized I was becoming a junkie, but I didn't care by then."

Deidre sat attentively, listening to Naomi's story without taking notes. "Did you know what you were taking?"

"After several times, Aaron asked me, 'Well, what do you think of cocaine?' By that time it didn't matter to me what it was."

"What was the favor you were to do for his friends?"

"We were driving around one evening, and Aaron said he wanted me to meet a friend of his. He started up Highway 2, north out of town. We didn't stop until we were up around the Pines Picnic Area. Do you know where that is?"

Deidre nodded. It was a popular stop for families to show their children the towering white pines that had for some reason been spared when lumber barons stripped the area in the early 1900s. The giant trees invoked a sense of peace and calm, and there was a short, self-guided nature trail carpeted with brown pine needles. It wasn't far from the Whyte Road.

"A small man was waiting by his pickup in the parking lot. Aaron introduced him as Skinny. He kind of gave me the creeps, but he said if I wanted, I could work for him. All I had to do was deliver a package to Duluth once a week.

"I would pick it up where he instructed me to and deliver it to an address in West Duluth. As payment I would get a week's supply of cocaine. At that time, I hadn't had any for a while, and I was beginning to feel nauseated and agitated. Skinny gave me a small amount to help me feel better.

"I agreed to do what he was asking. Aaron said he'd go with me the first time. Before we left, Skinny gave me a packet of cocaine for my own use and a plain box that was taped shut. He said, 'Don't waste that stuff,'" and he pointed to the packet in my hand.

"Skinny told me, 'You won't get any more for a while. Meet me outside Friendly Jane's a week from today at this same time, and I'll have another package to deliver and a packet for you.'"

Deidre was still not taking notes. She didn't want to do anything that might make Naomi not feel like talking. Besides, Skinny was dead, she knew who Aaron was, and she knew where the shack was located.

"How many trips did you make for them?" she wanted to know.

"I don't know. Eventually, all that mattered was that I received my week's supply. It was then I knew I was in serious trouble, and I told Aaron I wanted to go to detox and be done."

"How did he react to that news?" Deidre quietly asked.

"He just looked at me and smiled. Then he said 'There is no quitting. Remember Jill Moore? She was going to quit. Well, she did, but I don't think you want to quit the way she did, do you?' I knew what that meant, so I kept making deliveries to Duluth even though I didn't want to do it."

"Did Skinny ever mention anyone else to you, anyone you'd recognize?"

Naomi thought for a moment. "Once he said he had to get back to somebody he called Elias, but I don't know who that is." Deidre immediately thought of the fax she had received from the police in Elgin, Illinois. It must have been Elias Howard, she would bet her retirement on it, all six-feet-four of him evil.

"Can you give me the address of where you delivered the packages?" Deidre took out her notebook.

"I never really knew the building number, but it was above a tavern off Superior Street, somewhere around Seventy-fifth Avenue. The tavern was called Diver's Find."

Deidre jotted that down, and thanked the Jacksons for their help. As they were walking her to the door, Pastor Jackson asked, "Are we, especially Naomi, in danger? Should we be doing something to protect ourselves?"

"If you have a place to go, to stay for the next week, I would do that. Don't leave town without telling me where you will be, though. It'll be important I can contact you. Naomi, you may be called upon to testify if things go as I hope they do. Good luck."

Pastor Jackson broke in, "I can give you the information you need right now. This morning, I called a friend who owns a small cabin in northern Wisconsin. It is on a lake that borders on the Chequamagon National Forest, very secluded and accessible only by a rustic gravel road.

"If we stay there, no one will know where we are."

"Perfect," Deidre agreed. "If you leave this evening after dark, so much the better. I'd like to have an unmarked car parked down the street. The officer will follow you out of town to make sure no one's trailing you. Okay?"

"Thank you," Pastor Jackson said, his voice a little unsteady. "I don't know what we would have done without you."

ON HER WAY TO DULUTH TO MEET with Mac, Deidre wondered how she would react if she ever came in contact with John's killer. Inside, she was a ball of grief and anger that was very near the edge of rage. She didn't know if she could show mercy to the person who had destroyed her world.

As she approached the outskirts of Duluth, she glanced at her speedometer and saw she was doing ninety miles an hour in a sixty-five. Deidre realized her emotions were causing her to be distracted from what she wanted to accomplish.

Mac was waiting for her. "How you doing, friend?" he greeted her.

"Mac, I feel like I'm about ready to come apart at the seams, but I know I want to see this through to the end. I hope you can help, because I can't do this alone."

Mac patted her on her shoulder. "Sit. We'll get our plan set, and by tomorrow evening, we'll have some answers. At least, that's what we're hoping for."

"There is one more thing that's come up. I talked to Naomi Jackson this morning. She's dried out and is home with her parents," Deidre said. Her voice was so tired the words were flat.

Deidre went on to tell Mac about what Naomi had told her about being a mule. Not only that, but Naomi was sure there were others, although she had never talked to them about their involvement. Several other students had been friends with Jason and hung out with him. This revelation presented a problem. If they found what they were expecting up north when they served the search warrant, most certainly the recipients of the drugs in Duluth would be alerted and the drug conduit they were looking for would be broken.

"I'll have a petition for a warrant drawn up right away," Mac said, and he called in his secretary. "I want a request for a search warrant drafted right away and sent to Judge Davidson. Make sure he is the one who gets it. The warrant is for the purpose of searching Diver's Find, 7531 West Superior Street. We want to enter the building on October 12, 2012 at 2:00 p.m." He hung up the phone and turned to Deidre.

"We have a very efficient judge who I'm sure will help us. I ordered it timed to coincide with our work in Isabella. If we don't get it, and I'm sure we will, at the very least we'll have Diver's Find under surveillance."

For the next two hours he and Deidre put together their strategy. Deidre's chosen deputies had been put on notice of what they would be asked to do tomorrow, and Mac had selected three members of his task force. With themselves, that would form a group of eight, enough, they believed, to handle almost any situation they might find. The element of surprise would be on their side.

It was agreed that all of them would meet at the Law Enforcement Center in Two Harbors at eight the next morning. They would lay out the group's strategy and by noon would have driven to Pete's cabin. From there it would be up to Pete to guide them to the lake the way he had taken Deidre the first time.

"What do you know about this guy, Pete?" Mac asked, a little skeptical of the man he had never met. "Are you sure he can be trusted? I don't want us walking into an ambush. He's not the kind who would sell us out for a few bucks and a six pack of beer, is he?"

That thought had never crossed Deidre's mind, and she tried to picture that scenario.

"Pete is one of the most straightforward persons I've ever met. He's a retired logger who lives alone, except for his dog. He's old and looks worn out, but you'll have a tough time keeping up with him in the woods. I'd be surprised if you have any qualms after meeting him. I'd trust him with my life."

Mac stared at her for several seconds. "You will be, Deidre. You will be."

CHAPTER
THIRTY-NINE

BY EIGHT IN THE MORNING, the members of the team who were to execute the search warrant were gathered in the meeting room in the Two Harbors Law Enforcement Center. Mac and Deidre took turns outlining the plan they had drawn up in his office the day before, sometimes one finishing a sentence the other had started. By ten o'clock they were ready to roll. The plan was for them to travel up Highway 61 at scattered intervals and then follow Highway 1 to Pete's place. That way, they wouldn't be traveling like a convoy past the road into April Lake. Deidre and Mac rode in her vehicle. The other six officers paired up and came with three more squads.

Shortly before noon Deidre pulled into Pete's driveway. His old lab came limping out to greet them the way he always did, and she took time to stoop and scratch his ears. He flopped on his side and looked up with his eyes begging her to scratch his belly.

"Looks like you have a lifelong friend there, Sheriff." It was Pete, easing his way down the rickety steps from his cabin.

"This is the guy who's going to guide us through the woods?" Mac whispered incredulously.

"I warned you," Deidre whispered back. "Wait until he gets in the woods, then see if you can keep up."

"Hey, Pete, you ready for some excitement?"

Pete laughed. "I suppose you'll have enough rifles so I won't have to carry mine."

Deidre caught the glint in his eyes as though he were wishing she would say, "No, we need you to back us up," but she knew that could never be. Instead she said, "Pete, we can't take a chance on you getting shot, better leave your rifle home this time." She could see the disappointment in the old man's eyes.

"Pete, I'd like you to meet one of the people who'll be going in with us, Mac McApline. Mac, this is my friend, Pete."

Mac extended his hand. Pete looked him square in the eye, and placed his boney mitt into Mac's. Deidre could see the surprise in Mac's eyes as Pete shook his hand.

As they followed Pete into his cabin, Mac bent close to Deidre's ear. "My God, he's got a grip like a vice. Where does he get that kind of strength?"

Deidre kept walking behind Pete, a smile on her face.

By the time everyone had arrived, Pete's dog had had more attention in the past few minutes than he'd experienced in the last six months. He was in his glory, going from person to person with his tail wagging.

"Mac, will you ride in one of the other SUVs? That way Pete can ride with me and get us to the spot where we'll start walking. It's not too far from here. So you won't be surprised, it will seem like we're heading away from our target. Don't worry. Pete knows where he's going."

The caravan bumped along the same backwoods road that Pete and Deidre had traveled a few days before, eventually ending up in the small clearing that served as their parking area.

"This is the place where we start to hoof it," she announced to the others.

Mac added, "Each of you, make sure you have a rifle. Deidre and I are only taking our sidearms, because we'll be the ones who will move in the closest."

"Double check to make sure you have everything you need, because it's at least a mile to where we're going," Deidre warned.

"A mile-and-a-half," Pete broke in, and he smiled at Deidre. She didn't think she had ever seen him with such a spring in his step.

He took off through the woods, ducking under low-hanging branches, skirting downfalls, and nimbly stepping over rotting tree trunks lying on the ground. After twenty minutes of walking, he turned to the group. "From this point on you'd better be quiet," he whispered. "The wind's behind us, and sound will travel a long way today." Then he looked at one of the officers who had come with Mac. "Try to pick up your damned feet. You've stumbled over everything on the ground." Pete's look and tone assured the man he wasn't joking.

From then on they walked in silence, single file through the stand of pine trees. It took the group longer to reach the rock outcrop than it had when just Deidre and Pete made the trek, but Pete was moving slower, more cautiously. Everyone picked up on his actions and watched where they placed their feet so as not to create more sound than necessary.

Pete turned to them and whispered, "The sheriff and I will crawl to the edge of the rock and take a look before the rest of you come up. When you do, crawl on all fours and don't rise up to look over the bluff. The sheriff will tell you what to do when you join us."

Chapter
Forty

Together Pete and Deidre began making their way up the gently sloping rock sheet. It took less than a minute for them to be in position to look down the other side. The anhydrous ammonia tank was still sitting under the pines off to the side of the clearing. However, there were no vehicles parked in the crude turnaround. Neither of them spotted any sign of human activity. Pete beckoned with his hand for the others to join them.

Again keeping his voice just above a whisper, he said, "There ain't no sign of anyone down there. I think the sheriff can take over now. She'll tell you what she wants."

It was evident to Mac who Pete thought should be in charge. Deidre made sure the others knew this wasn't totally her show. "Mac and I talked this through yesterday, but we counted on there being somebody home. I don't think this turn of events changes anything, though. We'll assume someone is inside as we approach the building. What do you think, Mac?" He nodded his approval.

Deidre continued. "The back side of the building has only a couple of small windows, and they are high up on the wall. You and you," she said, pointing at two of Mac's people, "I want you to work your way down to the back corners of the shack. Position yourselves so you can cover both the back and the sides. Don't become so focused on the building that you forget to watch your own behinds. Whichever of you is on the far side, move into position by walking well south of the shack so you can cross the driveway out of sight from inside."

She singled out one of her deputies and the last of Mac's team. "Make your way down to the front of the building. Stay about fifty yards away, but be ready to stop anyone who might make a run for it. Also, be alert to anyone coming down the driveway. Stop them before they get to the cabin. Jeff, you go with him," and she pointed at Mac's officer who would be crossing over the driveway. "Help him through the woods so he gets into position without being spotted."

The officer looked at Deidre with chagrin, but decided to let Jeff lead the way.

The last two officers were stationed further up the driveway, closer to the highway. They were instructed to allow any vehicles entering the compound to pass but to not allow anyone out.

Mac, Deidre, and Pete watched the six work their way down the bank toward the tarpaper-covered building. It took them a good twenty minutes to get in place, and Deidre appreciated the caution with which they moved.

"Pete, you stay here. If anything goes wrong down there, you get out right away. I don't want you getting involved. Got that?" Pete just grinned and slightly nodded his head to indicate he had heard but had no plans to comply.

With that, she and Mac started down the incline, the warrant in hand. It was almost two o'clock.

Mac stepped to the door but didn't stand directly in front of it. He reached around the frame and rapped sharply on the crude boards that formed the barrier. There was no answer. He pounded on the door and yelled, "Police, open up!"

They heard something being scraped across the floor and the sound of breaking glass. From behind the building two voices called out in unison, "Police, put your hands against the building and spread your legs." Then all went silent for a few seconds. One of the officers who had been stationed in the back came around the corner of the building, escorting a handcuffed young man. Deidre looked at him and her eyes opened wide.

"Hello, Jason," she said in a tone that wasn't really a greeting. "It seems things haven't gotten a whole lot better for you since we last met. How long has it been since you posted bail, a week? Two weeks?"

She looked at the officers who had nabbed him coming out the back window. "Did you read him his rights?" she asked.

"As soon as I had the cuffs on him," He pointed to his partner. "Jim was witness to it."

"What do you say we go inside where we can talk?" Deidre suggested. "Is anyone else in there?" Jason shook his head, and Mac escorted him to the door. Deidre took him inside, while Mac reposted the deputies and SWAT members. He moved two of them closer to the highway, two others were sent halfway up the driveway, a fifth was placed in the trees where he could watch the front of the shack, and Jeff was stationed where he could keep an eye on the back. By the time Mac entered the ramshackle building, Deidre had Jason Canton seated on a metal kitchen chair and had used her handcuffs to make sure he couldn't leave it.

"I'll watch Jason," Mac volunteered. "Why don't you begin to search the other rooms while he and I have a conversation?"

Deidre pulled aside the curtain hanging over a door opening. She walked into what evidently served as a bedroom. It held two small beds, their blankets balled into disheveled messes.

"Have you found anything?" Mac called from the other room.

He heard her fumbling with something, and when she came out of the bedroom, she held a ragged sweatshirt wrapped around an object. She took it over to where Jason was shackled, and she slowly unwrapped what it was covering.

"Well, look at this," she said as she waved a pistol in front of his face. She looked at the markings on the handgun's breech. "Twenty-five caliber. You know, Jason, we've had a number of slugs of this same caliber cropping up inside people's heads."

Jason's face blanched, and before Deidre could say any more, he blurted out, "That's not my gun! I didn't kill anybody!"

"Why Jason, I didn't say you had," Deidre responded, forcing her voice to stay low and calm. "But you must agree that this looks a little suspicious, don't you? You're the only person I can see, and this gun was found in the same building where we found you. I mean, it certainly looks suspicious, wouldn't you say?"

Mac spoke up, but his voice was not gentle like Deidre's. He growled, "It looks to me like you're in pretty deep, Jason. Of course we don't know if this gun is the same one used to kill Aaron Sarstrom in Elgin, Illinois. I suppose it could be a coincidence that you chose to use the name Aarom Sarstrom as your alias. But that would be quite a coincidence, don't you think? Then there are the remains of the seven people we found executed, all killed with the same caliber gun. It looks pretty suspicious to me. How does it look to you, Sheriff?"

"Pretty suspicious, I'd say," Deidre almost crooned in her soft voice.

"It's not my gun!" Jason screamed.

"Then whose is it?" Mac barked.

"Look, Jason. Right now we have little against you, only a charge of fourth degree possession of cocaine. That carries a sentence of what, zero to five years? For you that probably means probation, or at the most, six months at the Northeast Regional Correction Facility." Again Deidre used a soft, caring voice.

Mac interrupted Deidre with his rasping voice. "But if you're looking at possible murder charges—eight of them—well, throw away the key. You won't get out of prison in three lifetimes."

Deidre picked up the one sided conversation with her more gentle way. "If you know anything about who owns this gun and this shack, I'd advise you to tell us. It'll be a lot easier on you in the long run. I'll tell the county attorney you cooperated with us."

Jason hung his head in despair and shuffled his feet on the floor. Deidre thought she knew what he was thinking. If he ratted out the others, his life wouldn't be worth much. On the other hand, if he said nothing he could end up taking the hit for whoever owned the gun.

"Listen, Jason, I know you're in a tough spot, but if we can put away the others who are responsible, maybe we can work some kind of deal, segregation from them, a shortened sentence, something like that. We can't promise you anything, but it'll go a lot better for you if you cooperate with us. You're young. You've got a lot of life ahead of you. Maybe it's time to make some changes. Who owns this gun?"

Jason continued to look at the floor, and Deidre could see his jaw muscles clenching.

Mac bellowed, "Tell us who owns the gun!"

Deidre turned to Mac. "Let's just tone it down a little. I think Jason was about to tell us something. What about it, Jason?"

Hearing those words, Jason raised his head, and they could see in his eyes that he was defeated.

"The gun belongs to Elias Howard. He and Joseph Durante built this place about ten years ago. They're the two you want."

Deidre did the talking. "Where are they now?"

"Checking on what they call the line. There are sixteen shacks like this built in the woods on Superior National Forest land. They're squatters. They throw up sheds where nobody goes, near swamps or bogs, like this place. They check on them once a week."

Deidre gave Jason a forced caring look. "What happens in these sheds?"

"They've got what they call cooks. They're mostly flunky chemists who make a fresh batch of meth every week. Once a week, Joseph and Elias take a cylinder of ammonia and other ingredients to them. They pick up the manufactured meth and bring it back here. That's why we can stay in here. We—they don't cook it here."

"Where do they store it?" Deidre asked, her eyes sweeping the room.

Jason nodded at the barrel stove standing against the wall. "That stove can be easily moved. Disconnect the stove pipe and slide the stove over. The metal mat it's sitting on can also be moved. You'll find a trapdoor under it."

Mac had already begun to move the stove, and it took only seconds to slide the mat away. He lifted the metal ring attached to a trapdoor. In a lined hole under the floor he could make out what looked like shoeboxes stacked on each other. He lifted one out and removed the lid, estimating that the plastic bag inside the box held about a pound of a substance that resembled large salt crystals. Some of it had flaked off and formed a white powder.

"This is what we came looking for," Mac understated. "I'm going to put it back the way it was for now."

He turned to Jason, "How long do you think the other two will be away? Do they follow a schedule?"

"Usually they get back about three-thirty. Will you take me out of here before then?" he pleaded.

"We will," Deidre promised. "But there are a couple more things I need to know. Will anyone else be with them, and how heavily are they armed?"

"There are four of them: Elias and Joseph, and two others I don't know. I've seen them only a few times, and no one called anybody by name. They're from Chicago, I think. They aren't the kind you talk to unless they ask a question. Elias always carries an assault rifle, the others usually have handguns. All four will be armed."

"Did they leave in one vehicle or are there others?" she wanted to know.

"Two. Elias and Joseph are in a black Dodge pickup with a camper top. The other two guys are driving a black Cadillac Escalade."

"One last thing," Deidre wanted to know. "Do you know the location of these factories you say Elias and Joseph are checking on?"

"Most of them, I guess all of them."

Mac unlocked the cuffs holding Jason to his chair but left the cuffs on his wrists. He motioned for the person guarding the front of the building to come over.

"Take the prisoner to the rock outcrop where Pete's waiting. Keep him out of sight, and don't let him make a sound.

"When you get behind the rocks, have Pete guide you to where the cars are parked. You know, where we started walking from. Tell Pete to return to his rocky outpost overlooking the shack as soon as he can. We may need him to get us out in the dark."

Deidre stepped outside and joined Mac. They didn't want the four they were waiting for returning while they were inside discussing what to do next. The two of them moved off to the side and stood under the cover of thirty-year-old red pines. Three of the remaining deputies joined them, and the two hiding near the highway entrance were left in place.

Chapter Forty-One

Four suspects would be returning to the shack, and there were seven officers left to confront them. Deidre thought the odds were pretty much in their favor, although she didn't like the idea of facing an assault rifle. For an instant, the thought of the night when John had been killed flooded her memory, and she shivered at the remembrance of the spray of bullets that had shattered her dreams.

She felt herself begin to perspire, and her heart began to race. She took a deep breath and tried to be calm, but a rage was building that she feared was growing into something beyond her control.

Mac brought her back into the present. "What do you think, Deidre? How should we handle this situation?"

Deidre looked up from her thinking, befuddled for a second until she realized they hadn't planned for this discovery. Mac gave her time to gather her thoughts, and he watched intently as she grappled with her emotions.

"My opinion is that we should back off and let them go inside. Give them a couple of minutes to begin doing whatever they do and then crash their party. If we sweep up the broken glass from the back window, maybe they won't notice right away. Let's try to put everything back the way it was when we went in."

"That sounds right to me, but what about Jason? We can't disguise the fact that he isn't going to be there. That'll tip them off right away."

Three deputies were left outside to watch for anyone coming down the drive. Deidre and Mac went inside and started to straighten up what had been disturbed by their search. As she passed the doorway to the bedroom, she said to him, "What if we stuffed some pillows under these covers? We could pull the curtain shut over the doorway. There's no window in there, and in the darkness, they might be fooled. It might buy us a second or two if they think Jason's sacked out."

"Worth a try," Mac answered, and he joined her in making a form that somewhat resembled a human shape curled into a fetal position with his backside to the door.

They took one last look around the main room and decided they had done the best they could at restoring it to its original condition. Now they had to wait.

Mac contacted the officers guarding the driveway entrance. "Be sure to stay hidden, and don't stop anyone from entering. Let them in without your being seen, but don't let anyone out. These men are extremely dangerous, so have your rifles ready, and don't hesitate to use them if the situation warrants. When they do return, warn us they're coming, but I don't want you to speak to us. Hit the page button once on your two-way. We don't want to tip them off to the fact that they have visitors."

Deidre and Mac thought the best way to position themselves would be similar to how they surprised Jason. This time Deidre would be near the back window with her deputy, Jeff. That left Mac, one of his officers, and one of Deidre's deputies to cover the front. They each took their positions, hidden from view, but close enough to be able to reach the cabin in a few running steps. It had been agreed that Mac and his two deputies would make the first move. All of them had brought along bulletproof vests, and they tightened the buckles, feeling the confinement of the padding. Deidre knew that a vest was no guarantee that she wouldn't be injured, but it gave her a sense of security.

She hunkered down behind a pile of rotting lumber stacked behind the cabin and was only yards from the window through which Jason had bolted. She envisioned at least one of the others trying to make the same exit.

She repeatedly looked at her watch, and it was as though time had been suspended. A few end-of-season mosquitoes buzzed around her face and neck.

She had just shooed the pests away and adjusted her position when she felt her pager vibrate. They were coming!

Now time became irrelevant as Deidre crouched behind the decaying pile of wood, and she wondered how the others were feeling. *How will I react to the sight of Joseph and Elias?* Her hand involuntarily squeezed the handle of her pistol. *Maybe I will get the chance to get even for what has been taken from me.*

Before her thoughts could go any further, from the other side of the building she heard vehicles coming down the driveway. Pebbles crunched under their tires, and she could hear the sounds emitted by the trucks' suspension springs as they rocked back and forth over the ruts and holes of the gravel entry. There was a moment of silence and then the slamming of doors. She heard profanity-laced banter. Evidently the men were in good spirits. Things must have gone well on their route. The door to the shack made a scraping sound as it swung inward, and then she heard it close.

"Where the hell's Jason? Elias, get that stove moved and stash the stuff. I'll go find him."

Deidre heard the sound of someone moving toward the door mixed with muffled conversation.

"Check the bedroom first. He's probably sleeping after the night we had. He must have one hell of a hangover."

Deidre heard more sounds of movement and then, "What the . . ." At the same time she heard the door splinter as it was broken down.

Mac's voice bellowed, "Police!" but before Deidre could hear anymore, a body came hurtling through the back window, landing only feet from where she squatted. Her first image was of a man, a very large man, rolling over to lessen the impact of hitting the ground. He had an assault rifle in his hand.

She immediately jumped forward and stepped on his forearm. At the same instant, Deidre thrust her service pistol at him until its barrel rested against his temple.

"Don't try to get up. Release the rifle." She looked down into the face of Elias Howard, and he glared back at her through contemptuous eyes.

For a moment the image of John lying dead in her arms flashed before her, replayed like a bad dream. She focused on Elias's face, on the scar across his cheek, on his sneering lips, and within her, hatred welled up beyond her comprehension. She had read of people's lives flashing before them when they confronted death. With her it was different.

Images of John holding her, giving her an engagement ring, of them laughing at silly jokes, of nights they had spent together rushed through her mind. She was not thinking, not processing the situation. Her total focus was on the man in front of her and hate, hate deeper than any emotion she had ever experienced. Deidre felt the pressure of her gun's trigger against her finger, and she began to squeeze.

From behind her, a calm but forceful voice said, "Deidre, don't," and she felt the firm grip of Jeff's hand on her shoulder. The tension in her trigger finger slowly eased, and she felt energy drain from her body.

Jeff eased her away from Elias and trained his pistol on the suspect, who was still lying face up on the ground. He no longer resembled the arrogant thug Jeff remembered from his picture.

Instead, his eyes were pleading, and he knew he had been a millisecond away from having his brains scrambled by a shot from Deidre's service revolver. He didn't move a muscle while Jeff talked her down from her irrational emotional state of mind.

"Back away, Deidre. I have him covered. Grab your breath while I read him his rights."

Deidre sat down on the pile of rotten lumber, unaware of the moisture from the wood soaking through her pants. The muscles in her legs trembled so that she doubted she could stand. She laid her gun down and covered her face with her trembling hands, not yet fully comprehending how close she had come to committing murder. Unable to control her emotions anymore, she sobbed.

Jeff ordered Elias to roll onto his belly and place his hands behind his back. Then he put his handcuffs on wrists that were nearly too large for the shackles. Sounds of a violent struggle came from inside the shack, and they heard a body slam into the wall. Glass shattered amid curses and grunts. Within minutes the noise stopped. By this time, Jeff had recited the words of the Miranda Act and ordered Elias to get to his feet. It was a struggle for the big man to gain his balance, even with Jeff's help. By that time, Deidre had regained her composure and stood in front of him. She glared but said nothing.

As she, Jeff, and Elias walked around the building, they could hear more recitations of the suspects' rights being read, and by the time they were to the door, they could see the aftermath of the ruckus.

Mac was sitting on a chair, blood staining the front of his vest as it seeped from a gash above his right eye. One of his officers sat on the floor holding his forearm, which had a growing lump where a purple hematoma darkened his skin. The two remaining officers were holding their handguns by their sides, and on the far side of the room, against the wall, stood three suspects, hands secured behind their backs.

Joseph seemed to have gotten the worst of the brawl. His nose was crooked as though it had been violently struck from the side and blood trickled from his left nostril, splashing in large drops at his feet. His forehead was marked by a large contusion. He stood defiantly, looking at Deidre while the other two handcuffed men hung their heads in resignation.

Using her two-way, Deidre summoned the officers who waited at the entrance to the driveway. It took several minutes for them to make their way back to the cabin, and by the time they arrived, the entire group had moved outside and was waiting.

Mac and Deidre moved off to the side and discussed their many-headed dilemma. Jason had to be kept separate from the others. As long as he remained talkative, they didn't want to give Elias or Joseph any opportunity to intimidate him. They wanted to make surprise visits to the meth factories hidden in the woods, but they didn't know if they needed search warrants, considering that the shacks were built illegally on federal land. Finally, they wanted their searches to be surprises to whoever was minding the store at each site. The logistics were rapidly becoming a law enforcement nightmare.

"I think we're in the clear if we just barge in and confiscate evidence at each of the factories," Mac argued. "It isn't their property. The feds aren't going to question if we had a search warrant or not."

Deidre put her hands on her hips to keep from jabbing a finger at him. "I don't care what the feds would do or not. All I can see is a lawyer requesting that all evidence we'd find be disallowed. You know yourself that they'll be grasping at any straw they can. If we use your logic, then we didn't need a warrant to bust into this place either, but we got one, because we didn't want to compromise the situation. So what has changed?"

"But, Deidre," Mac continued to argue, "If we don't act now, they could be tipped off and destroy all the evidence."

"Aw, come on, Mac. How will word get out? They have no landline service up here, cell phone either. We have the bad guys in custody, and we can have a warrant by tomorrow morning. Look, I'm as anxious to bust them as you are, but let's not compromise our case in any way. A few more hours won't matter."

Mac caved.

One deputy had been sent with Pete and Jason. That left five deputies and Task Force officers with Deidre and Mac. They decided to send three of them up to Pete, hoping he had enough time to have escorted Jason and his guard out and make it back to the rock shelf. Pete would have to guide them back to where the vehicles were parked. The one who had been in charge of Jason would take him to the county jail where he would be sequestered from the other prisoners. The three other officers would bring the remaining SUVs around to the cabin with Pete acting as guide. Deidre doubted if they could find their way out alone.

Deidre, Mac and two deputies were left behind to guard the prisoners and gather evidence from inside the shack. Jeff and the remaining deputy from the Drug Task Force were to stand watch while Deidre and Mac bagged up the boxes of meth they'd uncovered.

The pair took photos from every conceivable angle, being sure to capture as much evidence as they could with the digital camera.

They were especially cautious when handling the twenty-five-caliber pistol Mac had again retrieved from its hiding place. By the time they had made a sweep of every cupboard and storage possibility in the place, they could hear the SUVs making their way down the rock-strewn drive.

It was dark by the time the units returned to Two Harbors and well past nine when the bookings had been completed. Together they went to the cell where Jason was being held. He looked up at them from where he sat on the bench that would serve as his bed. Deidre wondered if he'd be able to sleep or if worries about his safety would keep him pacing his cell all night.

"Hello, Jason. Are you still willing to talk to us?" He nodded. "And do you realize that our visit will be recorded on video? Again his chin went down almost imperceptibly. Deidre asked in her quiet, collected voice. "Please say 'Yes' for the record."

"Yes."

Jason, totally cowed, agreed to point out the locations of the sixteen meth factories on a county map she and Mac had brought with them. They walked away with their targets identified.

Deidre immediately phoned the judge. She answered the phone with a voice that reeked of irritation at being interrupted at home.

"Judge, this is Sheriff Johnson . . . Yes, I know what time it is, but I need a big favor . . . Yes, another . . . Yes, this is imperative." Deidre went on to explain what had transpired, and the judge's disposition changed considerably. She asked Deidre to meet her at the courthouse in fifteen minutes.

Deidre returned to her office with the signed search warrants she so desperately had sought, and Mac met her at the door.

"Let's get this thing set," she said with a weary voice.

By midnight, they had put together a force of sixty-four officers, including every deputy Deidre had at her disposal, Mac's entire force, and several officers borrowed from the St. Louis County Sheriff's Department.

The group would assemble at the Law Enforcement Center at seven the next morning. Deidre decided to sleep in her office and borrowed a blanket from the jailer. The sofa in her office was short, and at first she had a difficult time falling asleep. When she did, she had frightening nightmares.

She was standing over Elias Howard, her pistol barrel to his temple, and she could feel her finger tighten on its trigger. In her dream, she continued to squeeze and heard and felt the gun's discharge. Elias's head exploded, sending pieces of tissue flying in all directions.

Deidre woke with a start, sweat soaking the uniform in which she slept. She found herself madly trying to brush the mess from her clothing before she could orient herself. Then she realized it had all been a very bad dream and that Elias was alive and in a cell down the hall.

She dozed off again, and this time her dream was about John. He stood in front of her without saying a word. He looked as handsome as ever. He only smiled at her, a loving smile. Then he turned his back and walked away.

Deidre turned, trying to get comfortable. By six in the morning, she decided sleep was out of the question.

Chapter Forty-Two

It was beginning to become light when Deidre went to the washroom and tried to straighten her appearance. She called the one cafe in town open at that hour and ordered a takeout breakfast. Mostly, she craved strong, black coffee.

It was a short drive to the cafe, and when she arrived, her order wasn't quite ready. She waited impatiently at the counter until the waiter brought her a bag. She had ordered one bagel egg sandwich, black coffee, and a caramel roll.

Back at her office, Deidre quickly devoured the sandwich. She was eating the roll when the first members of the team began to arrive. Mac strode into the room, looking rested and ready to go.

"Good morning, Deidre," he sang out, his voice all too chipper to suit her. "We're on the home stretch. I can feel it. Can't you feel it? Man, this has been a long haul." Deidre wished she could share his enthusiasm, but she felt deflated and defeated.

"Wait until you hear what happened in Duluth yesterday," he continued, almost bubbly, but that term was hardly ever used to describe Mac.

"At the same time we were surprising Jason, my guys were serving the warrant at Diver's Find. They're a good bunch, professional. Anyway, they surprised three men and one woman in the apartment above the bar, and there was no resistance. They found almost eight thousand grams of meth in various-sized packages. It looked like the four were about ready to transport it elsewhere, Minneapolis and Chicago, I suppose.

"When we ran checks on the four, we found that three of them were from the Minneapolis-St. Paul area. The fourth was traced back to Chicago, Elgin, actually.

"They were interrogated separately. The three men lawyered-up right away, but the woman was another story. She claimed she was being held against her will, and she started turning on the others almost before we could read her the Act. She claimed one of them, the one who seemed to be in charge, was forcing her to have sex with him and his buddies.

"I think by the time we have everyone rounded up and get their stories straight, Ben and his FBI buddies are going to be busy for a very long time." He grinned at the thought of what they were uncovering.

"We have enough evidence of gang-related activity and of interstate drug trafficking to place it in their jurisdiction.

"And if the woman's story holds up, we have the added charges of kidnapping and human trafficking."

By that time, the meeting room outside Deidre's office was crammed with more people than it was built to hold. As she and Mac emerged from her office the chatter quickly died down, and the mood changed to a serious silence.

Mac turned on his laptop and projected a Powerpoint image on a screen. When Deidre saw the display, she thought he must have gotten no sleep last night. On the projected map of Lake County, he was pointing out the location of each of the sixteen targets. He had assigned four officers to each location. Because of what they knew of the drug operation, he and Deidre expected to find two or three wasted individuals cooking the meth.

Mac concluded his talk. "We want to synchronize our movements so we all hit at the same time. Each team will have a search warrant in their possession. The raids are set to take place at noon, so that gives you three hours to get into position. It is imperative that you do not make a move until then. We're thinking these factories won't be well guarded. That would take too many people on the inside. Each probably works independently of the others, and the cookers aren't aware of any of the other sites, at least that's what we believe." He closed the laptop.

"Don't take any chances," he said. "If you meet any resistance at all, call for help. Deidre and I are going to stay here and monitor your calls. Don't call us if things are going as planned. Keep the lines open for emergency calls only. Oh, and don't forget, each of you has been issued a hazmat kit. We suspect the workers won't be staying inside the labs. It's too toxic even for them. After you secure the site, you'll have to gather evidence. Be sure to suit up and use the proper safety protocol when you go inside."

He wished them good luck, and sent them on their way. It was difficult to disguise their movement as thirty-two law enforcement vehicles made their way out of Two Harbors up Highway 2. As they passed the golf course, a foursome of old duffers, enjoying one last round before snow, stopped play and gawked at the caravan speeding past them.

One remarked to the others, "Something big must be happening up north. I've never seen anything like that before in my life." Little did he know how prophetic his statement would be.

Mac and Deidre had some serious logistical plans to make. If the raids went as planned they would have far more prisoners than what the jail could hold. She called the sheriff in the county to the northeast of them, Cook County. The sheriff there assured her that, if needed, they could house up to ten inmates.

Then she called the sheriff of St. Louis County. They had room for another twenty. Next it was a call to Carlton County. They agreed to house another dozen, and so by the end of the hour, Deidre had enough cell space prepared for when the teams returned later in the day.

Deidre and Mac paced the meeting room, drinking coffee and trying to stay upbeat. At times one or the other would sit down for a few seconds but then would become restless and begin pacing again. Deidre didn't know about Mac, but she could envision a hundred things that might go wrong and end in disaster.

Finally, the clock's minute and hour hands lined up vertically, and the bells of the Catholic Church down the street chimed the first of twelve strokes. It was time. Without thinking, Deidre moved closer to the radio, waiting for a frantic call for backup, but none came.

By twelve-thirty, she and Mac suspected that the operation had succeeded. She thought that the tension would have been over by that time, but it only increased. Deidre compared herself and Mac to fishermen who had thrown their nets into the water and had begun to drag them in. They knew something was in the trap, but they didn't know what.

"I don't expect we'll hear anything. It's been almost forty minutes and no calls. Assuming all went well, I suppose our personnel are gathering evidence. That will take at least an hour, probably more. The closest lab is at least an hour from here." Mac thought for a minute. "The earliest anyone will return is two, more like two-thirty. What say we go grab a bite to eat while we can?"

It suddenly dawned on Deidre that she was ravenous. They decided to walk the three blocks to Seventh Avenue. The fresh air would clear their heads and wake them up, they thought.

The waitress in the small restaurant was extraordinarily talkative, and Deidre's nerves were frazzled. She was reminded of a cartoon she had seen, a drawing of a woman who was definitely at her wits end. The caption under the picture read, "I have only one nerve left, and you are standing on it."

She was able to control herself and politely ordered a burger basket.

Neither officer ate more than a few bites of food after it was placed on the table. It was as though their digestive systems had become paralyzed. Nevertheless, Deidre was glad she received no calls to interrupt their meal.

Chapter Forty-Three

The walk back to the center took a little longer. What little they had eaten had been swallowed too fast, and they were suffering for the way they had forced the heavy food down. The nervous ball in the pit of their stomachs didn't help much. They climbed the stairs to Deidre's office and had just sat down when they heard the tread of several pairs of feet moving up the stairs. Both of them jumped from their chairs in anticipation of who was arriving first.

Two of Deidre's deputies flanked a disheveled man. She tried to judge his age, but it was impossible. His eyes were rimmed by lids that drooped, most of his teeth were missing, and he was emaciated. Behind the trio, two other suspects were escorted by Mac's people. They were in better condition than the first, but not by much. Deidre began the paperwork required to hold the three.

After that, a steady stream of officers and the arrested individuals returned to the center. When the entire booking process was completed, the cells were packed with thirty-four persons who had been picked up in the sweep. Five of them were women and needed to be segregated from the men. Several appeared to be agitated and needing medical attention. There were a few who were alert and healthy-looking. Deidre thought maybe they were higher ups in the organization, supervisors of a sort, who knew to take precautions when working with the toxic ingredients of methamphetamine. Or else they were new to the business and hadn't had time to sink to the level of the most wasted. The others, she thought, must have been expendable junkies who, when they were too used up to perform anymore, could be replaced. She didn't know whether to be elated that the sting had gone so smoothly, or to be sad because of the waste of humanity she held in the cells.

She and Mac began to separate the names of the prisoners and determine which would be shuttled to other area jails. Calls were made to inform jailers how many inmates to expect. Officers were assigned to prisoners they would escort to other jurisdictions. By early evening, the population of the jail had returned to a more manageable number. Elias Howard and Joseph Durante remained in Two Harbors, as did Jason Canton, although he was sequestered from the others.

It was late when Deidre was able to return to her temporary home at Inga's. She was relieved to see the kitchen lights on when she pulled into her parking place and even more relieved to find Inga sitting at the table waiting for her.

"Oh, my Lord," she exclaimed when Deidre entered the kitchen. Inga jumped up and ushered her to a chair. She poured a cup of steaming coffee and placed it on the table before her.

"Deidre, are you all right?" she asked, her voice quivering with shock. Deidre shook her head, and her long-pent up emotions gushed out in a flood of tears. She buried her face in her folded arms and allowed her body to convulse as she wept openly and long. Inga stood behind her rubbing her shoulders, never saying a word, or even offering her a box of tissues. She did nothing to stifle Deidre's need for catharsis.

How long she wept, she didn't know, but eventually there were no more tears to shed. Deidre felt totally spent. For a long time she rested her head on her arms, and Inga continued to knead the knotted muscles in the back of her neck. Eventually, Deidre sat upright and wiped her nose. It took several tissues. Inga offered her a cool, damp washcloth, and Deidre placed it over her eyes for a few seconds.

"Thank you, Inga. You've been so kind."

"I'm fixing you a light snack. Here's some fresh coffee, and then I'm putting you to bed."

While Deidre ate the cheese and crackers Inga put out and had a few pieces of fruit, Inga went upstairs and turned on the shower. By the time Deidre joined her, the bathroom was steamed up like a Turkish bath. The hot water washing over her skin felt as though it was washing away the dirt from what had happened to her the past weeks.

By the time she toweled off and put on her nightclothes, Deidre could hardly crawl onto the bed. Inga had turned down the covers, and she literally tucked them in around Deidre's chin. Then she bent down and kissed her forehead, retreated to the door, and turned off the lights. Deidre was sleeping so soundly she was aware of nothing.

Chapter Forty-Four

It was almost noon when Deidre woke, and the bright, late October sun was shining through the crack between the window shade and the frame. She jolted up, her heart racing. Then she rested back on her pillow and took a deep breath. It was Saturday, a day off. The Lake County Jail and the jails of surrounding communities held more prisoners than they were built to hold. John's killer was locked up, forever she hoped, and the state hazmat team had already been deployed to begin the cleanup of sixteen meth labs.

Deidre made her way downstairs, and not to her surprise, smelled the aroma of good food emanating from Inga's kitchen.

"I'm so glad you could sleep, my dear. I've fresh caramel rolls in the oven and coffee ready. Sit down now. Let me wait on you."

Deidre eased herself into a chair at the table. Even though she had not had a physical confrontation, her body felt as though it had been pummeled. She ached all over. She heard the spatter of hot grease as Inga cracked two eggs into the frying pan. Then Deidre noticed the morning edition of the local newspaper lying beside her plate. The headlines blared, "Massive Drug Bust!"

She turned the paper over to hide the news, but under it was a copy of a Minneapolis newspaper. Its headlines were in even bolder print, "Northern Minnesota Drug Bust Largest in State's History!"

Before she could make any comment, her phone rang. She had left it on the table before she had gone upstairs last night. Inga snatched it up before Deidre could reach it.

"Your phone's been ringing every ten minutes since early this morning. I peeked at the caller IDs. I hope you don't mind, but I wanted you to sleep as long as your body called for it. The news networks are trying to contact you. My advice is to turn off your phone, have a nice breakfast, and then get cleaned up for the day. These people aren't going to go away. You can face them this afternoon."

Deidre smiled at her friend and held the END button on her phone until she heard the sign-off tone play. Once she started eating, she realized she was famished.

Later, Deidre began returning calls. She had decided to hold a news conference the next morning in the high school auditorium, the only place in town large enough to accommodate the crowd she expected. It took her more than two hours to return all the calls.

By late afternoon she was feeling exhausted but made one more call, to Naomi Jackson's parents to inform them that it was safe for them to return. She asked how Naomi was doing and was assured she was still committed to helping any way she could.

It was a few minutes' drive to Deidre's office, and one more vital piece of work had to be completed. She met the district judge in her office. It was easier for Deidre to meet there than the other way around, considering the volume of paperwork the judge was going to have to sign.

Deidre's office staff had worked overtime to type up formal complaints against each of the suspects. They had been arrested on Friday and by law could only be held for thirty-six hours. To prevent them from leaving, a written list of facts against each individual, a complaint, had to be drawn up and endorsed by a judge. There was no way Deidre was going to allow even one person to walk.

After the judge left, she made the error of opening her e-mail. Some one hundred-ninety messages clogged her inbox, almost all requesting information about the case.

It was late when she finished answering most of them, and she slowly drove home.

Again, Inga was waiting for her.

"Tomorrow is Sunday. Would you take me to church? It's lonely going alone all of the time. It'd please me to have someone to sit with tomorrow."

"I'd love to, but I have a press conference scheduled for eleven o'clock."

Inga didn't skip a beat. "But the early service is at eight-thirty. You'll be out of there by ten, which gives you plenty of time to get to the conference. Besides, I always go to the early service."

Deidre knew that Inga always attended the late service, and she knew she was being manipulated, but the thought of some peace and quiet appealed to her. Perhaps the music would calm her, although she didn't know how she would react to a sermon. She had never put much stock in religion.

That night, as she and Inga sat at the table, Deidre didn't cry, didn't even get misty eyed, and she hoped that last night's crying jag had been the result of her utter exhaustion.

SUNDAY DAWNED RAINY AND GRAY. As Deidre drove to Inga's church, she wondered why she had agreed to attend. She had no desire to be around people or to be in such a confining atmosphere.

By the start of the service they were seated in a pew. Inga had marched down the aisle to near the front, and Deidre had been obliged to follow. As they sat in the quiet of the sanctuary and she let her thoughts mimic the tempo of the organ, Deidre felt a flood of relief. Although people had looked at her as though they wanted to talk, she was thankful they respected her space, and now she let herself sink into the maroon velour-covered cushion of the pew.

The service began with the traditional Lutheran liturgy: a pimply faced acolyte carrying a lit candlelighter, a cross bearer struggling to keep the icon vertical, and a pastor walking behind, a slight smile on his lips.

Deidre stood when the others did. She didn't know the words to the songs and didn't sing along, but the rhythm calmed her. She felt a peace begin to grow within her. Her mind began to wander, and she thought of facing Elias Howard. She pictured herself on the witness stand, testifying against him, and she wondered how she would hide the hatred and contempt she felt.

The pastor began to read from the Bible prior to presenting his sermon. First he read from the book of Isaiah. "For the Lord is a God of Justice." Deidre felt her back muscles contract, and she sat more upright.

Next he read from Psalms. "The Lord loves righteousness and justice." She sensed a pattern beginning to develop.

The pastor continued, "Our Gospel is from Matthew, 'but you have neglected the more important matter of the law—justice.'" He had Deidre's total attention. By the time he finished with his sermon defining the difference between vengeance and justice, Deidre's mind was clearer than it had been for a long time.

Vengeance was not to be her duty. Instead, she was acutely aware that she had done her job. Now it was the court's responsibility to make sure that justice was served. She felt a weight had been lifted from her shoulders. Justice would be served, of that she had no doubt.

As the two women left the church with Deidre supporting Inga as they walked down the steps, Deidre asked, "Did you know this was what he was going to say?"

Inga looked at her with her watery blue eyes and said, "No, dear, sometimes things just work out this way."

Chapter Forty-Five

THE HIGH SCHOOL PARKING LOT WAS PACKED. Motor coaches were lined up, each growing a satellite dish from its roof. The major networks were represented, and Deidre noticed several vans painted with the logos of local stations. By the time she fought her way through the crowd of reporters and curious bystanders, she felt as though she had run a gauntlet.

Approaching the microphone on stage, she motioned for quiet, then calmly stated, "If you'll please find seats, we'll begin. First of all, I want you to understand that I won't be able to answer every question, because this is still an ongoing investigation. Let me begin by giving you the background of what has happened."

She took a deep breath. "Early last summer a juvenile female was found to have either taken or been given a lethal dose of methamphetamine. At about the same time a person named George Tomlinson went missing. Many of you knew him as Skinny. Also, about then, an undercover drug informant moved into the community."

The room was abuzz with whispering and looking at each other in surprise, wondering who that had been.

"In both cases, the disappearance of Skinny and the death of the girl, we couldn't find a lead. Then, the first day of grouse season, two hunters reported finding what looked like graves on a ridge far back in the woods by Whyte.

"With the help of the BCA, we unearthed the remains of seven people. One of them was Skinny Tomlinson. The others have been identified, and their relatives have been notified. Evidence indicates that the sale of drugs was a contributing factor in all the cases. Along those lines, our informant came forward with the names of three individuals who may have been involved. They were traced back to the Twin Cities, but more than that, to the Chicago area.

"On Thursday, my deputies, along with the Gang and Drug Task Force from Duluth, executed a search warrant to the residents of a cabin by April Lake near Isabella. Five suspects were arrested and are being held in the Lake County jail on the basis of complaints signed by the district judge. A warrant was drawn up to allow the Task Force to search an apartment in Duluth in connection with what was going on in this county. Four persons were arrested there. They are under St. Louis County's jurisdiction and are being held in its jail.

"Finally, on Friday, sixteen meth labs were seized. They were scattered throughout the southern part of the Superior National Forest. A total of thirty-four additional suspects were taken into custody. The arraignment of all parties will be tomorrow in the Lake County Courthouse, with the exception of the four arrested in Duluth. It will be a very busy day. Do you have any questions?"

A middle-aged man jumped from his seat. "Why didn't you do something to prevent this from happening?" he demanded. Deidre recognized him as Gerald Colter II, the father of the boy she and Mac had taken home on the day of Jason Canton's first arrest.

As calmly as she could, Deidre said into the microphone, "Mr. Colter, because of time constraints, I'm going to accept only questions from the media at this time. I promise you that in the very near future, I'll conduct an open meeting where the public will be invited to voice their concerns."

"How near?" he demanded.

"Please be seated, Mr. Colter, or I will be required to have you removed." He grumbled and sat down.

A woman in the front row raised her hand, and Deidre recognized her. "Mary Lopp, Channel Fourteen out of Duluth," the woman identified herself. "Do all of these arrests have anything to do with the murder of FBI agent John Erickson?"

Deidre was stunned. Although she should have, she hadn't expected that question. After a lengthy pause, she said, "At this time we really aren't sure. The investigation may move in that direction if the evidence points there." She hoped no one noticed her eyes tearing up.

"Peter Sanger, WMIN out of Minneapolis. Along that line, is the FBI involved in this operation?"

"All of the arrests on the north end were carried out by Lake County deputies and members of the Task Force. The search in Duluth was a function of the Task Force. We're attempting to make a connection between the apprehended individuals and members of a gang in Chicago. When and if we can make a connection between gang activity and any interstate trafficking of drugs, Agent Ben VanGotten will be brought in. He has already been apprised of what he might expect."

"John Driden, St. Paul *Crier*. What evidence do you have to hold these people?"

"I'm sure you realize I can't divulge that kind of information here. Tomorrow, if any of the suspects have attorneys present, we will have to make full disclosure to them. However, it would be premature to divulge what we know at this time."

There was another show of hands, and Deidre pointed to a young lady in the front row. "Jillian Cable, St. Paul *Free Press*. Why are these people being charged in state and not federal court?"

"So far the evidence we have concerns crimes committed in Minnesota. When and if it is determined that interstate activity is involved, the federal government will issue separate charges."

The questioning lasted more than an hour, and by that time Deidre said, "I'm sorry. I'm going to have to end this session. You are free to view the proceedings at the courthouse tomorrow. Thank you for your time and your cooperation." She walked off the stage and exited the school through a back door.

When she pulled into the parking space behind her and Inga's houses, Deidre had an urge to walk through her own place. It was the first time that thought had come to her since John's death. Hesitantly, she inserted her key into the lock and turned it. The door swung inward, and Deidre was greeted with the smell of emptiness.

She quietly walked through her kitchen, almost tiptoeing as if she were afraid to wake someone sleeping. She stood in the doorway between the kitchen and dining room. The window through which the fatal shots had come had been repaired, and the sun streamed in.

Deidre looked at the spot on the floor where John had lain. A cleanup crew had removed any evidence of the trauma that had taken place. Deidre tried to find the places in the wall where the spent bullets had carved out holes in the wallboard, but they too had been filled and repainted. She felt almost as though nothing was wrong, except for the nothingness.

Deidre was amazed that she had no other reaction. It was as though she were in a stranger's house, wondering what had happened to cause it to be abandoned. Nothing, not even a memory, was alive.

After walking through the upstairs and ascertaining that everything was in order, she left the house as quietly as she had entered. Inga wasn't home, and Deidre went up to her own room. As she lay on her bed, a wave of uncontrolled sadness swept over her, and again, her tears flowed with no restraint. It was more than a half-hour before they stopped, and she felt spent.

At that instant she knew she would have to sell her house and find a new place to live. There would be no going back to what had been home. Her mind wandered to the meeting she had earlier in the day, and she wondered what awaited her when she held a public meeting. Certainly Mr. Colter was planning to stir up issues, and she began to question where she had failed her community, her department. She wondered how the pending trials would play out. Who would find loopholes, who would have none, who would get off with their hands being slapped?

She slept.

Chapter
Forty-Six

The bailiff's call, "All rise," greeted Judge Trembly as he took his seat. His gavel slammed down on its wooden block and the courtroom came to order. The clerk of court announced the first case.

"The State of Minnesota verses Joshua Harris."

Judge Trembly asked the defendant to rise. "You are charged with fourth degree possession of a controlled substance and with the manufacture of said drug. Do you have an attorney present?"

The defendant nodded.

"You must make a verbal answer for the record, Mr. Harris. Now, do you have an attorney present?"

"Yes."

"If I have been correctly informed, you have been appointed a public defender. If that is so, please answer yes."

"Yes."

"You have the right to plead guilty or not guilty at this time, or if you make no plea, the court will assume it is a not guilty plea. Do you wish to plead at this time?"

"I ain't saying nuthin'," Joshua replied.

"Enter a plea of not guilty. Bail is set at fifty thousand dollars."

The judge's gavel slammed down. "Next case."

The morning was a series of similar scenarios, one pretty much following the other. A few of the defendants had attorneys to represent them, but the majority of them had been assigned public defenders. Deidre wondered where they had all been found. The court recessed for lunch. She would have to wait for the two she most wanted to observe.

During the recess, Deidre walked down to the breakwater. The air was blowing in off the lake, fresh and cool. She leaned on the restraining cable and listened to the waves lap against the concrete. Her hair was tousled in the wind, and she shook her head to allow it to be arranged as it would. The words the pastor said yesterday in his sermon kept repeating themselves, "But you have neglected the most important part of the law—justice."

Not today, she thought. Today, justice will be served, but then in her mind she added, *And maybe a touch of vengeance as well.* She stood for several minutes looking at the docks, seeing gulls wheel against the blue sky, and hearing the actions of the workers as they filled an ore boat. Walking back to the courthouse, she wondered how she would react to the sight of Elias Howard facing the judge.

For the afternoon session, the courtroom was again packed. A few more of the lesser players were charged with little formality.

It took several days to get through the cases involving those manufacturing the drug. Finally, the words came she had been waiting to hear. "The State of Minnesota verses Elias Howard." Deidre's heart missed a beat when she saw the hulk of a man rise and face the judge.

"You are charged with nine counts of premeditated murder in the first degree, one count of possession of a controlled substance, and one count of drug trafficking.

"How do you plead?"

"Not guilty, your honor."

"Are you represented by legal counsel? If not, the court will appoint a defender."

A woman sitting at the defendant's table stood. "My name is Melanie Jenks. I'm a member of the Minnesota Bar Association, and I will be representing Mr. Howard.

"Your honor, in light of the notoriety my client has received because of this case, I believe he has little chance of fleeing without being recognized. As such, we are asking for bail to be set at an amount that is reasonable."

The judge looked at her for several seconds, and without comment declared, "Mr. Howard will be held without bail. Deputies, please return Mr. Howard to his cell."

Deidre felt a tear trickle down her cheek, then her neck, finally to be absorbed by her uniform collar.

Next on the docket was Joseph Durante. Deidre had heard that his attorney had met with the county prosecutor, telling him that Joseph was ready to tell all he knew about the murders and the drug operation. In turn, he was asking for a reduced sentence. Deidre wasn't sure how she felt about that possibility. Perhaps in the long run it would be for the better.

His bail was set at one million dollars, hardly an amount he could easily raise.

Jason was escorted into the courtroom by two deputies. He looked rather scrawny in his orange jumpsuit. The judge read the complaint.

"How do you plead?"

"Guilty, your honor," he replied.

"You will remain in protective custody until the trials of Mr. Durante and Mr. Howard have been completed. Do you accept those terms, or do you want me to set bail so you can be released?"

"I accept your terms," Jason said, his words barely audible.

The day was over, and Deidre was spent, as if she had been involved in a six hour tug of war. Perhaps she had.

CHAPTER FORTY-SEVEN

DEIDRE HAD DECIDED IT WOULD BE BETTER to hold a public informational meeting sooner rather than later. She scheduled it for Friday so the announcement could be placed in the local newspaper. Her office was getting back to some semblance of a routine, and in the days after the preliminary hearings, she was able to begin catching up on a backlog of paperwork. Friday came too soon.

The forum was scheduled for seven o'clock in the evening in the high school auditorium. When she pulled into the parking lot, she was more than a little surprised at the number of cars. She hoped a volleyball game was going on and that most of the visitors were spectators. As she walked past the entry doors to the gymnasium, she was a little dismayed to discover it was empty. That meant only one thing.

When she walked into the auditorium, she heard the mumblings and whispers of over a hundred-fifty people. The place went silent as she walked down the isle and stepped up on the stage.

"Most of you know this has been a very trying week for law enforcement in Lake County. The happenings have been so thoroughly reported I don't believe I have to repeat the details to you. With your permission, I'll go directly to answering questions you might have."

There was murmuring, and Deidre saw many heads nodding their assent.

"All right then, so this remains an orderly gathering, I will ask that you raise your hand until you are recognized. I promise everyone who wants will get an opportunity to speak. There are three microphones available to you. Please use one of them so everyone can hear what you say. First question."

There was a hesitation, and a lady sitting near the front raised her hand. A mic was handed to her. "Sheriff Johnson, can you guarantee that all of the individuals involved have been arrested."

"Of course there are no guarantees, but we are quite confident that all loose ends have been tied up."

The ice was broken, and a number of hands shot up. Deidre started to single out the questioners as methodically as she could.

"How many students in our school were involved?"

"We won't know that until our investigation is complete. Perhaps we'll never know for sure."

"Have any of the students spoken to you about this matter?"

"For several reasons, I can't answer that question at this time."

"Does this drug trafficking ring extend beyond our area?"

"Yes."

"How far?"

"That I can't say. The FBI will be in charge of any investigation concerning movement across state lines."

Deidre called on a man sitting farther to the back, and she had a difficult time seeing his face. The bright lights were in her eyes, and the house lights were not turned up high. He stood and took the microphone.

"My name is Gerald Colter II, attorney." The audience turned to look in the direction from where the commanding voice emanated. "I have several questions. First, how did something of this magnitude escape your attention, Sheriff?"

Dreidre could sense that she was about to be targeted. "Mr. Colter, this is a very large county with acres and acres of wilderness.

My deputies do their very best to cover an impossibly large area. This was an organized group who knew our vulnerabilities."

She still couldn't see her questioner's face very well.

"I see. Well, can you explain how you allowed our schools to be infiltrated?"

There was no way she could answer that question without putting her foot in the trap. After all, the school had been infiltrated. She was on the defensive and she knew she was. A buzz of agreement swept through the crowd.

"Believe me, Mr. Colter, when we first began to suspect that students were involved, we made every effort to act expediently."

"You make it sound like you had no clues before this fall that something was amiss. Am I safe in assuming that is what you are saying?"

Deidre felt as though she were on the witness stand. "Yes, that is what I'm saying."

"Tell me, Sheriff, why didn't you investigate the disappearance of Jean Dickerson more than three years ago? If I am not mistaken, she was reported missing, and her disappearance went uninvestigated for several weeks. And when you did investigate, it was to track down a runaway. If my facts are not correct, please set me straight." Colter's voice dripped with sarcasm and ridicule. The crowd stirred restlessly.

"No, you are correct."

She was dismayed to hear the sound of voices of discontent arise from those in attendance. Gerald Colter II was not finished.

"Yet you say that you were on top of things. It seems that this has been going on for several years, right under your nose. How many teens have died since you misjudged the disappearance of Jean?"

Deidre was left speechless for several seconds. "Mr. Colter, I am aware of the consequences of my misjudgment. Sometimes facts and perception do not coincide, and we have to pick up the pieces. That is what we're trying to do."

"One more question, Sheriff. Why did the investigation surge ahead in the past two weeks? Did that have anything to do with the fact that it was your fiancé who was gunned down and not someone's child?"

Tears formed in Deidre's eyes, and she nearly shouted at her tormentor, "That statement is not worthy of an answer. Please be seated and allow someone else to speak."

She looked around the auditorium. No one raised their hand, but she could sense the hostility that had overtaken the meeting.

"Good night, then." Deidre stalked off the stage and up the stairs, exiting before anyone in the audience could leave.

Chapter
Forty-Eight

THE WEEK AFTER THE TOWN HALL MEETING at the high school, the local newspaper ran the first of a series of articles tracing the history of the drug operation in the Two Harbors area. It talked, too, about the trials that were going to be held. Some would begin in a few weeks, but the most serious, those of Elias and Joseph, would not take place until late spring at the earliest.

For Deidre, it was bad enough that her actions were going to be under scrutiny by the paper for the weeks to come, but there appeared several scathing editorials questioning her willingness to have tackled a difficult situation until she had been affected personally. Attorney Gerald Colter II was leading the charge.

As the weeks went by, and the questions of the way she had handled the case kept being raised, each round getting more direct and vicious, Deidre wondered how much longer she could hang on.

The emotional numbness caused by John's death had lingered for weeks after his murder, but little by little the reality of what had happened hit her. One day, she could do nothing but sit on the edge of her bed and cry out, and for the first time she faced the fact that she was alone. John was never coming back. A wave of emotion too much like panic swept over her.

Deidre's days became little more than an attempt to make time pass. Work, walk, eat, talk to Inga, and then repeat the same sequence the next day. She realized she was drawing into her own shell, but she didn't know how to pull out of it.

Shortly before Christmas, the first case involving a suspect captured during the sweep was heard. It was a man who had been picked up in one of the labs. He looked far more human than the day he had been apprehended. He spoke clearly and politely to the judge.

The trial concluded almost before it began. The judge, sitting high up on his bench, addressed him and his attorney.

"I have been informed you wish to plead guilty to a reduced charge of possession of a controlled substance. Is that correct?"

"Yes, your honor."

"And as a part of this agreement, you will consent to being placed in an inpatient facility to face the issue of your addiction."

Again the man answered, "Yes, your honor."

"I hereby sentence you to time served. In addition, you will be placed on five years' probation, and you will enter an inpatient program for drug abuse. I understand a spot is open for you at one in Minneapolis, and that you will be escorted by your attorney immediately upon your release."

The man looked at the judge with tears in his eyes. "Yes, your honor."

"Then the sentence stands." The judge rapped his gavel.

EACH DAY, DEFENDANTS paraded before the judge. Most followed the precedent set by the first trial. However, some of the suspects had prior convictions, ranging from misdemeanors to felonies. These factors complicated the cases, because state guidelines dictated a mandatory minimum incarceration of one year. In some cases the suspect had been previously involved in violent crimes. For these, no plea agreement was on the table, and they required a full-blown court trial.

By May, all of the individuals picked up at the meth labs had been sentenced. All were found guilty. The county jail population had shrunk to its usual size. The three more serious suspects remained to be tried.

Jason Canton had waived the right to bail and had chosen to remain in the safe confines of his cell in protective custody. Elias Howard had fought to have bail established, but because of his past record and the severity of the crimes of which he was accused, he remained behind bars. Joseph Durante failed to make bail.

Joseph was the first to be tried, and on the first day of his trial, Deidre sat in the back of the courtroom. She tried to focus on the prospective jurors, tried to read their faces, but they all wore expressions difficult for her to interpret.

The opposing attorneys filtered through the list of jurors, questioning some, excusing many, until the number had been pared down to twelve plus two alternates.

"Mr. Duarnte," the judge began, "You are charged with one count of first degree possession of methamphetamine, one count of manufacture of methamphetamine, and seven counts of accessory to murder. How do you plead?

"Not guilty, your honor," he replied. And so the sparring began.

Each attorney made their case in their opening statement to the jury, Joseph's contending that his client was a victim of society and deserved to be given a chance.

The prosecution called their witnesses. Jason, looking pale and shaken, testified that Joseph was not the owner of the .25 caliber pistol. He spelled out what his own role had been in the operation, and how it was he who had recruited Jill Moore. In detail, he described how she had been given a lethal dose of meth by Joseph and Elias.

Under severe questioning from the prosecutor, he told what he knew of the seven graves that had started the whole investigation. It took the prosecuting attorney two days to get through with his witness. By the time the defense had their chance to cross-examine, Jason looked beaten.

"Mr. Canton," Joseph's attorney started, "Just what are you getting out of this?"

"I don't understand your question," he mumbled. The judge ordered him to speak up and answer the question again. "I don't understand your question," Jason repeated, defiantly.

"Haven't you agreed to testify if you are granted immunity?"

The prosecutor sprang from his chair. "Objection, your honor, no such deal has ever been proposed to the witness." The judge sustained the objection and warned the defense counsel to limit his questions to the facts.

"Well, then, you are at least anticipating receiving leniency from the court if you cooperate, are you not?"

Before Jason could answer, the judge pounded his gavel on his bench. "Sir, you are trying to put up a smoke screen with what-ifs and suppositions that you know the intent of the witness. If you continue with this line of questioning, I'll hold you in contempt of the court. Now proceed in an acceptable manner."

After the warning, Joseph's attorney attacked Jason's testimony head on, questioning him over and over about various aspects of his story. In the end Jason's testimony remained consistent throughout his cross-examination.

The prosecution called Naomi Jackson as a witness, and she presented herself as a poised and articulate young lady. The defense attorney acted as though he didn't quite know how to handle her. In the end he backed off, thinking it would be too easy to make her a martyr in the eyes of the jurors.

The defense really had no one to call for a witness. Their best shot was to call in a character witness from his days growing up in Chicago. Deidre sat through all the hours of testimony, and she couldn't believe that the witness would have any bearing on the case whatsoever.

After seven days of testimony, both sides rested their case, and the jury was dismissed to reach a verdict. It took them six hours of deliberation, and when they filed back into the courtroom Deidre was there. The forewoman stood and faced the judge.

"Has the jury reached a decision?"

"Yes we have, your honor."

"On the charge of first degree possession of methamphetamine, how do you find?"

"Guilty, your honor." Deidre saw Joseph's shoulders slump.

"On the charge of seven counts of accessory to murder, how do you find?"

"Guilty, your honor."

Joseph buried his head in his hands.

"And on the charge of one count of manufacturing methamphetamine, how do you find?"

"Not guilty, your honor." Joseph didn't react to that minor victory. It really didn't matter one way or the other. He was going to spend many years in prison.

Chapter Forty-Nine

EVEN THOUGH JOSEPH'S CONVICTION was going to put him in prison for a very long time, Gerald Colter II kept up his relentless attack on Deidre in the community. It was as though he had become obsessed with destroying her because his son had suffered the humiliation of being caught in the drug business, even though he had never been charged with a crime. Deidre quit reading the editorial section of the newspaper.

Even she was surprised by his vitriol. The day after Joseph's trial ended, Gerald Colter II showed up at the courthouse carrying a petition with enough signatures to demand an election to recall Deidre. She was numbed by the prospect of having to face another election that would be hostile beyond what she thought she could go through. She put the issue out of her mind until the matter at hand was completed.

Two weeks after Joseph's trial, it was time for Elias to face a jury of his peers. In his case the stakes were even higher. At his trial, he was charged with nine counts of premeditated murder, possession of several pounds of methamphetamine, possession of a firearm by a felon, and a lesser charge of trespassing on federal property.

For days, the defense and the prosecution sparred back and forth, the prosecution making thrust after thrust, and the defense trying to parry the moves that often came too quickly to avoid.

Deidre was called to testify only about the circumstances of John's death. The prosecution had decided to use Mac as their arresting officer witness, taking away any appearance of bias.

Again, Jason testified for the prosecution, looking more haggard and frightened than he had during Joseph Durante's trial. As had been attempted before, the defense attorney tried to plant in the minds of the jurors the idea that Jason was testifying for personal gain. Deidre couldn't tell if the jury was buying the argument.

Many days, Inga attended the trial, sitting beside Deidre, sometimes holding her hand. *Strange how we make false judgments of people without really knowing them,* Deidre thought, and she appreciated Inga's quiet support more and more.

It took two weeks to reach the attorneys' closing arguments. The jury, after deliberating for two days, came in with their verdict, guilty on all counts.

Deidre walked out of the courthouse unsure of her feelings. She had expected to feel elated, or at the least satisfaction. She felt neither. Instead, she harbored a growing feeling of peace.

She didn't return to her office, but instead walked down to the harbor and leaned on the restraining cable designed to keep people from falling into the frigid waters of Lake Superior. She watched the gulls soar and dive, watched them bicker with each other, watched them skim the water, looking for food. She marveled at their freedom. It was then that she made her decision.

Chapter Fifty

From the deck of her new home, Deidre looked out over the water of Cedar Lake. In the distance two loons called to each other, and near the water's edge she saw killdeer running up and down the sand spit, searching for tidbits of food that the waves deposited.

She leaned back and let the breeze ruffle her hair. The same breeze made a faint *sshh* sound as it blew through the white pines that towered over her home. A black lab thrust its muzzle under her hand, demanding to be petted. He reminded her of Pete's old labrador. She inhaled the fresh air and dozed off to sleep in her lounger.

After Elias had been convicted and sentenced to enough lifetimes in jail that he would never get out, Jason had to face the consequences of his actions. He was found guilty of being involved in trafficking cocaine but not being a part of the murder of the seven. He was sentenced to five years in prison with the chance of parole in three years.

Most disagreed with the leniency of his sentence, but a few saw a person who might stand a chance of being rehabilitated.

After Jason's trial, Deidre resigned from her office, convinced she never wanted to work in law enforcement again. She was positive she didn't want to face a recall election, and she wasn't sure she even wanted to stay in Two Harbors.

Her house had been on the market since May, and to her surprise, a young couple with children offered her almost what she was asking. They occupied the house in August. Deidre had smiled when she saw Inga go over with freshly baked bread and cookies and when she saw the children hug her in thanks.

Deidre had looked for a place removed from the bustle of society. John had carried a large life insurance policy, which to her surprise was to be split between her and his mother. When she found a lake cabin several miles off Highway 1, she had cash in hand to purchase the property.

It was difficult to say goodbye to Inga, but she was sure the new neighbors would brighten her days. Jeff had been appointed by the county board to be the interim sheriff until the fall elections, and she wished him well. There had been the usual round of farewell parties, some sincere, some not so.

By the time she was ready to pack up a U-Haul truck to move to her lake home, the town had settled back to its usual humdrum pace. The football team played its first game at home, and the band marched to the field. Students were enjoying the last days of summer before school began, and the front page headlines of the paper read, "SCHOOL SUES OVER LEAKY ROOF."

Deidre looked in her rearview mirror as she drove out of town. She had no remorse.

That was over a year ago, and now as she lay dozing in the late summer sun, she was at peace.

Her phone rang, jarring her awake, and Deidre rushed into her cabin trying to locate it by its sound. Just before the last ring, she hit the receive button.

"Hello?" she answered questioningly. Few people knew her number, and even fewer cared.

"Yes, is this Deidre Johnson?" a stranger's voice asked.

"Speaking," she hesitantly responded.

"Ms. Johnson. Allow me to introduce myself. My name is Max Fostton, and I'm the chairman of our town board. Our police chief has had a medical setback. We would like to speak to you about filling in for him until he gets back on his feet. It should be for only about six weeks."